THAI HONEY

'Sexy man!' she purred, the cigarette dangling from the corner of her mouth, in perfect sluttishness. 'You want me to dance for you?'

She sprang on to the bed and began a slow sensuous gyration to the music, spreading her thighs, and alternating between back and rear view, always with her finger rubbing inside her chatte. She twisted herself into revealing yoga positions, all showing glistening pink: the crab, the archer, the hare. She was animal, a body of pure sex, intent on the display of her vulva, with a female's solipsism, absorbed in her own self. Finally, she balanced on her head, quivering thighs spread, with her sex gaping open.

Squatting, she demanded a coin, which she placed under her bottom. She lowered herself until her sex lips enclosed the coin, then sucked it into her pouch. She ordered him to open his mouth, and her belly heaved, as her sex spat the wet coin into his mouth. He kissed her petals before handing her the coin in mock solemnity and saying 'your tip, miss'. She squealed with laughter. She sat facing him on his lap, clamped his erection between her undulating thighs, right at the lips of her chatte – *so near, yet so far* – and pushed a foot into his mouth.

THAI HONEY

Kit McCann

This book is a work of fiction.
In real life, make sure you practise safe, sane and consensual sex.

First published in 2006 by
Nexus
Thames Wharf Studios
Rainville Rd
London W6 9HA

www.nexus-books.co.uk

Typeset by TW Typesetting, Plymouth, Devon
Printed and bound by Clays Ltd, St Ives PLC

ISBN 0 352 34068 1
ISBN 9 780352 340689

Contents

Prologue

This is a work of fiction, but the events described are not fictional. Everything you read here has happened, and happens. It's all about sex. Don't be surprised. Ask anyone who knows Thailand. Or ask yourself.

1

Rules and Rituals

It is true that the English are a nation of hobbyists, fond of crossword-puzzling, train-spotting, bird-watching, pigeon-racing, potholing, dog-breeding, jam-making; collecting stamps, antique typewriters, bottles, motorcycles or biscuit tins, while some extreme hobbyists, devoted to 'body art', pierce themselves with pins, gaud themselves with tattoos, and dye their hair in alarming pastel colours. They play games whose appeal and rules are mystifying to outsiders: shove-ha'penny, cribbage, skittles, darts, often in a local exclusive variant. Each pastime must have its club, with rules the more arcane the better, or, preferably, several rival clubs.

No exception is the world of corporal punishment, or 'flagellation', a quasi-sexual enthusiasm known as 'the English vice', its practitioners organised in societies with intricate rules of procedure, and their own private jargon of masters, slaves, tops, bottoms, thud and sting. This world accommodates collectors, too, who accumulate punishment tools made from exotic timbers or hides, and enjoy arcane discussions of their quality and provenance. There are even more would-be adherents, who pruriently enjoy press exposés of deviant spankers and caners. A body of pseudo-scientific literature, mostly salacious, gloats on the grim facts of corporal punishment throughout human history, especially that of England: boys whipped on the bare buttocks in school or service, girls less frequently.

It would be idle to pretend that the British public is not eternally fascinated by smarting bottoms, of either sex. Yet English deviance, like English budgerigar-fancying, is nothing if not respectable. It is best explained by the English love of games, rules and rituals, and the thrashing scenario is all those things. Like dog-breeding or potholing or rugby football, with their messy or even painful aspects, it is a game easy to get used to and enjoy. Everyone gets a pleasant shiver when they think of spanking; the account rendered below is of a typical Scene gathering.

Why do we do this? Mitch Barnett mused, wielding his cane as his heart pounded both in exertion and excitement. *Why do we get such pleasure in our strange sport? By inflicting pain in fun, are we trying to protect ourselves from the real pain of the world? Or are we simply addicted, like train-spotters?*

He was a whipper of submissive or masochistic girls, part of the subculture known, cumbersomely, as 'bondage, discipline and sadomasochism', or BDSM. So were all his friends. They looked indulgently on his parallel fascination with girls' underwear, and female clothing in general, while BDSM purists despised any fetish that departed from the strict path of ritual pain, considering lovers of, say, colonic irrigation as mere dabblers in deviance or, that most shocking word in the erotic lexicon, *timewasters.* He explained that in fact a girl's bra, panties, stockings, and the elaborate arrangement of nylon stockings, suspender belt and garter straps (pantihose being unspeakable) were a second skin, inviting the admirer to peel them off and reveal the bare flesh beneath, ready for spanks or the cane. Women accused him, not without admiration, of being oversexed.

Underthings, particularly her panties, smelled of a girl, of her very essence, and were the key to truly knowing her. So he claimed, but his spanking friends laughed that he was a dreadful pervert. They all were, then: nice middle-class people, with the codewords of fetishism as their common currency. But such arcane language is rather crude, demanding ironic smiles; no language can truly

2

explain the tender affinity of strokes. Even in the liberal Scene, where spanking was a healthy communal sport (no chains and dungeons, no blood, or the more lurid painful exotica beloved of the tabloid press), Mitch kept his underwear fetish discreet. He didn't consider himself a pervert, just a typical *homme moyen sensuel*.

It was a late summer Saturday morning in Wimbledon. Girls sunbathed and dogs were walked on the tree-girt common. Comfortable villas sheltered behind hedges; the Barnetts' buckthorn hedge rose to twice an adult's height, affording total seclusion to Mitch and Shannon Barnett, their house, and lawns. Outside the mock-Tudor mansion blossomed roses, lupins and peonies, tended by Shannon's green fingers, under a shady canopy of elms, larches and oak, and a grove of silver birch trees, many denuded of twigs, while – unseen by even the most determined hedge-peeper – she liked to work wearing only espadrilles and a ribbon in her hair, to *épater* any prying bourgeois. Eschewing expensive products, she would pluck a branch to fashion a rod for her own back. Sometimes she would net butterflies – peacocks, red admirals, painted ladies – and keep them in a fine-mesh terrarium.

The bright flowers and the green of the immaculate lawn illumined the shady dining room with its gleaming Victorian rosewood table in pride of place. Shannon's guests were assembled, cradling copper goblets of champagne and smoking cigarettes. Scene people smoked a lot. They were Greg Tobin, the globetrotting Aussie, and his English girlfriend Wendy Ruminaw; Alan Kean, something in computers, and his wife Deb; Matthew and Prue Acker, both civil servants; Derek Wantrill, a history lecturer, and his mistress Jane Bellingham, a sociology lecturer (for Derek's wife Amanda would not accept invitations to the Barnetts'). All considered themselves, with more or less smugness, superior to the unliberated common herd; Shannon's nude gardening modestly expressed her disdain for the 'stuffies'. Yet they chatted of house prices, the latest TV cookery goddess, rail stoppage, or shortcut to beat the London traffic. Chopin tinkled discreetly: consensus music.

3

A buffet luncheon lay spread on the sideboard, to be savoured after the preliminary *hors d'oeuvre* thrashings. There were bottles of champagne from Sainsbury's (not top of the range, but not cheap either – somewhere in the middle) in crushed ice, and wines in crystal decanters. Over the display presided Giselle, the maid, dressed for the occasion in a scandalously frilly (as Alan said) black French maid's costume with black fishnet nylons, a tiny skirtlet that bounced up and down to show her black thong panties, and a white blouse two sizes too small, under which strained her ripe braless breasts, squashed together by the tight straps holding her skirt to her like a schoolgirl's pinafore. Teetering high stiletto heels supported Giselle, thrusting her buttocks into inviting prominence as she moved amongst the guests with a tray of canapés. Her Scene costume excited the approval of the company and drew compliments on Shannon's excellence as a hostess.

'A French maid cannot be scandalous,' she said, licking a sliver of smoked salmon, 'for Giselle *is* French. She's something quite grand in the French Embassy. *And* she shops at Strips. Mitch gives her a very decent discount on knickers and nylons.'

Mitch Barnett's ashplant rod landed sharply on the bare buttocks of Wendy Ruminaw, Shannon's best friend, whose turn it was for a tickling. Shannon herself, as hostess, had taken a warm-up thrashing from Greg. Like all the Barnetts' guests, the drubbed Wendy belonged to the discreetly named 'Wimbledon Commoners', who prided themselves on being one of the most exclusive clubs in the BDSM Scene; keeping the chavs out. They enjoyed visiting arrangements with many others in Britain, as far afield as Inverness, all devoted to the recreational arts of flagellance. Once a club member, serene in expressing and accepting deviance, a flagellant found him- or herself in a cosy freemasonry of the lash. Few wanted any other, and most secretly dreaded expulsion or ostracism. The Commoners, part of the 'liberal Scene', shunned the sleazy side touted in the trash news media. They practised spanking as others made quilts or tea cosies. They were triumphantly middle-class.

Nevertheless, the Scene permitted its adherents, including loyal spouses and girlfriends, an orgiastic moment outside their more or less respectable lives. It was in fact unjust to call flagellance an English vice, for was not de Sade a Frenchman? In the days when upper-class boys were flogged through their public schools, theory had it that as flagellant adults, they sought to recreate their boyhood. These days such explanations no longer applied, and BDSM was a broad democratic church. For some, spanking was an enhancement of the sex act; for some, a substitute; but to all, the spectacle or sensation of bare buttocks whipped made the pulse quicken with an almost religious ecstasy: a shared ecstasy, with the satisfaction of belonging to a secret elite.

Within the formal structure of a punishment scene, they explored fantasies unthinkable in the everyday, while assured of discretion. There were boundaries not to be crossed: no whipping to blood, no continuance, once a victim cried stop, no romantic attachments. Women enjoyed role-playing scenarios of master/slave, teacher/pupil, king/serving wench for, in a game, they could express their innate impulse, impractical in reality, to obey (and be thrashed by) an authoritative male. To play the part of a slave girl, beaten for her errors, signalled comfort and reassurance. Mitch would not dream of inviting Wendy to be whipped one-on-one outside the club rules, and Shannon would not dream of letting him. Yet they lived for whipping, sometimes with the willing victim trussed in intricate cords of bondage, and welts on raw flesh were their vim, their sap. Not sex – though obviously sexual – it was a realm beyond sex, of which many dreamed, but hesitated to enter.

Mitch had always spanked his girlfriends, cheerfully explaining his fondness for (literally) slap and tickle, to find most took it willingly, with artful joy; they understood the erotic stimulus, or physical relief, of a spanking. Others, though fond of him, needed a little casuistry:

5

'You like mustard on your hot dog, and horseradish on your steak, don't you?'

'Yes.'

'Well then. Spanking's just like pepper, for extra taste. It's all good.'

Some were ahead of him, suggesting stronger spice, the strap or cane, and thus was he introduced to the Scene, finding that women were its guiding lights. His svelte appearance helped, for girls felt he understood their need for spanking, and their coyness about admitting it. He was non-threatening: not some hairy beer-bellied oaf, piggy eyes glittering with lust, but slim, boyish, smoothly muscled, with a feminine curl to his lips. Shannon would tease, saying 'my sweet hunky well hung girl' at which they laughed. He was unsure whether his penis (*her* possession) was bigger than others, but all men like it said.

Like their social, spanking life, their private sex life was uninhibited. She liked to fellate him, and also liked them to masturbate separately, watching each other, or have him masturbate her while he licked the whip weals he had raised on her bottom; then suck her long prehensile toes, which she would wiggle in his mouth. She liked his fascination with cunnilingus, for he never tired of kissing her orchid, and also anal sex, which allowed her to wallow in exciting shame. Those were intimacies not for the club, whose members would have been embarrassed at such display, just as the most ardent libertine is dismayed by teenagers gushing over each other in bus or tube.

He remembered no time when he had not been fascinated and frightened by corporal punishment: browsing over descriptions of savage naval floggings, the birching of schoolboys and cadets on the bare buttocks and, especially, the flogging of girls and women. Shannon in turn had always relished a powerful man turning her over for a spanking on the bare, and that love progressed to a taste for the whip and cane, her pleasure heightened by ogling in the mirror the dark coruscations left on her raw flesh. Friends said they were the perfect Scene couple.

Some clubs permitted 'switch', that is, male members could take punishment from females, but most, woman-driven, like the Commoners, had a policy of girls-only submissives. Their solemn, perhaps tongue-in-cheek, rule book stipulated that punishments must be agreed, indeed demanded, by the victim; that each member had her code word, whose utterance signified that she really could not endure further pain, upon which the cane would be still, although a truly submissive girl would rarely diminish herself by using it. By an unwritten rule, members had to be youthful.

Couples, or single girls, coyly discussed and revealed their secret desires for whipping, scared that others would think them perverted, then delighted to find that throughout the country decorous homes sheltered nice like-minded folk. As they edged their cautious toes into the rippling waters of discipline, they realised how many people shared the same tastes. Celebrity autobiographies were these days unashamed to admit a spanking fetish. Slap and tickle, a grand English tradition. *There are more of us than the unenlightened know.*

It was axiomatic that *everyone* had fetishes, had they but the courage to admit them, and that the world would be healthier if they did. They came to the Scene in various ways: through contact fetish magazines, through clubs and spanking parties, often experimenting with the bizarre gamut of ropes, rubber, leather, hot wax, clothes pegs, pins, whips and canes, until those who craved the joy of masochistic submission and the stimulation of pain found the right mix of giddy play-cruelty to suit their needs. Once they were part of the Scene, it became their life.

As well as several fetish magazines, the Barnetts took the glossy *Chance*, which specialised in photos of readers' wives and girlfriends, with fervid stories of couples who picked up a stud on some holiday beach, or in a club, and took him home to give the wife a 'good seeing-to' while the husband watched, then finally joined in, once the newcomer had ejaculated into his wife. The deposit of a stranger's sperm was the essence of the husband's masochistic excitement, and it was always the female adulterously pleasured, never the male. Shannon thought this intriguing, while he dismissed it as caveman *ur*-memory, an inbred tribe requiring foreign seed to refresh its gene pool; although he read the magazine as avidly as she did.

Wendy's naked buttocks were by now well marked from the cane. The girl was bent over Shannon's immaculately polished dining table, her knuckles white as she gripped its edges. Her big pale breasts, squashed against the table in their scalloped pink brassiere, quivered like jellies as the cane struck her bottom; her splayed legs, shining in pink nylon under her matching suspender belt, jerked rigid, with her pink knickers stretched taut between her ankles and the ribbon in her hair fluttering as her bottom quivered. Even in abasement her nudity exercised power for, while a male's clothing impresses by concealing his body, a woman captivates by how much skin she reveals. His cane lashed her again, cruelly deepening an existing welt, and her buttocks squirmed as she exhaled in a loud gasp of pain. Derek Wantrill's video camera whirred as he recorded her ordeal for their archives, with copies for sale to associate clubs.

'Lovely jubbly,' (Mitch winced), drawled Shannon, nude but for stockings and garter straps, and sitting with her freshly caned bottom in a basin of crushed ice while she rubbed her nyloned toes together and sucked on a cigarette held in the same hand as her wine goblet.

The cane gouged Wendy's welt to a sullen purple, and the girl began to shake.

'Oh! God, that's really hard,' she panted. 'You're in fine mood today, but I can scarcely take any more.'

'You've only had five,' Mitch growled. 'I thought we'd agreed on a dozen. Shannon took a full twelve without moaning.'

'You'd better tie me, then,' gasped Wendy. 'I don't think I can go the distance otherwise.'

'It'll be a sentence of an extra two strokes for that privilege, Wendy,' Shannon intoned, with magisterial gravity.

'All right, then,' said the caned girl. 'You're an incorrigible dominatrix, Shannie.'

'How cruel.'

Shannon rose, to reveal the patchwork of crimson welts on her buttocks now shaded blue from her ice bath.

'My bum says otherwise. *You*, miss, are such a *corrigible* sub,' at which Wendy pouted; it was the sort of banter Scene people enjoyed.

Shannon fetched coarse twine with which she deftly knotted Wendy's wrists and ankles to the table legs, until she was stretched flat across the varnished wood. The girl's splayed thighs exposed her shaven sex, glistening with moisture. Mitch licked his lips. Like the other males, he wore only black latex shorts, called a 'skin', which moulded his budding erection.

'Careful, darling,' said Shannon. 'Strictly whops, remember? No you-know-what.'

'Why?' said Greg, leering. 'We'd be doing nothing wrong. I like seeing Wendy squirm under a good shafting by a mate. Aussies get around the world – the things I've seen, and seen people do, and done myself!'

He chuckled slyly.

'Brazil, Gambia, Cambodia, Thailand . . . Now, Thailand's the place,' he mused. 'All those luscious brown girls, and some of them weren't always girls, know what I mean? Under that sun, in that heat, your brain melts. Anything goes, and nothing means anything, except having fun. Normal and abnormal, right and wrong – they don't exist. What are girls anyway? In the east, girls are just meat for pleasure.'

'Are boys not meat?' Shannon drawled, baring her teeth in a lupine smile.

'Assuredly,' purred Derek Wantrill, his reedy lecturer's voice tinged, as always, with irony. 'Flogging of boys occupies an honourable place in our island history. In the Victorian navy, midshipmen and first-class boys, fifteen to nineteen years old, were punished with the cane, the cat, or the birch, often publicly, strapped to a gun, which they called "kissing the gunner's daughter", and always on the bare arse. Two or three dozen strokes were usual, the lashes on the five seconds, for maximum pain. The offences were laughable: pilfering food, drunkenness, fighting, masturbation, or the quaintly named "skulking". It all went on record and, significantly, a boy wasn't considered officer material if he hadn't taken a few floggings. That separated the toffs from the proles, for the decent classes were used to punishment on the bare; the lower classes resented it. In fact, I'm not sure I shan't write a monograph on the subject.

'Or consider ancient and noble Eton College, bircher of aristocratic bums. The ceremonial parade to the birching block, chaplain in attendance, the trousers down for swishing, and the victim got to keep his bloodied birch as a proud souvenir. Remember that fellow with the double-barrelled name, one of the great headmasters? Died a few years ago, just as somebody wrote a most learned definitive history of Eton. Suggested that our chum was too much the sadist, liked caning boys on the bare, and was always drunk. Furious correspondence in the *Times*! Old buffers wrote in from Hampshire defending or attacking him. Half cried foul, he hardly ever flogged anybody, he wasn't drunk, his upper-class drawl just made him sound drunk. The other half said he bare-caned boys all the time, served a glass of sherry afterwards, did me the world of good, caning makes a man of you, and all that. They seemed to be talking about two completely different individuals. Point is, the entire scholastic history of Eton College was ignored, for the public only cared about the flogger.'

'*Bien alors!* Perhaps it does make a man of you,' said Giselle, pouting.

2

A Depraved Adventure

Deb, Prue and Jane shifted nervously in their seats, for their bottoms had not yet been seen to. Deb and Jane wore only stockings, and Prue as well, but for the addition of a corset in boned white satin that pushed her breasts into gourds and squeezed her twenty-three-inch waist to an abnormally thin nineteen inches. All three had their mounds fashionably shaved smooth, like Shannon's.

'Come on, Mitch,' whined Wendy, straining against her cords. 'Do me properly. You're making me fruity.'

'Subs,' laughed Matthew Acker, sipping his champagne. 'Such demanding creatures.' And his wife put her tongue out at him.

Mitch lifted his cane. He lashed Wendy on the sensitive skin of her top buttocks, just under the nubbin of her spine, and a new weal blossomed on her skin.

'Ooh!' she gasped, her bottom clenching hard. 'That was tight.'

'Pile it on, mate,' said Greg. 'Make her squirm. My lovely little English fox can take all you give her.'

'Brute,' pouted Wendy.

Mitch lashed again.

'Ohh!' she cried. 'That's sneaky. I wasn't ready.'

'Is a sub allowed to be ready?' he said, and continued to cane Wendy, inspiring her to theatrical squeals.

'Oh! I'm sorry,' she whimpered, but Shannon told her not to worry about smearing her table as she used a brand of wax polish that was resistant to such things.

Mitch spaced his canestrokes at intervals of five seconds, thus allowing maximum pain, which only just began to ebb before a new cut overlaid the existing weal. Wendy's long ribboned tresses danced on her back at each cut. He began to swish the insides of her splayed thighs.

'*Ahh!*' Wendy shrieked, as her legs jerked rigid and her feet stamped the parquet floor, polished by Shannon to a gleam. 'Not so hard! I mean, yes, hard . . .'

He took the girl's caning to the ordained fourteen strokes. Gasping, she was released from her cords and stood stiffly, face crinkled, as she rubbed her bottom, a glowing tapestry of red welts, many crusting to ridges where the cane had bitten more than once. She snuffled and wiped tears from her eyes as she turned to inspect herself in the mirror. A smile curled her lips.

'Mm . . . I really took some punishment, didn't I?' she purred. 'Shannie, may I borrow your ice tray?'

'Of course.'

Gratefully, she lowered herself into the crushed ice and sighed with relief, after accepting one of Shannon's cigarettes and a frosted goblet of champagne.

'I'm hot enough to melt the ice,' she boasted. 'I'm really sizzling.'

She blew an air kiss to the sweating Mitch.

'That was *super*,' she murmured. 'I feel so cleansed. My poor bum will be like hardboard all next week.'

Next up was Deb Kean. Smiling shyly, and trembling, she stretched over the table. Greg took the cane, lifted it to the full length of his arm, and brought it down with a crack on the taut croup. He applied several strokes to the same weal, deepening it to purple.

'Oh . . .' she panted. 'This is tight! Greg, you're a beast.'

'Want to be tied?'

Deb looked at Wendy, with the ghost of a smile creasing her drawn-back lips.

'Umm . . . no. No. I don't need . . .'

'Thud or sting? I can use a wider cane if you like.'

'No, just sting is fine.'

Vip!

'*Ahh!*'

Wendy laughed.

'You'll wish you'd taken cord,' she said.

Greg gave Deb her full twelve strokes, and she did not cry out again. When her beating was over, they all applauded. She rose, wiping tears from her face, and accepted the dish of crushed ice which Wendy held out to her.

Prue Acker took her dozen from Derek, who used a four-tongued rubber quirt, hand-crafted, with the tongues a foot long, while her husband Matthew wielded the video camera. Then, Matthew was to whip Jane Bellingham, who demanded special treatment. Derek, her 'master', trussed her in leather strips, which bit into her pouch lips, and bound her feet, breasts, arms and belly, then fastened clothes pegs to her sex, mouth, earlobes and, most painfully, armpits and nipples (the art of pegging was admired in the Scene). At last, she was strapped face down to the table top by a rubber flange round her kidneys, with her ankles strapped to its legs. Derek handed Matthew a short-thonged leather cat-o'-nine-tails.

'Please, not the cat, Derek,' mumbled Jane, rattling the pegs clipped to her lips. 'You promised cane only.'

'I had my fingers crossed,' purred Derek, shrugging.

Jane was helpless. She squealed, struggling in her bonds, until, after three powerful strokes, spaced at ten seconds, her skin was crimson. Matthew ended her whipping at the half-dozen, and Derek ripped the clothes pegs one by one from her body, causing her to shriek. To applause, Jane stood stiffly, smoothing her hair, then scanned her welts in the mirror. Shannon emptied the ice tray over her. She smiled, and rubbed the cubes over her body.

'Wow!' she gasped. 'I needed that.'

'I think we all need some lunch,' said Shannon.

Giselle served them food and refilled their wine goblets as the members perched on their chairs, the females sitting on their masters' knees. All looked expectantly at the maid, teetering clumsily on her high heels. As hostess, Shannon would ensure an incident happened. Sure enough, when

Giselle poured her wine, Shannon jogged the maid's elbow (a time-honoured ritual) so that wine spilled over her belly and thighs.

'Naughty girl,' she declaimed. 'You know what happens to naughty girls.'

'*Mais oui, Madame*,' pouted Giselle.

All knew what was to follow, in the drama of role-playing: crime demanded punishment. Without bidding, the French girl lifted her skirt, lowered her panties, and bent over the table with her legs splayed. Mitch wielded the cane. As her flesh wealed, she wriggled her fesses wildly.

'Ooh! It hurts so,' she gasped in her musical little girl's accent, and enjoying her pouting charade. 'How many must I take, *madame*?'

Shannon waited until she had emptied her mouth.

'Until I say stop,' she said. 'A dozen for members, anything for guests.'

'Oh! Ooh!' squealed the French maid, as Mitch beat her; to the sound of her mewling little gasps and moans, her stiletto heels danced, clattering, on the parquet.

'I've . . . I've often wondered what it would be like for girls to thrash men. They do it in the switch clubs, don't they?' Wendy said abruptly.

All the males laughed.

'Not for us,' chortled Derek.

'Only wimps like taking it from girls,' Mitch said. 'Not real men.'

'It's not unknown, Mitcham,' said Shannon. 'Would you really object if I, or another girl, caned your arse? *We* like it, why shouldn't you? You could wear one of my thongs, a nice yellow one, for shame. Maybe a pair of sexy nylon stockings. That would be fun.'

'I certainly would object,' he growled, hating it when she addressed him by his full forename – the embarrassment, to be named for two places at opposite ends of London! His Mitcham-raised dad's idea of a joke, although he would say Mitch was lucky, it might have been Croydon.

'Lots of real men like being flogged by a woman,' said Jane, sucking on a salted stick of celery, then noisily biting

14

its end off. 'You've only to look at the ads in the fetish mags. And lots of men look sexy in girls' panties.'

'Not here they don't,' Mitch declared. 'That comes close to insolence, Jane. Are you ready for another basting? You can take this miscreant maid's place.'

His voice was melodramatic.

All laughed as Jane blushed and, after swallowing a mouthful of celery, whispered she couldn't take another.

Shannon swallowed an oyster.

'You boys are excited,' she said to the ogling males. 'Giselle does squirm nicely. But no touching.'

'I could really do with a seeing-to,' blurted Wendy, munching asparagus, and licking her lips of hollandaise sauce which threatened to run down her chin. 'Aren't we a quorum? I mean, we could vote to change the rules. I'm so fruity! I could use . . . *you* know.'

'Just this once, perhaps,' Shannon murmured.

'You shouldn't have served oysters and asparagus, Shannon,' said Deb. 'They get a girl horny.'

The final canestroke descended on Giselle's bottom.

'Please, *madame*, let *me* be tupped,' the maid pleaded, once released. 'I am so wet in my *chatte*.'

'Tupped, *moi*?' said Derek, and everybody laughed.

It was agreed by unanimous vote – after Matthew had threatened the reluctant Prue with a strapping at home – that any girl who wanted tupping might accommodate any male member. They looked nervously at each other, aware they had crossed some kind of Rubicon.

'Well, let's get on with it,' said Mitch.

What followed extended the bounds of a typical scene, and the Commoners' rule book. It was, let us not be coy, an orgy. Bodies writhed, rubbed, penetrated, interchangeably. This was the Scene at its best, Mitch thought, flesh and friendship, unpossessive, sharing. Fucking, no more or less than a handshake. Giselle proved the most lustfully inventive. '*Ooh là là*,' said Derek several times, watching her. Those French! Mitch reminded him that he was half-French, and one of his ancestors was a drinking mate of de Sade (he made that up).

15

Several women ostentatiously smoked, cigarettes dangling from slack lips as they were pleasured: a symbol of their detachment from the event. Giselle did without a smoke as her lips were occupied. Shannon and Mitch watched each other, complicit in their sport.

'It's all good,' she panted. 'Pity men can't have their brown wings, without being gay.'

'There are strap-ons for girls to use,' said Greg.

'Yuk!' said Mitch. 'Not on me.'

'Don't knock it till you've tried it.'

He felt like a zoologist, watching an experiment with rabbits or rats. His panting wife was no longer a household chattel but a ravenous sexual animal. But this was a scene, not real life. It was like lending a friend the keys to a new sports car for a spin round the block; the friend had to give back the keys. Just like in *Chance* magazine. It was theatre. No names, no packdrill. They continued, all drinking heavily of the champagne, until, at last, the sated Commoners resumed their conventional clothing and, with much backslapping and air-kissing, said goodbye until the next scene. They were back to normal, to humdrum London, where such things didn't happen outside the Sunday papers. Each felt the next scene would be different again, a new world of depraved adventure glimmering on the horizon.

'I thought that went quite well, considering,' said Shannon, for a hostess must not boast: her success must always be *considering*. 'It's nice to have friends. I had some lovely fucks.'

'So did I, right?'

Alone with his wife, he resumed the estuary English he adopted in deference to her proletarian – if lavishly moneyed – origins, and which he sometimes dropped, reverting to his upper-middle lilt when playing a master's role, or reminding her he had married rather beneath him.

'You really got off on Prue's corset. Do you think I should wear one? It would make my bum stand out.'

'That would be super, but you don't need one,' Mitch said, pinching her waist. 'Your waist's perfect. So is your bum.'

He knelt and placed the tip of his tongue deep in her bottom cleft, letting it rest there. She shivered.

'Flatterer,' she murmured.

Late pink sunlight outside. Amanda Wantrill was in her kitchen in Norbiton making a lamb casserole, and wearing only her butcher's apron, when her husband Derek returned home and startled her. He placed two fingers in her bottom cleft and applied gentle upwards pressure.

'Derek! You frightened me,' she cried.

'May I not goose my lovely wife?' he murmured.

'I wasn't expecting you back so soon,' she said, blushing. 'I suppose you're feeling fruity after visiting those appalling Barnetts.'

'It's not what you imagine, darling,' he purred. 'I do wish you'd come along one day. Just an agreeable luncheon with old friends.'

'*I'll* bet,' she snorted. 'There are girls there, aren't there, who want spanking? I'll never understand. What do you see in it? You, a man on his own, doesn't that make you some sort of voyeur? Or do you join in? I suppose you must. Then you come home all randy, like some horrible wanker. It's disgusting.'

'Love invites death,' purred Derek. 'Spanking is a way to cheat it. It's healthy fun. You should let me . . .'

His fingers were still between her buttocks, kneading her anus bud.

'Oh, don't! That tickles.'

'Don't you play spanking games with Tara Lee and your other lesbo girls?'

'Certainly not,' retorted his wife. 'And don't talk like that, or I'll bloody spank *you*. You knew about my friendships when we married. We agreed . . .'

'Of course. It's just that I'd love to . . .'

'No, you can't watch. And no threesomes, you horrible pervert.'

Derek stroked her naked bottom, sniffed the cookpot, and licked his lips.

'Mm,' he said. 'My favourite. Don't forget the oregano.'

'I never forget the oregano,' Amanda said. 'I got some more, it was on special offer at Waitrose, buy two, get one free. And I got some haricots and *confit de canard* for a proper cassoulet I'll make tomorrow. The lamb was reduced too. But it won't be ready for a while.'

'My clever, wonderful girl,' he purred, goosing her again.

'Hmph! I suppose you think flattery will . . .'

He silenced her with a kiss. She unfastened her butcher's apron, and let it drop to the floor.

In Wimbledon, Shannon said coyly, as she cleared away the luncheon things: 'So glad the sex part went well. You didn't mind me . . .?'

Mitch shook his head.

'Oh, good. I didn't mind you and Wendy. Or Prue, with that gorgeous corset you were drooling over. I must have one. Even if it hurts.'

'We'll be in *Chance* mag at this rate,' he said.

'It's the *Scene*. How can people be happy any other way? I'll put the kettle on.'

'You know, I've often dreamt of being a high-class call girl,' she declared over tea and cress sandwiches. 'Most girls do, to enjoy power over men, just as they secretly crave spanking. We walk that delicious tightrope between power and submission.'

'Well, you can forget Wendy's nonsense. Girls spanking guys! For wimps. No girl thrashes *me*.'

Shannon smiled her inscrutable smile, and licked her lips.

'Then there's no need to get worked up about it.'

After tea, he gunned his black BMW through the late afternoon sunlight to his boutique in Wimbledon village. He was the sole owner of Strips, a chain of women's boutiques spread across south London, with shops in high-end places like Richmond and Blackheath. Shannon had her own inherited money, not discussed, but Strips was all his, and of his making. They specialised in outré girlwear and accessories, especially stockings, corsets, basques, and ever skimpier grades of cache-sexe (bikini, thong, string or thread), in nylon, silk, satin and latex. The upmarket locations reassured women that Strips was respectable, not like some sleazy place in Soho or the East End. He scanned the hardcore fetish press for ideas, considering his merchandise one step short of the Scene; he was proud of his own invention, a line of fruit-scented thongs and bikini panties with peach, banana and strawberry being the most popular. A parallel line, in edible wax, also sold well, especially as Christmas stocking-fillers, although they tended to melt in hot weather. Shannon sometimes wore them, and he would eat her discarded panties.

He parked and went into the airy whiteness of the shop, sniffing, as always, the delicious scent of female clothing, even unworn. Jacqui the manageress greeted him with cautious deference, for the high-rent Wimbledon shop barely made a profit. However, he liked to have a shop nearby, to exert his authority whenever he felt edgy or perplexed, as he did now. Their scene may have ended with the usual hugs and air-kisses, but Shannon's private smile disturbed him. The Scene required an open mind, and there was an exhibitionist thrill in publicly possessing your wife, but what was it about watching her service their friends that disturbed him?

He professed to have a modern marriage. A male could not be content with the same ageing female for the rest of his life, of course, but surely it wasn't the same for women? Indeed, was there any such thing as 'modern' marriage? Shannon didn't want children, which would spoil the romance, and neither did he, for gloomier, unspoken reasons: he saw no point in prolonging the human species. His fecund half-sister in Doncaster could do that. Promiscuity was pure pleasure, or irresistible need, and perhaps old-fashioned furtiveness kept things tranquil. He was certainly practised.

3

Zelda

He had never told his whole truth to Shannon, just as he respected her secrets. His bookish, rather academic father had kept a grocery market at the cheap end of Merton High Street, a long way down the hill from plush Wimbledon or their comfortable family home in Putney. It was a big successful shop, one of the few proper groceries surviving in Tesco-bloated Britain, selling organic fruit and vegetables, for which the Volvo-propelled middle classes would pay through their trendy noses. From his dad he had learned about stock control, accounts payable, personnel management, display techniques and the other intricacies of shopkeeping.

His half-sister, from his dad's previous marriage, lived with her brood in Doncaster, and he had cordial relations with his sibling, seeing her once or twice a year, despite feeling a little unnerved by her championing of everything northern and fertile against 'cockney wankers' like Mitch. His late mother was French, an ebullient handsome lady from the port area of Calais, quite the opposite of his dad, which was perhaps why they attracted each other. They had met in her family's café-restaurant, the very last before the docks, where Dad used to stop before boarding the Dover ferry, after his trips to the market in Calais or St-Omer. Where Dad spoke of organic farming and renewable resources, she called it all *ratatouille*.

He always enjoyed the childhood trips to France: the smell of fresh coffee and bread and wine, even in the damp beer-drinking north; the bustle of the café; the smell of French tobacco, and the bright summer dresses of the girls, sleek and fashionable in skin-tight undies, even though Calais was a smokestack town, with docks and communists, not like the smug English south. His female relations cooed that he was so good looking, *comme une jeune fille*, with a hint of the Midi. There were dark hints of Provençal ancestry, some ancestor fleeing a scandal of debauchery – more being unmentionable – to marry into the blue-eyed Celtic north. His mother made sure he could speak French and, though proud of being a Londoner, he was aware of being *other*.

Raised alone, a spoiled child, he was occasionally beaten by his mother for some misdemeanour. She would beat him with a heavy vegetable, out of Dad's sight, if not earshot. Through him, was she really spanking Dad? Pants down for a whopping with one of his damn cucumbers. It was silly, but supposed to be silly. His mother giggled; it was all a *plaisanterie*. She was making fun of the vegetables, her rivals in Dad's affection, as much as of him. The fake beatings hurt a bit, but also shamed; he was determined no one would ever tease him like that. If only she and Dad (who had passed on, with thankful suddenness, not long after his wife) were alive to see what a success he was at twenty-eight, having taken the commercial path in defiance of his university education, a bit of a lad. He was sorry at disappointing his dad, who wanted him to be a civil servant, but there was no security in that nowadays. And a fucking *arts* degree!

He had fallen in love for the first and only time, in the family café, with his mischievous beautiful blonde cousin, Sylvie Delatour. She was svelte, lithe: Sylvie the sylph. He was sixteen, she a few years older and, he guessed, experienced. She loved him too, she said but, though unconsummated, their love was not platonic: they French-kissed, and he could feel her breasts and buttocks through her clothes, but not her sex. Walks along the seafront, under grey skies and cawing seagulls. She chided him that he was not *sérieux*, not in love with her, but with the seaside. How on Earth, he retorted, could anyone be in love with Calais? Yet perhaps he was. He begged for one of the bright ribbons she always wore in her hair, and she gave him a pink one, knowing he would worship it. That summer, their intimacy grown, they would bathe at a distant beach, Sylvie in a microscopic bikini.

After swimming in the cold grey Channel – he furiously erect – she would stretch out her legs, keeping her distance, and, sweetly laughing, rub his groin with her toes until in seconds he ejaculated in his trunks as he breathed her scent mingled with sea and sand. Girl smell and sea air still wafted him to a thousand paradises, a thousand memories: the ocean, a woman. *Et voilà!* she would exclaim, a chore done. His orgasmic vision was her wiggling bare toes and the swelling hillock beneath her bikini; he wanted to be those panties, to taste her *chatte*. She let him kiss her bare toes, in adoring gratitude, after the caress, but would let him go no further. Sleepless, not eating, he feared she treated him as a plaything. He wrote her love letters in French, and masturbated overmuch in a vain quest for relief.

Once, his mother beat him with a marrow after she surprised him masturbating into a pair of Sylvie's stolen panties which she imagined were his half-sister's (another of his peccadilloes). He had Sylvie's pink ribbon knotted around his balls. Another *plaisanterie*; she did not take his passion seriously. Cyrano de Bergerac never got whopped with a bloody marrow! After a while, Sylvie, or the family, decreed he was too young, and an affair between cousins undesirable. A few months later, she married a ferry officer. Was she a tease? Perhaps she sensed his romantic rapture did not contain the soul of a breeder. He still thought fondly and sometimes dreamed of her, but vowed never to repeat the painful experience of love. Marriage was a convenience, based on good manners; an eighteenth-century noble sent his calling card to his wife if he wanted a tumble. When he lost his virginity, on his travels, to a whore in Nice, it was an anti-climax. *Et voilà.* That's that, then.

Sometimes Dad took him on a purchasing trip in the small hours to some organic fruit and vegetable supplier out in Surrey where he would prod and caress marrows, lettuces, apples or plums with a lascivious smile. He said he preferred plants to people, and now Mitch wondered if he didn't, too: beating a girl's bare buttocks was like lashing into a succulent melon, peach or tomato. He remembered the absurd slapping of fruits and veg on his own backside, which perhaps explained his love of beating girls: not a desire for revenge, but resentment that he had never been *properly* thrashed.

Entering Strips did not soften his edginess. He felt he had in some way lost authority in the Scene gathering. Damn that Greg with his carefree voyeurism as his girl was pleasured, and hints of wilder debauchery in exotic lands! Smart in slacks, blazer and open-necked designer shirt, Mitch avoided eye contact with the fragrant young ladies who thronged the shop. You never knew if they would be embarrassed, seen feeling a pair of split-crotch panties, or the latest minuscule string or thread, although Jacqui and the new assistant, Zelda, like all his staff, wore the latest creations. They were demure enough not to shock the customers, but had a hint of naughtiness, and always the proper apparatus of high heels, nylons and suspenders. He longed to caress the displayed shiny fabrics which would soon grace female skin. Zelda flitted among changing rooms, talking volubly, and Jacqui said she was pleased with the girl though, at nineteen, she was still a bit 'bubbly'.

He examined the itemised sales roll from the cash machine, to see what lines were moving. All the sales had Zelda's code number, and a glance told him something didn't quite add up: a cash shortfall. He asked Jacqui to take over the sales duties while he had a word with Zelda in the back office. The blonde girl widened her eyes and paled a little, with a pleasing tremble of her jutting breasts, neatly encased in a skimpy scalloped bra in peach satin under a translucent matching blouse *en décolletage*. She turned, and he followed her to the office, ogling the ripe swell of her bottom wiggling in her too-tight white skirtlet over peach stockings in shiny glassine nylon. Her long blonde tresses, ironed flat, shimmered down her back, reminding him of a younger Shannon, and her cheeky snub nose made her superbly elfin.

She sat on the sofa facing his desk, smoothing her skirtlet after it had ridden up to afford a glimpse of suspenders, stockings and panties. Her thread, worn over the garter straps, scarcely covered her hillock, which looked shaven smooth. Her stocking tops were an inviting pattern of flowers and fronds, like antique Calais lace. Seated imperiously behind his desk, in the heat of the office, he felt himself stir, and he knew that despite his prowess at the scene, it had failed to satisfy him. *Women, like Chinese meals. An hour later, you want another. Maybe every woman is an appetiser for the ideal one.*

He opened the sales roll, but his eyes were on Zelda's breasts, shivering, and beaded with sweat. Sunbeams slanted through the open window, striking her smooth skin, and making the dewdrops of moisture sparkle. Like most males, he could not resist a blonde. It was all in the genes. Blonde hair darkened with age, so that back in caveman days, choosing a blonde mate guaranteed she was truly youthful. *What if the ideal female is herself an appetiser for some platonic form?* An idea, an impulse, gripped him. Corny, but life was corny. He might get away with it.

'There's nothing wrong, I hope, sir?'

He replied with a sharp intake of breath, through pursed lips (yes, corny!), and a shake of the head.

'I hope not, Zelda,' he said at last.

He opened his gold cigarette case, and offered her a Gauloise Blonde.

'Oh – I don't often – well, yes.'

With nervous fingers she took one, and allowed him to light her with his gold Dunhill. As he did so, his knuckles brushed her bare breast skin. She inhaled nervously while he leaned back in his chair and toyed, puffing, with his cigarette. He explained the discrepancy in her sales amounts.

'An unkind boss would think you were pilfering from the till,' he said.

'Not me!' she gasped.

'I hope it's simple carelessness.'

She drew hungrily on her cigarette.

'It must be,' she said. 'I don't think I've got the hang of that computer till yet. I would never, *ever* ... you know. The right money must be there somewhere.'

'Maybe you rang up a no-sale by accident, Zelda. Let's assume that, for I can't imagine you would do anything wrong. Pure in body, pure in heart.'

She blushed, and his pulse quickened: his own little scene! You *could* do it. Master and erring maid. Life imitated art. You had to dare to be outrageous.

'You have an enchanting name, by the way.'

'Thank you. Mummy loved the novels of Scott Fitzgerald, so she called me after his wife. If I was a boy, I'd have been Scott. But ... I'm not a boy.'

'No, you are very much a girl. And a careless one.'

'You're not going to fire me, sir?' she stammered, brushing a hair from her forehead.

He looked at the elfin blonde trembling before him and his penis hardened fully. Fabulous! The primaeval hunter, licking his lips over his quivering prey. He sucked on his cigarette, and stubbed it out; Zelda did the same.

'No, I'm not.'

'I'll pay back the money from my wages.'

'Not that either,' he replied. 'It would only make you sullen. You can pay it back with a really hard sales effort – sell a few more frocks or knickers, and you're clear. But you must *feel* clear.'

'Yes, I see,' she said, not seeing.

He lit another Gauloise – she demurred – and sucked deeply.

'Don't be shocked when I say this.'

'I'll try.'

'You should have a spanking. It's what careless girls get. Plenty of people do it, especially married couples. It's not kinky. It clears the air. Penance without blame.'

'You mean' – eyes wide – 'you'd spank my bottom? Sounds a bit kinky. I'm not shocked, but ... well, I'm a big girl.'

'No girl's too big for a spanking,' he said. 'Not even Mrs Barnett. No funny business, just a little discomfort.'

'I *know* what it feels like. My dad was a detective inspector, you know, zero tolerance. We're all prisoners of our past, aren't we? But I'd hate to lose this job. I love the clothes so much. It's like ... like my fantasy world, for real. If I agree to it, I can go back to work, and not worry?'

'Scout's honour.'

'Okay, then,' she pouted.

'Good,' he said, inhaling smoke; he had never been a boy scout. 'Just bend over my knee, I think, with your bottom up, and your legs apart. We'll get it over with quickly.'

It worked! Gingerly, Zelda obeyed, draping herself on his thigh, and flattening her breasts on the sofa, with her bottom up. He told her she must raise her skirtlet and lower her panties. She looked alarmed.

'A proper spanking is on the bare,' he said. 'If you've been spanked before, you should know.'

'Yes, always bare,' she sighed, 'and it hurt like hell. But surely I can keep my thread – I'm almost bare already.'

'No, lower it to your knees. True spanking is the *idea*, the embarrassment.'

'Or,' she said cheekily, 'you just like watching a girl strip. Your power, as she peels off. That's why men are fascinated by undies, they want to peel off that second skin. I think they really want to peel off her *first* skin.'

Who's in charge here?

Frowning, she rolled up her tiny skirtlet and impishly twanged her panties before rolling them down her stock-inged thighs, to reveal her bottom and an untrimmed pubic fur.

'You don't mind me being so hairy?' she said nervously. 'The customers can't see.'

'Of course not! It's quite a novelty. Ready?'

'Ready, sir.'

He liked her 'sir'. Smack! His open palm landed in full centre of her croup, leaving a pink imprint. She gasped and her bottom clenched slightly, but she did not protest. As the slaps continued, ever harder, and her buttocks reddened, she began to squirm, her bare sex rubbing his thigh. Her breath was hoarse and she swallowed, gulping air, after each smack.

'Oh!' she panted. 'You do it much harder.'

'Harder than what?' he demanded.

Smack!

'Oof! That hurts,' she gasped.

'Sorry, but you've earned it.'

'Yes, I have. It's silly really. I spent last year backpacking around Asia and Australia, and I ended up in Thailand with an Aussie boyfriend. The beery oaf! Well, I didn't know any better, and I really fancied him at first. We stayed on this island, Ko Lanta, on the beach, a colony of girls and guys, like in that weird movie, you know? There were some Thai men there, they drink too much whisky and treat their women like dogs. They are pretty, no body hair, almost girlish, and a few of them were wannabe girls, they call them ladymen. *Katoeys* in Thai. Some Europeans, boys or girls, used to sleep with ladymen. I don't know what they did together, but I can imagine. Yuk.'

She shivered; he continued to smack, each time she paused for breath.

'I thought it would be real freedom, but the girls were forced to be servants – slaves, really – and if they were lazy it was bikinis off for a public spanking by their boyfriend, or even someone else's boyfriend. It all got a bit too kinky, so eventually I left, with a very sore bum. Ahh! Please, not so hard.'

'It's supposed to hurt, you know.'

Her crimson bottom wriggled charmingly as he spanked her from top to haunches, his arm holding her shoulders down. Her chatte slithered on his thigh. Smack!

'Ooh! Surely that's enough,' she whimpered.

He asked if her beatings in Thailand had excited her.

'That's unfair. A girl can't help being excited by . . . you know . . . on the bare.'

'And now? You've taken forty spanks.'

He smacked her outer haunch, her recoil slamming her hip against his erection.

'Ah! Can't you tell? And *you're* excited. I felt it.'

He gazed at her puffy bare buttocks.

'You're nice and red, so you've had enough,' he panted hoarsely, and released her. Stiffly, she rose, rubbing her bottom.

'Thank you,' she said. 'Is there a mirror?'

'No. But I imagine you'll still be glowing when you get home.'

She kicked off her panties, coyly saying it would be too sore to wear them.

'I'm sorry for hurting you, Zelda,' he said. 'But we're quits now.'

'Are we?'

His erection was stiff to the point of discomfort. He felt helpless. Suddenly, she hugged him, and plunged her face in his hair to sniff it.

'Mm . . .' she gasped. '*Hom* . . . you smell nice, like a real man. Why the hell do we like brutes?'

She said that in Thailand people did not kiss, but if you wanted to give a compliment, you smelled someone's hair and said '*hom*'. He embraced her, stroking and squeezing her breasts, while burying his face in her mane. Adrift in the precious aroma of her spanking.

'*Hom*,' he murmured, stroking her bottom.

'Oh! Don't,' she whispered. 'I want it so. *You* know. But we mustn't. If I deserve spanking, okay, but anything else . . . oh, it's so dangerous. You're too sweet . . . *sir*.'

4

Nampoong

That evening, and every night for a week, he made love to Shannon, her bottom sheathed in a split-crotch nylon thong from Strips, with a wad of cotton wool soaked in zinc ointment pressed to her weals. The thong made a sticky noise if peeled off, and she left it on for convenience. It thrilled him to tup a woman actually wearing her panties, a wonderfully furtive and sleazy invasion of her privacy; as a prelude to coupling, he breathed the perfume of her hair, then went to her crotch, to sniff and kiss.

'You can't get enough, can you?' she gasped, giggling.

'Don't say you don't like it.'

'I do like it. I can never get over your control of that damn todger. But I wouldn't be surprised if you're seeing some bloody girl. You never used to smell my hair. And you're so ... *vigorous* ... as if you're atoning for something.'

'If I were, which I'm not,' he lied, 'it would never affect *us.* What's a zipless fuck? Office party stuff. And I don't have an office to have a party in.'

'If it were *only* a zipless fuck.'

'You know I don't cheat.'

She put her hand over his lips.

'Sauce for the goose, sauce for the gander,' she murmured dolefully. 'I knew I married a sex maniac. Men are always on a quest, aren't they? Looking for the ultimate, without knowing what it is. Women *know* what they want.'

Well, he wasn't exactly seeing another woman. He avoided Strips in Wimbledon Village, scared of enthralment by the bewitching innocence of Zelda. Instead, most afternoons, he drove down the hill to Merton where he frequented Valentino's sauna and massage parlour, sandwiched between a chip shop (also Valentino's) and a bookie's. Relief massage was just that, for you didn't need to impress, or chat up. The smell of steam and fragrance, elegantly Italian, put him at ease, as did the greeting of Signora Valentino, a lady of a certain age whose twinkling eye hinted at still-bubbling passions. He had never seen Signor Valentino, but she hinted he was big in finance in Milan and Zürich, and indulged her profitable hobby of the massage parlour. Mitch imagined he really commanded the sizzling vats of chips and haddock next door. If he was real.

Shannon's words, and her newly secretive air, puzzled him. The sweltering sauna, and the massage afterwards by the dyed-blonde Trudi, dissolved care. She knew him, and how to turn him on, for he tipped well, and as she pummelled him she would do a coy striptease, until she wore only black suspenders and stockings, bra and panties: corny, but effective. She invited him to unhook and remove her bra before his 'special massage'. She lived somewhere with her parents, who thought she was a shop assistant – 'If they knew what I really do, they'd skin me alive.' Eyes closed, and flat on his back, he dreamed of Zelda's blonde hair and squirming bottom as Trudi's deft fingers rubbed his penis, then sandwiched it between her breasts for his ejaculation. It was clinical, efficient: 'That's you done for today!' she would say.

He spent most of each morning driving among his various shops. Business was not so good; there were rumours that Girl Kit, the discount store, almost as risqué as Strips, was planning to invade his territory by opening branches south of the river. They could afford a price war, and he could not. So, even after Shannon's voracious draining every night, he still craved the relaxation of the sauna, and Trudi's thoughtful unhurried fingers.

One afternoon he found her absent, replaced by a brown Asian girl in a silk sarong artfully draped to suggest that

30

her slim body, with ripe breasts and buttocks, and long sleek thighs, partly uncovered, was nude underneath. Over bare dainty feet she wore jewelled sandals in gold and pink with sparkling stones, and the nails of her fingers and toes were painted gold. Her face and nose were long and slender, the big oval eyes brown and heavily lashed; her lips parted in a smile, half welcoming and half menacing, which raised her high cheekbones and revealed perfect white teeth, unlike Trudi's, which were stained by nicotine.

As the Asian girl scanned him with her big eyes, he felt guilty that his own teeth were stained too. Her long hair was a glossy raven black, and swayed at her bottom cleft, as if to tickle her peach, moulded by the clinging sarong. Her breasts were laden with gold neckchains, nestling in their deep fold; her nipples hard berries, almost bared. She could have been no older than Zelda; twenty at most. The other masseuses, sitting listlessly with magazines and make-up, smiled at him without offering their services. He established from the Asian girl that Trudi was on holiday, as was Signora Valentino, whom she was replacing as cashier. Down Merton High Street was a Thai restaurant, its dinginess in contrast to the upmarket cars parked outside, and he supposed this girl worked there but, when he asked, she sneered.

'I am not a waitress or service girl.'

'Well, do you do massage?'

'I am the cashier.'

The girl spoke confident English in a sing-song slightly American accent. She leaned forward at her desk, resting her breasts on the counter and – unconsciously or on purpose – letting the sarong fall slightly away so that he could see her big brown nipples. She yawned, then smiled, fluttering her eyelashes, a perfect mixture of brass and beguiling innocence, and said that one of the other girls could be cashier for a while if he really wanted a massage from her. She only gave special Thai massages.

'How much you pay Trudi for special massage?' she barked.

He told her, and she smiled.

'Thai massage is more expensive.'

'How much?'

She shrugged.

'Up to you,' she said, teeth glinting and her eyes mockingly wide. 'You like massage, you give tip.'

The other girls looked envious as he followed the Asian girl to the back of the salon where the sauna, plunge pool and massage rooms were. She handed him a rubber wristband with the key to his locker; towels, slippers, a bathrobe and a little brass bell, then inclined slightly in a bow, with her hands clasped in front of her face, before disappearing, telling him to ring the bell when he was ready for his massage. There were no other customers. He undressed and took his time showering, already stiff at the thought of her body. A plunge into the icy pool reduced his erection, but he was still tumescent when he entered the sauna and threw water on the stove to produce a sizzle of steam and rushing heat. When his body was dripping with sweat, he rang the bell. Promptly, the door opened and his masseuse slipped in, to sit opposite him. Her hair was pinned up with a red ribbon and she wore only a red towel, demurely knotted around her breasts. She bore a sheaf of birch twigs, which she waved at him.

'It's for your circulation and heart,' she said. 'A proper sauna.'

She looked straight at his half-stiff penis with a quizzical smile that returned it to full hardness. He had always prided himself on his control, willing it to or from erection. But in the presence of the Thai girl, it obeyed its own commands, or her unspoken ones. She pouted, looked away, and threw a whole bucketful of water on the stove. He gasped as the heat washed over him. She smiled, seeing that his erection did not wilt.

'You do need special Thai massage,' she purred, her own body now lathered in sweat. 'In Thailand, it is hot all the time. Men get excited by heat.'

They sat in silence and sweat – soaking him, but on her, a mere dew – until he asked her name.

'Nampoong,' she said. 'It means "honey". "Poong" is a bee. Sometimes I am just called "Poong" because I sting.'

She bared her teeth and laughed.

'It's a charming name.'

'Thank you,' she said coyly.

'You sound American.'

'I was schooled in Surin by the Sisters of Mercy, from California. Surin is near Kampuchea, which you call Cambodia, and Khmer is my first language. I do not have the round face of the Thai rice-pickers. We Khmers are descended from princes. But that is in the past, and I do not like to speak of the past. Now I must birch you. Please bend forward.'

'It won't really hurt, will it?' he said. 'I don't usually . . .'

'Up to you,' Nampoong said.

He obeyed, as she flexed the birch twigs, with a loofah sponge in her other hand. She raised the twigs and began to whip his back, quite gently, and sliding the birch across his skin in a slithery motion after the first sharp crack of wood on skin, and following each stroke by a slopping wipe from the loofah.

'Hurt?' she said.

'No, it tickles,' he murmured untruthfully.

The birch made a crackling sound as Nampoong lashed his bare skin, harder and harder with each swish.

'Good?' she said after several strokes.

'Yes,' he gasped. 'It doesn't hurt much. It feels nice and tingly.'

She made him turn over and lie on his belly, and began to beat him on the legs and buttocks. She lingered mostly on the buttocks, and he groaned as her strokes became much harder.

'Steady on,' he gasped as the birch lashed his buttocks quite severely. 'Anyone would think you were thrashing me.'

'Well, am I?' she panted. 'It's all in the mind.'

Swish! The birch crackled on the top of his buttocks, and he cried out.

'Ow! That hurt!'

'Honeybees sting.'

Swish!

'Oof! You're vicious.'

She giggled, and told him to lie on his back. He did so, the pole of his erection swaying beneath her gaze, and she said he seemed stiffer than ever; perhaps he liked having his bottom birched.

'No way,' he said, his arse smarting quite painfully.

She recommenced her swishes, on his chest, belly and upper thighs, the strokes no more than a gentle caress. When he crudely tugged at her towel, urging her to take it off, she flinched and snapped that Thai girls were brought up to be modest. 'You pay for massage, not pussy.' She let the birch twigs rest between his legs, as if by accident and, licking her teeth, briefly caressed his balls with the tips. He said he was sorry, then wondered why. She finished swishing him, and threw another bucket of water on the stove. When he gasped that he was frying, she took his hand and led him outside to the plunge pool. Her own breasts and shoulders were delicately beaded with glistening pearls of sweat.

He dived in and the Thai girl demurely slipped into the water, swimming around him in a breast stroke, but miraculously keeping her towel on. When they emerged, the wet towel clung to her body, showing her breasts, nipples stiff from the cold water, and the outline of her swelling pubic mound. To his own surprise, he looked bashfully away. They took a hot shower together – Nampoong still wrapped in her towel – and she soaped him all over, his penis joyfully, shamelessly standing. Then she led him to a massage cubicle with a steel-framed padded table that was much stronger than the usual couch. She ordered him to lie down on his back on the table, draped in an absorbent paper sheet.

She turned away from him, and he watched the towel slip from her shoulders, baring her back; then her firm young buttocks, and the coltish brown legs, gleaming smooth. Her whole body was immaculately hairless and, having consigned their towels to a laundry basket, she

34

turned again to face him, her breasts, flat belly and shaven hillock a uniform brown, with pink glistening within her chatte.

'We are alone,' she said, 'and there is no one to disturb us, so I work in comfort.'

She selected a bottle from the table and poured an aromatic gel into her palm. She began to slap the gel all over herself, even deep into her buttock cleft, until her body glistened with the fragrant unguent. The bottle's gaudy label was in a strange script, with the image of an old witch-like woman leering. From a second bottle she anointed Mitch's body, her fingers not caressing him but brisk and businesslike, like a nurse's, even when she oiled his penis, carefully, for the fragrance of her moist body, the sway of her breasts so near his face, had him rigid. She said that her unguent was *yang*, or female, and his was *yin*, the male. Together they made harmony. When his front was done, she made him lie face down and slopped scented gel all over him, her fingers lingering, firm and nimble, at his scrotum, and delving into his cleft to smear his anus pucker. He told her nervously that it tickled.

She leapt on to the massage table and he felt her feet on the small of his back. She proceeded to march up his spine, stamping and kicking, while he gasped at the pain. She grasped his ankles and twisted his legs back, wrenching his thighs, until his feet nearly touched his shoulder blades; pulled his toes almost from their sockets; knelt on him, as she pummelled his shoulders. Thighs apart, she straddled the small of his back, her buttocks pressing heavily against his kidneys, her moist crevice against his spine; he felt her legs tense at each thump of her fist.

'Oh, that's good,' he panted redundantly.

The massage continued until he ached and glowed. Turning him to face her, Nampoong stretched her nude body on top of his, and pressed heavily on him. She grasped his wrists with her fingers, and his ankles with her toes, until they made the shape of a starfish. Then she began to wriggle, sliding up and down his belly, with her

35

oiled breasts and vulva rubbing him hard, to perform a slippery massage.

'Yes . . .' he gasped. 'That's *so* good . . .'

'I know,' she replied. 'It is special Thai massage.'

She slid down his body, rubbing her nipples on his, then stroking his belly with her breasts. She rose, her legs folded, toes rubbing his thighs, and he felt her toe in his arse cleft, poking his anus, which made him wriggle at her tickling. The toes of her other foot began to stroke his balls. At last she straddled him, to press his penis between her soft fleshy breast-pillows and rock gently up and down, hugging his stiffness. She pulled back his prepuce, brought her nipples to caress his glans, and he said she would make him come. Just when his gasps signalled ecstasy, she withdrew, bringing him again and again to the brink of climax, until he begged for relief. The massage seemed to have lasted hours, as Nampoong tantalised him. Suddenly, she squeezed her oily breasts firmly against his glans, rubbing hard, and he cried out as his sperm bathed her. She rubbed the ejaculate into her nipples, then put out her tongue and pressed a wet fingertip to it.

'You like special Thai massage?' she said.

'Yes . . . yes . . .'

Not bad for a titwank.

He lay, panting, while she showered and slipped into a fresh sarong. After his own shower, he fumbled in his wallet and held out crisp banknotes, twice what he gave Trudi, to the Thai masseuse. She did not take them but looked at the notes, then at him, in silence, with a stony face. He pressed more notes on her and with dainty fingers she accepted them, curtsying and bowing her head with her hands pressed together, clutching her tip.

'Thank you,' she said, with a flutter of her eyelashes, her big eyes pools of honey.

'Can I see you again?' he said suddenly. 'Not here, I mean. Dinner, drinks, then . . . whatever you like . . .'

'You mean you want bouncing?'

He grinned sheepishly.

'Up to you,' she pouted, turning from him.

5

Swinging *Londres*

Her cigarette pluming smoke, Shannon sat on the kingsize white tub, one foot in the steaming water scented from her bubble bath, and the other perched on the rim, spreading her thighs and sex as Mitch, kneeling, shaved her pubes. He used a cut-throat razor with a nacre handle, purchased in an antique shop in Thames Ditton; Shannon said she loved the thrill of danger as the blade slid across her hillock, scooping back the shaving lather. When she was shorn, she announced her news.

'I've decided to take a job,' she said, selecting a nail file and examining her toenails. 'I want something to do, and some fun money. Strips isn't doing as well as you pretend. Does "Girl Kit" ring a bell?'

'If you want a *job*, you can manage a shop.'

'No, you'd be my boss, and I couldn't have that. You might spank me if I was naughty.'

They laughed, and she kissed the tip of his nose before sliding into the suds. He dropped his bathrobe and followed her, crushing her body with his own. He gently slapped her wet bare buttocks.

'Ooh, you beast! Wet bum!'

Smack! Smack!

'Oh! Oh! Monster!'

They made love under the water, with the green froth spilling over the bathroom floor; a sea god, devouring his prey. She hugged him.

'No one could do me like you, darling,' she whispered. 'Most men have no idea what turns a girl on.'

Most men? Don't remind me. He asked what sort of job.

'Something respectable, with lots of lunches,' she drawled. 'Public relations. Or modelling. Like any girl, I've a taste for exhibitionism. Look at the photos in *Chance*. I've the bod for it' – she smiled smugly – 'and I might rocket to fashion stardom, sort of at the fetish end.'

Getting out of the bath, he lied that he had a dinner that evening with a lingerie distributor from Lausanne interested in marketing the Strips line, particularly threads, latex, nylon fine-mesh stockings and other exotica; he thought Swiss frillies a little too *embourgeoisées.*

'I suppose you'll take him to some sleazy club. Lap-dancing and so on.'

'Probably. You know these continentals, with their *sweengeeng Londres.*'

'Well, don't do anything I wouldn't do,' Shannon drawled, fingers poised above her mobile telephone; she required his absence before making her call.

Shannon was right: his fervent love-making was to conceal, or vainly exorcise, his bewitchment by the sultry Thai girl. Nampoong made him tense with desire, and in the restaurant that evening he could scarcely concentrate on his food with his penis stiff. It was wonderful, like being a horny teenager again. She sat demure, skimpy cocktail dress in black silk, balanced on her shoulders by the thinnest of spaghetti straps, and showing the proud swell of her braless breasts under her array of gold necklaces. She wore a bowtied black ribbon in her hair. Heads turned and she ignored them, faintly sneering, as she ate. Despite the languid movements of her fingers, and the stillness of her lips, the heaping plate of *spaghettini alle vongole* disappeared rapidly. Having doused her plate with an eye-watering quantity of pepper, she did not spit out the tiny clam shells but crunched and swallowed them.

It was an Italian restaurant in Fulham for discreet couples and braying foodies where he was known and interruptions were unlikely. *Reminds me of Aldo's marvel-*

lous little trattoria in Ventimiglia.. – Yah, so convenient for Chez Gilbert in Roquebrune. – Yah. Nampoong feasted, answering his questions with grunts or nods, as though afraid her food would disappear any moment.

'Eat first, talk later,' she said.

Only when her plates were cleaned, and he ate gorgonzola, washed down with a good Barolo, did she begin to talk.

'That is very smelly,' she said, wrinkling her nose. 'In my country, we like things to smell sweet.'

'But it's just the right creaminess. Do have some.'

'Thais cannot eat cheese. We have different stomachs.'

'And all that pepper?'

'That is good for the stomach, and with Italian food. I learned to like foreign noodles at the convent of the Sisters of Mercy, who were mostly Italian. But for bad table manners, they beat us without mercy! That's funny, isn't it? The strap, on the bottom, very shameful for a Thai girl, to show her underwear.'

She sipped her glass of San Pellegrino, then bit into a peach. Juice ran down her chin and she took a napkin to wipe herself, daintily pursuing the trickle of liquid between her breasts. She helped herself to one of his cigarettes, and conceded she had enjoyed her meal.

'But it will cost you a lot, and just to impress me. Foreigners always do that, buy us expensive meals and clothes when we just want money.'

'Do you always think of money?' he asked. 'In Europe, with a beautiful woman, we think about love.'

'We all think of what we haven't got,' she said, blowing smoke in his face.

He put his hand on hers, and stroked it. She accepted the caress without response, as her predictable due. He ordered coffee, while she wanted tequila. When her drink arrived, she ignored the paraphernalia of salt and lemon, but drank it in one gulp, and ordered another. She rewarded the handsome young waiter with a whore's come-on smile, and he felt a stab of jealousy.

'Tequila is what Thai girls drink,' she declared.

39

'Tell me more about yourself. Like, how did you come to be in London? I so want to hear your voice, Nampoong. You're special, you're different.'

She laughed.

'Every *farang* says that,' she replied. 'What he really means is, *I'm* different. It's called ego.'

'No – I didn't mean –'

'Farangs get so jealous, and weep, and make threats and promises, because their girl goes with other men while he is far away, sending her money. Or even when he is with her, but drunk and asleep. They do not understand that a Thai girl must work, and if she is not to break her back at rice-picking, she must tempt men to the honey between her legs.'

She lit another cigarette.

'Yet a girl is permitted to enjoy her work,' she said mischievously. 'The Buddha teaches us not to have an ego, that we are fishes swimming in the same sea, the waters eternally circling, and returning to their starting place. But fishes may have fun. Farangs think of love, without knowing what it is. If they had never heard the silly word, they would never invent it. I was married to a farang when I was a go-go girl, aged seventeen. I had to work as a dancer in Pattaya, to get money for my brothers and sisters on the farm. It is common for a farang to fall in love with a Thai girl half his age, especially a dancer who does tricks with her pussy, and lesbian shows, and things like that. A dancer is superior, because of her superb body, like mine.'

No trace of irony: a simple statement of fact.

'Farangs who live in Thailand a long time are not to be trusted, for they no longer believe in love, or think their girlfriend is different. They live for drink, and having short times, with a new girl every night. After a week, this man said he loved me, and we were married in the Buddhist temple. He got my visa, and brought me back to England, but there he expected me to be his slave while he was a butterfly, fucking other women. When he was drunk, he would beat me with his belt, like a Thai man, but sometimes gave me money to send to my brothers and sisters. We lived in Brighton where he owned video game and massage parlours, and he stopped giving money, and wanted me to work as a masseuse. I did so, and saved up my tips, and then he would beat me harder because I wouldn't hand over all my money. He said the beating was because I gave relief massage to customers – when that was the whole point of the massage parlour! So unfair!'

He agreed. Unfairness was not British.

'He had a black heart. One day, after I had serviced five customers and got handsome tips, he whipped me terribly. He wanted all my money for himself. I broke a beer bottle and smashed it into his face. I had to clean the blood off my shoes. I took all the money I could find, and my passport and papers, and got the train to London. I was at Victoria Station – so busy, like Bangkok! – not knowing what to do, when another man, very elegant, spoke to me in Thai. He took me to supper, then to bed, and gave me good money. I stayed with him for a few days, and then went to work for him as an escort girl. He had an escort agency where many of the girls were Asian, and we went out to dinner and shows and nightclubs with little old fat men who were very rich. I was the most popular, with the most repeat business, and the others were jealous. Sometimes we had bouncing with clients, but mostly they wanted a beautiful Asian girl, to show off – just as in Thailand. Many of them wanted us to cane them, which English men seem to like, and I liked it too, for I was getting revenge on men, and they tipped well. But some wanted to beat girls, and my employer said I would make more money if I took the cane on my bare bottom.

'I did that three or four times, but hated it for it was very painful, and made my bottom ugly, and those men always wanted to fuck my little hole. My heart was broken, and I wept every night! Also, I was worried that my husband would come after me, so I left and went to Valentino's, which I knew from a girl in Brighton, and Signora Valentino took me on as cashier. So you see, Mr Mitch, I am just a Thai girl like any other, another fish in the sea. I suppose you want to fuck me.'

'I . . . It's not like that.'

'Why not?'

'Of course I want to. But I want to get to know you. You're the most beautiful girl I've ever seen.'

'I'm *different*,' she sneered.

'Yes! Truly. I'd love you to dance for *me*.'

She smiled slyly.

'I haven't asked you about yourself, Mr Mitch. I assume you have money, and that is all I need to know. *No money, no honey*, we say. A man doesn't have to be different, just have money, and a good heart, and a powerful cock. I will cost you a lot.'

She slipped off a shoe and he felt her bare toes rubbing his penis under the table.

'Money's not a problem,' he gasped, his erection straining his trousers.

She snapped her fingers for another tequila, and swallowed it quickly.

'I think you have big power, Mr Mitch,' she said, impishly putting out her tongue as her toes tickled his balls. 'So where shall we go for bouncing?'

He took her to a friendly Hindu-owned motel he knew in Collier's Wood, and she greeted the desk clerk to another of her whore's smiles, gazing into his eyes, to Mitch's dismay, although he hoped she was teasing. In their bedroom – anonymous, like a million other motel rooms and, pointedly, with a large mirror facing the bed – his unease disappeared when he was faced with that slender colt-legged body under its clinging cocktail dress.

Her hair swayed over her breasts, and she did not resist his embrace, nor his plunging his nose to her scalp to smell the silky tresses. She put her arms around his neck and rubbed her nose against his, while grinding her crotch against his. *A fucking hooker, but I don't care.* Her tales of the countless men who had used her strangely excited him. His hands cupped her croup and found she wore no panties, her heavenly body covered by nothing more than the thin dress silk. He felt like a teenager on a first date. Did he dare . . .? He pushed up the dress and trembled as his palms felt her bare buttocks.

42

'Mm . . . that's nice,' she murmured.

He stroked the smooth peach, his fingers brushing her cleft, then penetrating deeper, to touch her anus bud.

'That tickles,' she cried, clenching her fesses to trap his fingers. 'Is that the part you like best?'

'I like all of you.'

'But my bottom – you're not feeling my breasts, like all the other men. I think you like my bottom best.'

He admitted he was an arse man, that his wife enjoyed a spanking. She pressed her face to his ear and nibbled his lobe, while his fingers crept to her chatte. It was moist. Biting his ear, she withdrew, saying she must shower. She disappeared into the bathroom and he stripped to join her, but found she had locked the door. Smelling steam and soap, as the shower hissed, he rapped with his knuckles, telling her to open up.

'No,' she said. 'I'm shy.'

'You weren't shy before.'

'That was work.'

He sat on the bed and lit a cigarette, angry at his still-rigid frustrated penis. He had consumed two cigarettes and a cold beer from the mini-bar by the time she came out of the shower, wrapped in a fluffy towel. She thrust a fresh folded towel at him.

'Now you,' she said. 'You're all sweaty, and smell of beer.'

She flicked his penis with the towel.

'Go and clean yourself,' she commanded, 'and use some perfume.'

'I'll smell like a girl.' *Like a whore's armpit.*

'Yes.'

Swirling in the shower steam, he imagined Nampoong in some fetid Asian brothel, on her back, thighs parted, to take one male after another, for grimy banknotes; then, her arse, squirming under the strap; anonymous males ramming her while he watched, a ghostly ectoplasmic presence. Her availability, opening her thighs to strangers, her . . . *whoredom* . . . was her mystery: a sordid wondrous thrill. Pink, steaming and erect, he emerged to find her sprawled

43

nude, beer bottle in hand and cigarette at lips, music playing in the background. She smiled at his erection.

'Sexy man!' she purred, the cigarette dangling from the corner of her mouth in perfect sluttishness. 'You want me to dance for you?'

She sprang on to the bed as he sat on it and began a slow sensuous gyration to the music, spreading her thighs, and alternating between back and rear view, always with her finger rubbing inside her chatte. She twisted herself into revealing yoga positions, all showing glistening pink: the crab, the archer, the hare. She was animal, a body of pure sex, intent on the display of her vulva, with a female's solipsism, absorbed in her own self. Finally, she balanced on her head, quivering thighs spread, with her sex gaping open.

Squatting, she demanded a coin, which she placed under her bottom. She lowered herself until her sex lips enclosed the coin, then sucked it into her pouch. She ordered him to open his mouth, and her belly heaved as her sex spat the wet coin into his mouth. He kissed her petals before handing her the coin in mock solemnity and saying 'your tip, miss'. She squealed with laughter. She sat facing him on his lap, clamped his erection between her undulating thighs, right at the lips of her chatte – *so near, yet so far* – and pushed a foot into his mouth.

'Shrimp me,' she commanded. 'You are experienced, and know how to shrimp, I expect.'

He obeyed, sucking her toes, as she continued her slow intercrural frottage, the soft skin of her thighs delicious as they rubbed his glans, with his balls and shaft touching her swollen sex petals. As he licked her toes, she would teasingly touch her clito.

'You're special, so special,' he gasped. 'You want it.'

She slithered off him, wrenched his hair, and ordered him to lie on his back, then straddled him, lowering her buttocks on to his face until she was squatting with her full weight on his mouth. She began to wriggle on his face, shifting up and down, so that his nose and lips were pressed in turn into her wet chatte, then into her anus.

44

Sweaty, smoky, damp meat, the perfume of a goddess. Her fingers masturbated her clito, sending a drip of moisture into his mouth as he drank from her.

'You naughty boy,' she murmured, and ordered him to raise his legs, then reached forward to spank him.

Her palm slapped hard and his arse clenched. Her bottom writhing on his face, she bent down and took his erection between her lips, sucking the glans, and sometimes swooping to take the shaft into her throat. He whimpered, his face crushed by the girl's scented brown buttocks. After a couple of minutes' spanking, she released him, removed her mouth from his groin, and slid up his belly. She spread her thighs and squatted over his penis, now glazed with her juices, then lowered her buttocks in a swoop, impaling herself. She fucked him hard, while masturbating vigorously before his gaping eyes. He looked not at her, but at their image in the mirror, as her tight wet chatte divinely squeezed his penis. Puppets, coupling. The mechanism of the thing: how do they do that?

'Make water inside me,' she panted.

He gasped as his seed flooded her womb, and her staccato cries of orgasm filled the air. He groped for a caress, a snuggle, but after their climaxes, she leapt off him and busied herself in the shower. When she emerged, she slipped on her dress, swigged beer, and lit a cigarette, then passed it to him before lighting one for herself. She put on her shoes.

'Aren't you going to stay the night?' he blurted.

She looked at her watch, and he realised that she had never taken it off.

'It's past four o'clock,' she said. 'You must go home to your wife.'

'I suppose so. Sometimes I wonder if it's only spanking that keeps our marriage alive,' he said.

'There are worse reasons to stay married,' she replied, handing him his wallet.

She waited while he peeled off banknotes, until her eyes lit up, and she nodded diffident thanks. He rubbed his smarting arse.

'You do sting like a bee,' he said.

'Next time, I'll bring my whip,' she purred, as she slipped out of the door and clicked it softly shut behind her.

6

Escorts

'An *escort agency*?' Mitch said, wrinkling his brow.

She was painting her toenails – *again* – sitting nude on a chaise longue, having just come in from the garden. Although she had showered, her fingernails were still muddy, which he had told her was rather sexy. In fact, why didn't she roll around in the mud, and come in dripping, he would love to fuck a muddy woman . . . She called him a perve.

'I mean, an escort just works for some pimp, as a . . .'

'A high-class hooker?' Shannon suggested.

Laughing, she tickled his chin.

'Apart from mud fantasies, you are so stuffy,' she purred. 'First, the money is good' – she mentioned her possible earnings, and he whistled – 'second, we need it' – Mitch nodded glumly – 'and third, it's not what you think. An escort girl with Chaperones is just that, a companion for some rich geezer, to dine with him, and go to the opera and so on, so that he can swank in front of the other business fatties. We work under a stage name, so I am the nice respectable Imogen Forbes. Fucking doesn't come into it.'

'Not at all? Pull the other one.'

'Well, maybe a bit, for some girls. You make your own deal, but *I* don't want to fuck some fat old guy. And *you* wouldn't want to do some Sloaney Imogen. Trust me, darling.'

'Seems I've no choice,' he said. 'Well' – kissing her – 'best of luck. When do you start?'

'This evening,' said Shannon. 'I've to meet my date at the Dorchester. We're going to dinner.'

'So it's a *date*, is it?'

'He picked me from my photo. We're all listed in the internet catalogue, together with a fake biography, like the models in skin mags. You know, "Imogen, show-jumping champion of Wiltshire", that sort of thing. Darling, you should be flattered. Of course, we get right of refusal, after seeing *his* photo. He's a short fat bald American millionaire, over seventy, complete with hairpiece and pacemaker. I doubt he'll have the strength to spoon his soup, let alone fuck. I don't know, I might possibly have to give him a wank. Like in a massage parlour, you know?'

'*Moi?*'

'Well, I'm sure you wouldn't mind.'

'Ugh. Cash in hand?' growled Mitch.

'Of *course*. Plus a tip.'

'So you won't be home for supper, then,' he said. 'That means I'll have to go out.'

'I can leave some things in the oven if you like, but – oh, go out. I know you will. You always go out when you want. Why shouldn't I, for a change?'

Her tone huffy, vaguely menacing. She switched to the toenails of her other foot, in the process parting her thighs to expose her quim, upon which a beam of sunlight slanted, making its lips glisten, and throwing into relief the curving hills and valleys of her nude body. He hardened. Grasping her waist, he pulled her to the floor, on to the Persian rug.

'Mitch!' she squealed. 'My toenails aren't dry.'

He made her squat, doggy fashion – Shannon desperately protecting her fresh nail varnish – and took her brutally in the vulva, from behind. She whimpered as her croup rose and fell to meet his thrusts.

'Oh . . . yes . . . it's so good . . .' she gasped. 'Harder . . . oh, you *beast*,' as he abruptly withdrew and pulled his studded leather belt from his slacks, then folded the thong in two.

He swished the air with the strap while holding Shannon by her hair.

48

'How dare you,' she panted. 'I forbid you to thrash me. This isn't a proper scene.'

Vap! The belt lashed her buttocks, which clenched tight as a thick pink weal blossomed on the smooth skin.

'Mitch, stop!' she wailed. 'Not the belt, not the studs! My bottom will be a terrible mess.'

'Your millionaire isn't going to see your damn bottom, though, is he?' he hissed.

He beat Shannon long and hard, not as a game. Shannon writhed and shivered, calling him names and sobbing as her skin, pocked with studmarks, turned crimson under the strap. Her bottom threshed helplessly, her thighs glistening with a seep of moisture from her sex.

'Don't tell me you don't love it,' he panted.

'Bastard!' she sobbed. 'You know I fucking do!'

He laid down the belt and grasped his wife's hips.

'Ahh!' she protested as he penetrated her anus; he grimaced, teeth bared, as his penis filled her rectum and he buggered her.

'Oh! Mitch, you're splitting me,' Shannon squealed.

'You love that too. Now wank off, *slut*, while I fuck your big bad arse.'

Shuddering, she obeyed, her fingers groping for her quim lips, and squelching between them to tweak her clito. Her whimpers turned to moans of joy.

'Ahh! It hurts,' she whimpered. 'Don't stop ... I'm almost there.'

He thrust harder until she panted in orgasm, and he released his sperm at her root. When he withdrew from her body, she groaned, rose, and staggered to the mirror, rubbing her bottom. She gasped, inspecting her skin which was peppered with welts.

'You *are* a bastard,' she murmured. 'That was fucking tight, and those fucking weals will last a long time.'

'It's what you like.'

'Yes, it is.'

It had been a fuck of despair, trying vainly to communicate, to possess a woman slipping away from him. Wiping away her tears, she grinned slyly.

'But now I'm so sore, I can't wear any fucking panties and I'll have to go on my date bare-bum . . . yah!'

Shannon, still nude, playing the cowed domestic slave, brewed tea for them both. With his teacup he went up to his den and logged on to the internet. Sipping his tea and smoking, he checked the sites of various lingerie suppliers and placed a few orders. When he heard a taxi draw up, and the door close, as Shannon went out for her evening, he keyed the Chaperones website and scanned the photos of the escort girls on offer. Sure enough, they were all called Felicity or Henrietta, fragrant from the shires, and were portrayed in elegant evening gowns.

There, too, was Imogen Forbes. Just as when he had watched her as a sex animal rutting in the scene, Shannon, his possession, was now someone else, a bauble for purchase, a love doll, *other*. Someone he didn't really know. Her joining the agency was a fait accompli, done behind his back, and that rankled, for did she think he wouldn't scan the website? Well (righteous indignation), her slyness obviously justified his own erotic adventures – albeit retroactively. The script was haughtily tasteful, making it clear that if a punter had to ask a girl's price, he couldn't afford her: 'Remuneration is by arrangement.' He wondered idly what Zelda was doing, then felt guilty at not thinking of Nampoong. Women were so complicated . . .

There were numerous links to other escort agencies, and he began to visit them, going to further links, in a descending order of respectability, and a rising order of smirking innuendo. The photos became more and more erotic until some of the sites featured girls in the briefest thongs and skimpy bras, often with high stilettos and fishnets, and occasionally caressing a riding crop. At last, he came to one called 'Asian Honey XXcorts'. The photos of the nude brown girls were cheesily erotic, with their legs apart, and their fingers busy at clito or nipple, feigning masturbation. Each girl had a full page of photos, showing her charms in every detail. He drew hard on his cigarette at the set featuring a voluptuous girl called 'Lek, the Thai Stinger Bee'.

Lek had no inhibitions about showing herself: legs curled behind her neck in a yoga contortion; squatting, buttocks raised and parted with masturbating fingers; tongue out, licking creamy fluid from her chin. In some photos she held a whip, raised for use. It was Nampoong. No doubt. Fuelled by angry desire, he reached for his mobile and punched the number of Valentino's massage parlour. He got Nampoong on the phone. Yes, she would see him. All right – yawn – straight away. Mitch would remember to bring sufficient cash for her needs? Of course.

He drove down the hill through the warm dusk with the glare of street lights flashing on his car. He licked his lips. Lek, the stinger bee, indeed! He walked into the massage parlour in jaunty mood to find Nampoong, wearing a white smock, sitting sullenly in the corner with some other massage girls. So much for being the cashier. *How many other men has she done in that back room?* She rose at his entrance and complained that he was late, that she was hungry and wanted food.

She doffed her smock to reveal a sleeveless shirtwaist mini-dress in bright crimson with gold sequins, its hem only a few inches below her crotch and showing a wide expanse of thigh sheathed in shimmering bronze nylons of fine glassine mesh. The dress was belted tightly in shimmering scaly leather, pinching her to adorable thinness. Cloth clung to her jutting teats, with buttons up to the neck, the first three hanging undone, to show brown breast skin and a sliver of silky crimson bra cup; the soft bra made a show of her nipples, standing firm.

Without waiting for an invitation, she hoisted her shoulder bag, marched out to his car, and stamped her foot, snug in fawn leather Grecian sandals with high heels, straps and buckles, until he opened the door for her. She slid inside and demanded a cigarette, which he lit for her. Frowning in a huff, she expelled smoke and told him to hurry up. When he asked her restaurant preference, she snapped that it didn't matter for when a Thai girl was hungry, she needed food straight away. It was obviously his fault she was hungry.

'Aren't you going to smile?' he said.

'I'm *hungry*,' she retorted, scowling. 'Nobody smiles when they are hungry.'

'I know just the place,' he said, turning left, then left again, and back on to the main road, to travel back up the hill.

'Ernie's Caff' in Putney High Street was a fashionable *faux* East End eel and pie shop in the Victorian mode, with *faux* gaslight, *faux* oak panelling, long-skirted waitresses in Victorian maids' uniform, and a large dining area, like an army canteen, surrounded by discreet private booths. Mehmet, the Lebanese owner, splendid in white tunic, chef's toque and ebullient moustache, greeted Mitch, in French, from behind his steaming tureens. They were early, before the evening rush of braying hoorays, and secured a private booth. Since there were only a few things to eat service was fast, and within minutes Nampoong was gulping down pie, mash and liquor, pig's trotter and jellied eels, washed down with brimming mugs of tea. Mitch ate slowly, gazing at the deft movements of the girl's fork and spoon, the glisten of juice on her lips as she swallowed. Buses grumbled past outside. There was a hint of rain.

'Better?' he said.

Nampoong nodded happily. He marvelled that the sulk of moments before had changed so suddenly into radiance, by the simple injection of food.

'I thought you said you were going to bring your whip,' he said jokingly.

She replied that she had indeed brought it. She pointed to the braided leather thong fastening her dress at the waist, then untied it, unwinding it round and round her hips, until she presented him with a heavy coiled whip, like a South African sjambok, seemingly of snakeskin. Its scales gleamed cruelly in the flickering light. Some hoorays glanced nervously, then sniggered.

'I had my palm read and fortune told today,' she said, 'and the *moh-doo* told me you would come. So I was angry you did not call sooner.'

Mitch shrugged helplessly.

52

'My wife . . .' he blurted. 'You know how it is . . .'

'Yes,' said Nampoong. 'The seer told me as well that you beat your wife, for she has a black heart, and is faithless to you. Even now, she is with another man.'

'With my consent! It's work. I told you I beat her, but it's a game, for fun. We have many friends who enjoy it.'

'Whipping is never for fun,' said Nampoong.

'Shannon and I, we . . . we understand each other,' he said lamely – *how to explain, to someone not in the Scene?* – 'But you can't believe all that fortune-telling rubbish.'

Nampoong's eyes glittered in fury.

'The *moh-doo* speaks to the ghosts who surround us,' she hissed, 'and they tell her the secrets of men and women. She can summon ghosts to punish any who displease her.'

She caressed her whip and refastened it around her waist before snapping her fingers for a cigarette, which Mitch obediently produced and lit, before passing it to her.

'I shall sleep with you, and spend the night,' she announced.

He felt her foot caress his erection, and she smiled.

'That pleases you,' she whispered.

'Of course it does,' he said hoarsely. 'I get stiff just thinking of you, darling Nampoong.'

'Darling? Isn't that what a man calls his wife?'

'Yes. It's a term of endearment.'

'Then I am your *mia noi*, your little wife,' she said. 'A man must treat his *mia noi* well, and reward her with much money.'

'Money and food,' he snapped. 'Is that all you think about?'

'Yes,' said Nampoong.

'I've already given you more money than you make in a week as Lek, the stinger bee,' he said coolly. 'I checked Asian Honey XXcorts on the internet, and there you were, in some very tasty photos, but a cheap deal. So don't mess me around, Miss Asian Honey.'

He regretted his words the instant he had uttered them, but to his relief, Nampoong just laughed.

'Oh, that,' she said. 'That is Lek, my sister.'

'But you said you worked as an escort.'

Nampoong, or Lek, shrugged.

'Maybe sometimes it is me,' she said. 'Thai girls often change their names, for good luck, or swap names with another girl. We are never what we seem. So sometimes I am Lek. Lek tells lies, and likes to hurt men. Do you want me to be Lek tonight?'

He breathed deeply.

'If that's what you want. Up to you, darling.'

7

Water Buffalo

They went not to the motel, but to Nampoong's flat, after
stopping at a Hindu mini-mart to buy drinks, various
foods in small tins or bottles and, at her insistence, sticks
of incense. She occupied the spacious top floor of a
converted Victorian terrace house off Balham High Street.
It was an ordinary apartment, cheaply but tastefully
furnished, with an eastern décor: rugs, lanterns, statuettes
of the Buddha, candlesticks for incense, and pictures of
moustachioed Victorian gentlemen, former kings of Thailand. On top of a dresser was erected an altar, like a doll's
house, with a golden statue of Buddha. She quickly said
she didn't live there, and was not going to tell him where
she did live. This flat was a working venue, for entertaining
only: so much for her quiet life in south London as a
cashier. Not that he believed her.

She clasped her hands and bowed to the altar, then
arranged her offerings, without opening them: tins of
sardines, corn and baked beans, cakes, bottles of beer, and
a glass of tequila. She filled candlesticks with sticks of
incense, and borrowed Mitch's lighter to fire them into
smouldering scented smoke. This done, she poured tequila
for them both and sat back, with the altar behind her, in
the sole cushioned armchair, raising her feet to rest them
on a footstool. She said that in Thailand you must never
point your feet, especially not at the Buddha, and the
Buddha must not see a girl naked, but she was now
shielded from his eyes by the chair back. King Rama could

see girls naked, for he had a hundred wives, and was the earthly counterpart to the spiritual Buddha. King Rama understood a Thai girl had to make a living, and enjoyed watching, too. They clinked glasses and drank.

'We drink to please the spirits,' she said gravely. 'In old times, Europeans thought that alcohol was the spirit of life, which could be friendly, or not.'

She put on some folk music of drums and twangy strings, with a warbling melancholy vocal. Carefully unwinding her snakeskin belt, Nampoong – *or Lek?* – let the hard thong play through her fingers while Mitch stood rather awkwardly, then snapped her finger and thumb. With an impish smile she crossed, then rapidly recrossed her nyloned legs, just long enough to show him that her sex was naked under crimson satin suspender belt and garters and above the stocking tops. The bronze nylons gleamed like the moisture at her sex.

'Take your clothes off,' she commanded.

Sheepish but thrilled, he did so, then stood with his erection trembling before her eyes, which seemed to feast on his hardness. She bared her teeth and licked them with the tip of her tongue.

'Kneel, and take off my shoes.'

He obeyed her. He fiddled with the complicated straps and buckles of the Grecian sandals, then reverently removed the shoes from her stockings and kissed the toecaps, then the instep, then the soles and heels, tasting and smelling the warm fruity aroma of her feet.

'Take the buckles into your mouth,' she ordered, 'and lick them with your tongue.'

He did so. The taste was acrid, metallic, over the tartness of leather. The points hurt.

'Thank you,' he murmured.

He clasped her stockinged feet, the nylon damp with her sweat, and nibbled her toes, then took each foot into his mouth as far as it would go, tickling his throat while he licked her sweaty fragrance.

'Your feet are divine,' he gasped. 'The scent of a goddess.'

'A goddess! I wonder what *that* is.'

He heard her laugh and looked up, to see her cigarette drooping from the corner of her mouth while she slowly hoisted her dress up to her navel, revealing her unpantied bare chatte. She commanded him to undo her garter straps and suspender belt, then remove them and roll down her stockings, but he was not to touch her skin with any part of his own. He knelt between her parted thighs, quivering ever so slightly as he fumbled with her underthings, while breathing in the heady scent of her vulva and flat muscled belly; he emitted little gasps and sighs as her musky freshness filled his lungs.

Wanting that creamy dark flesh so much, the honey welling in his balls, longing to kiss her and lick her and feel once again the warm wetness of her sex engorge him, he found it difficult not to touch her, but managed it, apart from a brief moment when his hand slipped while rolling down her left stocking and brushed her bare calf. She jerked as though stung and, abject, he said he was sorry. She rose, smoothing down her dress, and bowed once more to the Buddha.

'Doesn't he mind seeing me naked?' he asked.

'No,' she said in disdain, 'for you are only a farang, an animal, no more than a pig or water buffalo. You are my water buffalo tonight.'

She moved closer to him, repeating her order not to touch. She sheathed his head in her stocking and, breathing her fragrance, he exclaimed he looked like a bank robber, then she knotted the other tight around his balls. Using that as a leash, she led him into her bedroom by his tethered balls and tied the stocking to the bedpost. The bedroom was in darkness until she lit fat red ornamental candles, two feet tall, at each corner of the room.

They illumined a Spartan chamber with a bathroom to one side, and bare of decoration but for the gaudy plastic coverlet on the king-size double bed and a portrait of King Rama, who was looking towards two life-size nude photos of Nampoong, or Lek, similar to those posted on the XXcorts website. Beneath each portrait was a stereo speaker. One image was of her grinning impishly with thighs apart and ankles around the back of her neck; in the other, a rear view, she crouched with buttocks spread and her fingers parting her petals. Brown outside, wet pink within. Pure pornography. She flung off her dress and stood nude before him, flexing her whip.

'You touched my skin when I ordered you not to,' she announced.

'I said I was sorry.'

He knew where he was: a Scene game, like Giselle spilling wine.

'You allow your wife to go with other men, like the lowest worm in creation. You insulted the ghosts of the *moh-doo*. For all of those things you deserve punishment. It will please the ghosts if I inflict your punishment and spare them the trouble.'

'What do you mean to do?' he said. 'Come on, darling, can't you see how full of love I am for you – for *only* you – and how much I need you?'

'Can't *you* see how much I need to whip you?' said Nampoong. 'You do want to please me, yes?'

'You said we would sleep together tonight.'

'Afterwards,' she sneered, curling her lip. 'There is plenty of time for *bouncing*, handsome man.'

She untied the stocking from the bedpost and pulled him by the balls to lie face down on the plastic bed cover. Gasping hoarsely, he did not resist – no man resists a girl who calls him handsome, even in scorn – but clenched his buttocks as he heard the slither of the horsewhip. She lifted it over his body. The thong lashed his bare arse, and he groaned.

'Silence,' she commanded.

His buttocks began to clench and squirm as fire from her whip seared his skin. Gasping, he managed to take his beating in silence, though he could not prevent his eyes watering as the strokes proceeded past the sixth. She was good. She was *very* good, laying the whip neatly on every bare portion of skin, including the haunches, which he knew would stripe with the most livid welts, and cruelly laying two strokes to the same spot, transforming the welt into a puffy ridge of crusting flesh. He wriggled under the whip, with Nampoong occasionally jerking the stocking that bound his balls and ordering him to be still.

'Oh! God, it hurts,' he panted. 'Is this what you took from the Sisters of Mercy when they beat you?'

She paused, and wiped sweat from her brow and teats.

'What are you talking about?' she said.

'The nuns, in Surin ... where you got your American English.'

'Surin? Oh, yes, I remember,' replied Nampoong vaguely. 'Why, they flogged us much harder than this.'

Vap!

'Ahh! That's enough. Please stop.'

'When the spirits are satisfied you've been punished,' she snapped.

After a dozen strokes she desisted, flicking the leash to turn him on to his back and ascertain, with a cruel smile, that his penis was still rigid.

'You really know how to lay it on,' he gasped. 'I couldn't take another set like that.'

'But your wife and your whipping girlfriends, you beat them, yes?' Nampoong retorted. 'Is it different for girls?'

'I ... I suppose so,' he panted, his arse still clenching. 'They insist on it – subs are very demanding, always giving orders.'

'It didn't bother you, when you married, that many men had her before?'

'No, why should it? I wasn't a virgin, either.'

'A Thai man will not marry a girl who is not a virgin, or a girl with a tattoo, for that means she is a whore. Once a girl sells her body, she can never look back. Her only chance is to make some rich farang fall in love with her, and take her to live in his own cold miserable rainy land. You wanted me to dance for you, Mr Mitch. You may sit up and watch.'

She plumped pillows for him and he sank back into the soft down, grimacing, as he rubbed his bottom. She went into the bathroom and a thumping disco beat emerged from the speakers. She re-emerged naked, writhing to the raucous music, and placed two eggs on the bedspread between his legs. She jumped on to the bed and began to gyrate, crouching lower and lower with thighs parted, until her chatte enclosed the first egg. The large bed easily afforded her a stage; she rose, and clasped her hands above her head. With eyes shut, and lips mouthing to the music, as if in a trance, she shook her body, belly heaving, pelvis wriggling, and her hard-nippled breasts aquiver. She took a breast in each hand, forced it to her mouth, and chewed on her nipples, biting and sucking with a whore's moans of feigned ecstasy. Lowering her sweating body once more to a crouch, she sucked in the second egg. He gaped in grateful awe as her thighs approached his mouth, and she squatted over his face.

'Breakfast time,' she panted. 'Open your mouth wide.'

There was a muffled crack, and she squirted raw egg into his mouth. No sooner had he swallowed it, spitting out bits of shell, than another crack was followed by emission of the second egg. He gurgled, and wiped yolk from his lips and chin, then clapped his hands.

'Fabulous,' he said, but her serious face did not respond to his approval; she was a girl at work.

She revisited the bathroom, coming back with her hair pinned up and holding a towel which she placed by his feet; she took one of the red candles and held it over her breasts. Still writhing to the music, she upended the candle so that the scalding wax dripped on to her nipples.

'Uhh . . . uhh . . .' she groaned.

She transferred the candle back and forth between her teats, until each was crusted in a skin of red wax. He had seen this trick in home videos from other fetish groups, but it was too extreme for the Commoners. On video it seemed theatrical, and not entirely real, but in close-up Nampoong's body really was being seared by the wax. Her grimace of pain and tear-moist eyes were genuine. She smiled for herself through her tears, as if to show that, having inflicting pain on him, she was atoning for it with agony, and taking pride in her work.

She poured the molten wax over her belly and legs, then over her feet, until her toes were red waxen stalactites. Raising the half-consumed candle, she dripped wax down her back, to crust her shoulder blades and spine. Lowering the candle, and parting her fesses, she poured the hot red liquid into the crevice of her buttocks, baring her teeth in a rictus of pain with tears streaming down her cheeks to fall and glisten like raindrops on her waxen breasts. The only parts of her body unadorned by wax were her hillock and sex.

She advanced, stiffly, to straddle him with her quim petals above his eyes. Suddenly, she bent backwards and her head dived to the coverlet as she assumed the crab position. Flakes of wax broke from her arched spine and cascaded on to his belly. She held the candle a finger's breadth above her slit and parted the fleshy lips. She moaned as the searing droplets entered her pouch, filling her, until the candle, exhausted, sputtered to extinction and her chatte brimmed with congealing wax. She allowed her body to sink to the coverlet, then sprang to her knees with her lips pressed to his balls and her teeth unfastening the bronze nylon stocking which trussed them.

'Now you may fuck me,' she whispered.

'But how?' he gasped. 'You're full of wax! Ow!'

His fingertips recoiled as he felt the hot wax hardening inside her pouch. She swivelled and presented her wax-caked fesses to him. She pulled the cheeks apart, showering the bed with red shards, and began to clench the cheeks with her anal sphincter, making her anus pucker wink at him in invitation.

'There,' she said. 'In my little hole. That way, I am still a bit virgin.'

8

Girl Kit

'Surprisingly painless,' said Shannon, when he asked about her latest date. 'No hanky-panky, just dinner, rather a good one, and a few clubs, with lots of champagne. Quite the gent.'

His wife's acting as fantasy object for some wannabe sugar daddy did not distress him as much as he had expected; in fact, it was a secret thrill: *you can borrow her, but not possess her.* An escort girl was just acting.

'And how does Miss Imogen Forbes feel after her night of non-rumpy-pumpy?'

'He said he wanted to book me again. With that kind of tip, I'd be a fool to say no.'

He did not ask about the money, fearing Shannon would question *him.* Wives always suspected when husbands were cheating. Was he besotted with the Thai girl? Did his face carry a dazed ethereal glow, like the calf-brained teenager in love with Sylvie? He supposed so. When making love to Shannon, he imagined the Thai girl's belly and thighs writhing beneath his loins; or, sometimes, Zelda, her blonde tresses like his wife's. For Shannon's ritual beatings, he wore his black leather skin, stripping it off only before making love in the dark, for he was afraid Shannon would see the welts on his arse from Nampoong's whip.

'Mm ...' Shannon would gasp, 'I think my escort work turns you on, darling. You were quite brutal, my bum's like corrugated iron. We must have another scene soon.'

He mumbled that he was very busy just now with frocks, lingerie and undies.

'I'm sure you are, darling.'

'Also, I've a sort of spy in "Girl Kit". He tells me their plans, I think he has an office politics angle. They do cheap stuff, from the Far East, and they're torn between competing and ruining me, or buying me out to keep the two brands. I don't know if I want to sell or fight. That's why I'm so busy.'

'I do know what you're up to,' drawled Shannon.

For the last few weeks, he had called Nampoong daily, hating himself for seeming too eager, but always yielding to temptation, often to hear Signora Valentino's velvet tones telling him that Nampoong was 'with a client, dear' or out on a date, or simply would not answer the phone. Her teasing, sulking, and disdain only made his heart beat faster, and the thrill in his loins more electric, when she did consent to see him.

Her story was never the same: she had been a Buddhist nun, or the mistress of a government minister; she had learned English from a US Navy officer, spending a year in San Diego before she ran away. She had several brothers and sisters, or none, for they, along with her parents, had been killed by communist guerillas; she had been a Thai army commando, and killed Khmer Rouge with her bare hands, mutilating enemy corpses, the enemy seeming to be men in general. She changed facts, names, dates, places, denying what she had said previously, and accusing him of imagining things. Enchanted by his obsession, yet hating it, he was in love with the girl and her mystery. If you felt this way, it was *supposed* to be love. Otherwise, obscurely, you were under-performing. With all her lies and cruelty, she understood that he wanted to suffer. That was love.

Twice a week they would meet, sometimes at her flat, sometimes at the Hindu motel. He brought her gifts from his shop, and she received them with a pout; yet on their next session, she would be simpering in scarlet peephole bra and split-crotch panties, throwing her arms around him in a hug, and assuring him he made her feel 'so horny'.

63

She would whip him, after trampling on his body in a ferocious Thai massage; sit on his face, crushing his mouth with her buttocks, while she fellated him; crouch doggy fashion, thrusting her bottom up, and saying she could not bear to look at him, for she was so ashamed of her sinful life, yet begging him to encule her hard, as her punishment; during her period, masturbate him with a baby marrow sliced in two, which amused her, for he wanted to fuck her menstruating sex, and she refused, for modesty.

She let him lick her chatte, swaying and crooning, with her thighs locked around his head; that was perhaps his only power over her, for she adored cunnilingus. She shaved his entire body, saying that Thai men were smooth, and western men were dirty, and always had crabs, as if her shaven pubes could catch them. He enjoyed his smoothness, and continued to shave, telling Shannon that it was for her. Nampoong would not let him spank her – let alone cane her, which he longed to do – apart from a few playful slaps to her rump when he was in her from behind, and those made her howl and shiver, ordering him to stop.

'I can't stand pain,' she whimpered; yet as he slapped her fesses, she juiced.

She would let him strip off her clothing, piece by piece, and rub her fragrant garments over his body, with the moist panties and stockings wiped on his face and balls. She made him worship her by kissing her feet, his lips passing up her bare legs, licking every inch of her skin, to the parted sex, where he feasted on her juices as he tongued her clito to the brink of orgasm. If she passed the brink, she clutched his head with her thighs, moaning, as her belly heaved in spasm. But he never knew when she would laugh, break off his embrace, and order him to lie down for a beating.

He liked the cane least. There was something harsh and inhuman about the sting of the wood, and its dry slap on his unprotected flesh, with the unnerving silence between strokes. He could take twenty-one with the whip (three times seven, a lucky number), but mercifully she limited him to twelve with the cane (another lucky number), for her strokes were hard, taking him to the limit of his endurance. He wondered how girls like Wendy Ruminaw could take their tariffs so easily, although a playful Scene flogging was rarely as hard as it might be. When Nampoong beat him, her strokes were in earnest; the more his cries and squirming indicated his fear, the more she chose the cane for preference. She said she loved the cruel dry slap of a stick on a man's skin, and as Englishmen loved to be beaten by girls, she had plenty of satisfying work as an escort.

Did Dad ever spank Mum? Or did she spank him? Strange, you never think of your parents doing what you do.

Any curiosity about her work threw her into a rage, and led automatically to a caning, with his balls knotted in her stocking or panties – itself a pleasure – and the tariff taken to an agonising eighteen; twice nine, yet another number which presaged good luck. After such punishments he would shiver, sobbing, as she demanded more money, complaining he was a 'cheap charlie', even though every visit saw her reward increased. She abased him, knowing he would pay for degradation. At home, he scanned the XXcorts website, lingering over the changing photos of Nampoong. Jealousy stabbed him as he wondered what man took her photos, and if he fucked her. There was no address for the agency, so he could not spy on her, any more than he could spy on Shannon. He also began to read about Thailand, a place of which he had never thought before, save as a source of overpriced restaurants with simpering epicene waiters serving exotic food.

It seemed a place of contrasts: on the one hand, beach resorts with neon striptease bars and gaudy shows of sumptuously sequinned ladyboys, the tall voluptuous transsexuals who looked more like girls than girls did; on the other, a serene, mist-drenched landscape with temples, orange-clad monks and water buffalos plodding through the rice paddies. There were insurrections in the north and the Muslim south, and in the far north there was the Golden Triangle, ruled by warlords and drug gangs.

Everywhere, amid guns and flowers and whores, there was food, a Thai obsession: crustaceans, insects, luscious fruits and vegetables which he could not name; smiling brown girls, equally luscious, with Nampoong's grace. Effortlessly elegant in their bright costumes, they were fruits of the orient, creatures of dream. Vaguely, he thought he must see the place for himself, one day.

In contrast, Nampoong was neither jealous nor even curious about his home or wife or business. He thought her indifference was to his advantage, though it increased his frustration, for the love was all one-sided. She frequently gasped *I love you too much!* as they rutted, or, sarcastically, as he groaned under her whip, but the foreign words were a mere formula, learned parrot-fashion, to please or tease. He was another foreign animal with a bankroll, and an arse she whipped because paid to. Yet she guessed what he wanted – ecstasy at her smile, misery at her scorn – and she gave it to him. That was something, at least.

Their affair continued, with Mitch nervously aware what was happening to him: just as submissive Scene girls craved beating by a male, so he was coming to crave *her* whip. It seemed proper that his love of lashing girls should at last summon the whip to his own. And – it was *love*! – he wouldn't take it from any other woman. Their own secret. She demanded that he call her 'mistress' when she flogged him, which pleased him, showing she cared enough about him to cause him pain. One evening, with the rain lashing the motel windows, Nampoong whipped his arse and he whimpered as she took the beating past twenty-one.

'What happened to the lucky number, *mistress*?' he groaned, failing to make 'mistress' sound ironic.

'Does it hurt, darling slave?' she sneered. 'You should meet my friend Imogen. She's an escort girl who takes only real men, young studs. Escort girls know each other, just like bar girls in Pattaya, and all these agencies are the same one, under different names. Imogen does well, for she refuses nothing, opens her legs to them after taking the cane. The studs give her proper lashings, then fuck her in the little hole, *and* reward her well.'

66

Taunting him, teasing, hurting him more than with the whip. Vip!

'Ow!' Mitch whimpered. 'Imogen who?'

She did not answer, but took him to twenty-seven strokes.

'I gave three times nine tonight, for extra good luck,' she panted, laying down her whip as Mitch groaned that he had never known such agony.

'Agony will teach you not to ask questions.'

Then, one Saturday evening, as he had dreaded, Nampoong stood him up. When he arrived at the motel, the Hindu said she had left a message that urgent business had called her away. The bastard winked at him! They both knew what sort of business.

'She's the loser,' Mitch said with a shrug, but cold and sick to his stomach.

Furious, weeping, his heart in his throat, he drove home, mulling over ways to break off the liaison entirely while at the same time hurting her, making her realise how much she had lost by her teasing. Imogen – she had found Shannon's *nom de guerre* and used it to taunt him. Liaison? That was an illusion: there was no liaison, just a mug with his money, and his bit of greedy squirt. It was raining, a miserable night, with the suburban trash of fast-food takeaways, pubs, used-tyre dealers and mini-markets shimmering wetly against dark pavements. The wipers hissed over his windscreen, mocking him.

Relieved to be back in leafy Wimbledon, yet still lost in anger, he overshot his own driveway, shadowed by the tall garden hedge. He saw that lights were on in his house, more than the normal security lights, while an unfamiliar car was parked by his front door. That night Shannon was out on escort duty ('duty' making him less squeamish than 'fun'); surely she could not have returned so early from her date? Besides, she always travelled by taxi. *She's brought some fucking tosser home with her*.

He parked at a short distance from his home, his car invisible from the house. Keys in hand, he walked up the deserted footpath, letting himself through the high spiked gates, then, as silently as possible, the front door. He need not have bothered, for there was music and laughter, and the clink of glasses. He padded to the drawing-room, knelt and, feeling like a character in a Feydeau farce, pressed his eye to the keyhole. Shannon was nude but for a pale satin corset, which he had never seen before, pinching her waist pencil-thin. She sat – *his* sofa, *his* drawing-room! – on the lap of a young heavily muscled male, in his early twenties, and also nude. Mitch exhaled harshly, recognising Gavin Dern, his spy from the Girl Kit company. Shannon's fingers played with his erect penis.

'I'm so horny, Gavin,' she murmured, her lips nuzzling his ear.

He laughed and grasped her hair, winding it around his fist until Shannon complained he was hurting her.

'I'll really hurt you,' he said.

He forced her to kneel beside the sofa with her head pressed into the cushions, and began to spank her on the bare. She gasped as her buttocks reddened with his palm prints, then whimpered as he replaced his palm with a sports shoe.

'Ooh! Lovely jubbly!' she moaned, as the striated rubber slapped her fesses.

After a couple of dozen hard whops from the shoe, Gavin took his belt and strapped her for long minutes, until her squirming bottom glowed crimson. He put down the belt and at once she had her mouth round his engorged penis. He stroked her hair as she fellated him.

'Fuck me Gav,' she mumbled, his shaft filling her mouth. 'Fuck me hard.'

He withdrew, lifted her hips, and straddled her from behind.

'Oh! Yes!' she panted, as Gavin's penis penetrated her vulva. 'Fuck me, Gav, do me! Split my cunt. Give me cock! Nobody does it like you.'

Dirty talk, a turn-on. Mitch watched, breath bated, shocked that he was straining in erection even as her words bit his heart. Gavin pounded his wife, who writhed under his thrusts while she shrieked, hoarse with an animal passion Mitch had not heard in a long time. The man's arse quivered as he bucked with vigorous slamming strokes.

My wife, with his cock inside her cunt that belongs to me. What a lowlife. Imogen and Gav. Lovely jubbly. Yuk.

Yet Mitch could not take his eyes from the event; his penis throbbed rigid.

'Ah! Yes! I'm coming! I'm almost there!' she squealed. 'Oh, fuck me, take me, yes, yes, *yes . . .*'

Back arched and belly fluttering, she convulsed in orgasm while Gavin growled, ejaculating inside her. He let her slowly down to the carpet and the adulterers embraced with wet sloppy kisses as they sank to the sofa. Mitch's throat was dry, his heart racing.

'That was so *good*!' Shannon gasped. 'I've never come so hard before.'

'You're simply the best, lover,' Gavin said, and she laughed, a happy peal of bells. 'When are you going to get rid of the old man and put me in his place?'

Her finger tapped his lips.

'Now, Gav, you mustn't be in such a hurry,' she chided playfully.

'Hey, I'm action man,' he replied, lighting cigarettes for them both. 'I deliver. He bought that escort agency yarn, didn't he, *Imogen*?'

'Well, I *am* a Chaperones escort,' she protested, exhaling heavily. 'You monopolise my services, and my bum's a sight from your cane, and you tip miserably.'

'When I'm running Strips, and we've booted old Mitcham into touch, you'll stop being an escort girl.'

'Don't call him that,' she retorted. 'He's my husband.'

'Do you love him? Did you ever?'

She sighed.

'We love each other, in our way,' she sighed. 'We have a lot in common.'

'Apart from the Scene, what?' he said roughly. 'Don't tell me he doesn't fuck around.'

'If he does, I ignore it. Wives do, you know. It was the Scene that brought us together and, I guess, keeps us together. Spanking, not fucking, is central to our lives, and so we are central to each other. But with you it's different. I've never been given such a seeing-to. I don't know . . . oh, Gav, you're making me all trembly. I'm so confused.'

They kissed, and Gavin looked at his watch over his wife's shoulder. It was time either to depart or confront them, as the outraged husband of farce. *Corny, or what?* He chose to depart, as discreetly as he had arrived. He lit a cigarette with trembling hands and sat, smoking and sad, in his car, until he heard his front door open and the couple's smooching farewells. Before Gavin's car started, Mitch drove away quickly, into the dashing rain, uncertain where to go for the next few hours. Stood up by his mistress and cuckolded by his wife in the same evening. But 'mistress' and 'wife' were empty words, failing to penetrate a woman's otherness. Only a penis, or a whip, could do that. He could not lose his bitter image of Shannon, serviced by a strange male, and yet his erection still throbbed. *Like something out of* Chance *magazine. Shit happens, but why the hell does it have to happen to me? It's not fair. The evening's early. I need a drink.*

But he knew it was fair.

9

Accomplices

He drove to the Rose and Crown, one of his locals, parked outside, and entered the lounge, which was filling up for the evening. What secret impulse sent him there? The flagellant poet Swinburne, ruined by booze and flagellation, would walk down from Putney, for brandy-and-soda. But he was a sub, liked his own arse to writhe. Needed to be punished. Deserved to be?

> *I am weary of days and hours,*
> *Blown buds of barren flowers,*
> *Desires and dreams and powers*
> *And everything but sleep.*

Swinburne the sub of course became a grand old man. Thoroughly normal habits, for an English gentleman. Rose and Crown, a fitting choice.

To avoid the image of a solitary drinker, he gulped his double scotch with a Bogartish grunt, indicating that he was wet from rain after a hard day and needed a quick one. He lit a Gauloise and sucked smoke. The Australian barman (the pub was an Anzac Mecca) grinned sympathetically and poured him another. He nursed the second scotch, mindful of drink-driving, and felt the warmth of the first spread in his stomach. Thoughts of Shannon mingled with thoughts of Girl Kit. He had always suspected something crass and dodgy about Gavin, and now he knew not to trust anyone from Girl Kit. What was

Nampoong up to this wet London evening? He longed to take refuge in those silky breasts and thighs, breathe her warm musky scent – *hom* – and suck the life-giving juice from her quim. *Oh, fuck. Fuck it all.*

A woman's perfume invaded his nostrils, one he recognised, *Chatte d'Amour*, that they sold in Strips.

'Hello, Mr Barnett,' purred a voice.

He looked round and saw Jacqui, clutching a banknote.

'Won't you join us?' she said, pointing to Zelda who sat by a table in the far corner.

Both girls wore their shop uniforms which, in the thronged pub, were outrageously sexy instead of just sexy. He waved a regal finger and was served promptly, buying their gins and tonics, which he allowed Jacqui to carry, along with his own drink. He found himself seated between the two girls, bathed in delicious female scent – for Zelda was wearing the same perfume – and with envious male eyes giving him how-does-he-do-it looks, after scanning two ripe pairs of thighs, skirts hoisted and nylons exposed, *just so*, which cheered him up. Sniffing their perfume, he said *hom*, and Zelda smiled.

They exchanged do-you-come-here-often pleasantries, Mitch calling them Zelda and Jacqui, and the girls, unsure whether it was 'Mr Barnett', 'Sir' or 'Mitch', avoided addressing him altogether. Jacqui said they often dropped in here after Saturday late opening to unwind. Jacqui was eager, obviously preparing to say something important; Zelda demure, her wide eyes meeting his, then coyly turning away. His eyes drank in her shiny blonde tresses and elfin body with its cunning curves; dark Nampoong and blonde Shannon receded to the far corner of his mind.

Jacqui told him there were rumours of an impending sale of Strips, and naturally they were worried about their jobs. A Mr Gavin Dern, from Girl Kit, had visited the shop and quizzed them, although they had loyally avoided giving away secrets. Mitch scorned such rumours, but even if he was to sell, the jobs of two such lovely staff were secure. Scout's honour. Jacqui seemed content with that. He bought a few rounds, not letting them pay, and they made small talk, about films, TV, Strips. Both girls agreed they loved their jobs, for a girl working with sexy clothes was like a bloke working with motorbikes. Desire fuelled by drink, he longed to touch Zelda, slide his hand up her nyloned thigh, make her blush; finally, Jacqui looked at her watch, said she had a date, and must go. Zelda, dateless, was expecting a lift home, but he offered to take care of her. When Jacqui had gone, he smiled at Zelda, who bit her lip, then smiled bravely back.

'We last met in rather different circumstances,' he said.

'Yes, sir,' she murmured.

'Call me Mitch, please.'

'Yes, Mitch.'

'You're not angry with me, I hope,' he said.

'Angry! Oh, no,' she blurted. 'I hope you're not angry with *me*. I mean, I wouldn't mind if you were, you know, if I deserved it. In fact . . .' she stopped, her face flushed.

'Yes? Go on.'

He began to stiffen again.

'You'll think me silly.'

He clasped her hand, stroking it, and she submitted to the caress.

'I promise I won't. Tell you what, it's getting too noisy in here – tell me over dinner.'

'Yes, please. I'm famished.'

He was exultant: she said yes, and so fast! On a mischievous impulse, he drove them to the Thai restaurant past Valentino's. He glanced into the bright light of the massage parlour, perhaps hoping that Nampoong would burst through the doors and wave him to a halt, then, furious with jealousy, give him the tanning of a lifetime. Or else he could give her the finger and speed on, putting his arm around Zelda for the Thai girl to see, and eat her heart out.

She seemed pleased to sample Thai food again, and produced a few words of Thai, amusing the waiters. She talked him through the menu, and they feasted on small dishes of soup, crab, prawn and pork, with mountains of white sticky rice and laced with fiery chilli sauce, washed down with ice-cold 'Singha' beer, imported at a fearful price. He liked the food, liked even more the swell of her breasts, and her fingers brushing flakes of food from her lips and from the soft breast hillocks, a glimpse of skin rising and falling under her *décolletage*. She began to tell him her secret. Breathing hard, she said she had been thinking, since their . . . she groped for words.

'Our event,' he said smoothly.

'Since our event,' she agreed, 'and, you know, I've never felt like that before. I mean' – she blushed – 'I never thought I'd like being spanked, or anything like that, but it . . . it turned me on like nothing else has.'

He heard a clatter as she shucked off her shoes, and then felt her nyloned toes caress his ankles while she smiled mysteriously. He felt Nampoong and Shannon exit his mind completely, leaving a nice bare space for Zelda. Now was the moment.

'You turn *me* on, Zelda,' he whispered. 'I'll tell you why.'

She nodded and squeezed his hand, not letting go as he responded to the caress. Her manner was less oopsy, more confident, her lips slack, and eyes hooded in desire, as he told her about the Scene, the diversity of fetish clubs, and friendly flagellation for pleasure. He said her superb bottom begged to be spanked, an act of worship. Her stockinged toes clung to his calves.

'Do you find it a bit shocking?' he said. 'It isn't at all.'

Wordlessly, her face a glowing blush, she shook her head.

'Zelda,' he whispered, 'would you like us to make our scene again?'

She nodded.

'Yes,' she gasped. 'I've wanted it so much, ever since you did it to me. My bum was all burny. I had to go to the loo and, you know, play with myself. Bring myself off. God, you really must think I'm silly.'

He shook his head, smiling no. Her foot slid up his leg, over his thigh, and her toes pressed his balls, then stroked his erection. She giggled nervously.

74

'I *want* it to be a bit shocking,' she said.

She began a slow sensuous massage with her prehensile toes.

'Stop that, or I'll . . . you know, lose control,' he gasped, feeling deliciously foolish, and only half-joking.

'Mm . . . that's a turn-on, too,' she said, licking her lips, but stopped rubbing. 'In that case, we'd better go back to my flat, if you don't mind being cramped. It's so wonderful to hear all about the Scene. I feel I can speak freely, not embarrassed. I'm really hot for a spanking. There!'

Her blushes returned, fierier than ever, and his erection was proud. He slapped a credit card on the table and, when the waiter arrived, after an age, he scribbled a signature; another age, and he got his plastic back. His jacket obscured the bulge at his groin as he shepherded her to the door, the girl a precious lamb who might stray if he let her out of his grasp. She sank into the seat in the front of his car, sniffing the fresh leather upholstery, and told him what a fabulous car it was.

'You're only saying that because guys like to be complimented on their cars,' he said, laughing. 'Like, I'm the only BMW in town?'

'I know,' she murmured, her lips brushing his earlobe. 'Guys always want to think they're different, that they are the only one.'

'And girls don't?'

'Touché.'

Her flat was in a tree-lined street in Morden, less than fashionable, but friendly.

'Terrific,' she said, springing from the car. 'I'd have had to wait ages for a bus at this time of night.'

She explained that the downstairs flat was occupied by a lovely old couple, both quite deaf, while she had the upstairs. Their daughter, who lived with them, was scarcely ever home.

'I mean, no one will hear us,' she whispered.

She led him up the stairs, wiggling her bottom and showing pink thread panties under her swaying mini-skirt. She looked down and smiled, seeing him ogle her cheeks.

75

'I wear a thread to work because it gets me in a sexy mood for selling undies,' she giggled, as she unlocked.

The door swung open to reveal a tidy flatlet with kitchenette, living-room and bathroom and bedroom, and he said that it was very nice, and not cramped at all.

'Not for our purposes,' he added, receiving a delicious grin of complicity; that was the joy of the Scene, all were accomplices.

Zelda offered him a drink, saying she had gin or beer; he opted for beer, while she made herself a gin and tonic. They sat opposite each other at her kitchen table, their knees touching, and gravely toasted their new event.

'Well, to business, Mr Barn – Mitch,' she murmured.

'You're sure you want me to spank you?'

She nodded with silent eagerness.

'Better still, lash me. On the bare. God, I feel so naughty just saying that.'

'You're the boss.'

'We'd better do it in the bedroom, I suppose.'

He asked her what she would prefer as implement, offering his belt, and Zelda replied that the belt would be lovely, but she could find a suitable rod. Once inside her cosy bedroom, with its hot radiator, soft lamp with red shade and white dresser, Zelda looked him in the eye as she coolly stripped off her clothing and folded it neatly, to place it in the wardrobe. The single bed had an ornate brass bedstead, and Zelda said it had been her mother's.

'It's such a thrill,' she said, 'to be able to undress in a . . . a sort of businesslike way, for a good seeing-to. You know, no flirting or simpering or anything. Just say what you want, and get it. I think I should enjoy the Scene.'

Casual in her nudity, she disappeared into the bathroom and he heard the sound of a shower as he took off his clothes and wrapped his belt around his fist. She returned, her hair pinned up and her body steaming from the hot shower. Grinning coyly, she held out a bamboo cane, three feet long with split ends; she told him she had seen the bamboo in a garden shop and could not resist buying a dozen – 'very cheap' – for her hoped-for next event. He laughed.

'I've practised on my own bottom, but it's not the same. You do think I'm silly,' she trilled.

'Not at all,' he said, embracing her, with his erection stroking her belly.

'Mm . . .' she gasped, hugging him. 'I'm getting all tingly. You'd better do me before I fling you on the bed, *sir*.'

She crouched on her girly-pink floral-print coverlet and thrust her buttocks up and spread for her beating, with her head cradled in her forearms. He asked if she would like a spanking, to warm her up, but she murmured in a little girl's voice that she wanted pain, straight away.

'Please cane me hard,' she whispered. 'Make me all raw and stripy. Like in the films.'

He didn't ask what films, but raised the bamboo while gazing at the smooth pears of her buttocks, the gentle trench of her cleft, the winking little anus pucker, and the wet orchid, garlanded by her lush pubic jungle. He lashed her full across her bottom, raising a pink stripe, and was pleased to see them clench.

'Ooh!' she cried, pressing her face to her pillow.

Vip!

'Ahh . . . yes . . .'

Her bottom began to squirm as he laced the flesh, treating her buttocks as a canvas on which he was to paint a picture of crimson. He lashed her across the croup's full expanse, panting, as stripes marked her haunches and the tops of her thighs, making her wriggle with soft mewling cries. The bamboo cane was springy but firm, and the split tip left deep red snake's tongues on her skin.

'How many am I to get?' she sobbed.

'I think you could take a dozen with this,' he said.

'God! A whole dozen . . . all right, then.'

Vip!

'*Ahh!*'

With the clenching of her bottom, her chatte writhed, shiny with moisture. He flogged hard, and at the twelfth he put down the cane, asking her if she wanted to look in the mirror, but she remained crouching, buttocks presented.

'Later! God, it hurts. Take me, please. I'm all wet. I'm yours. Take me, *fuck me*. Now.'

A man with an erection is not taken aback. He grasped her hips and penetrated her, easily sliding into her wet sex. His belly slapped her buttocks as he thrust, and she orgasmed almost at once.

'Oh! Oh! *Ahh* . . .' she squealed, then whimpered that it wasn't fair, he must come too.

'Do me. Fill me up.'

When he came to his own spasm, not long afterwards, she climaxed a second time.

'God, yes!' she gasped. 'You know, before, when you spanked me, I was so horny, so wet, I needed you so badly, it was all I could do not to rape you.'

'I consider myself raped,' he replied.

'But it's not over. I want more,' said Zelda.

10

Pampered

He laughed, wiped his brow, and said he was due a rest before performing again. Even caning took it out of you, a fact submissives failed to appreciate. They were always telling you, do this, do that, *gimme*; it was usually the sulky sub who ruled the roost.

'You don't mind being called submissive?'

'No. It's rather thrilling.'

He said that a sub girl, the 'bottom', just had to lie there and wriggle, whereas the 'top' really had to exercise. Not to mention . . .

'You poor darling,' she said, licking the tip of his nose. 'I promise not to be sulky.'

She brought them fresh drinks, and they lit cigarettes and lay on the bed smoking and cuddling.

'This is nice,' she said. 'God, I've never had such a thrashing. My bum must look a treat.'

'It does,' he said. 'Lovely crimson. Was the rest of it good?'

'Mm,' she purred, licking her lips. 'That should satisfy your male ego.'

He explained that Scene events did not usually involve penetration (she made a *moue*). Strokes were a cleansing, giving fresh invigorating joy. The buttocks were a sexual zone, and their countless nerve endings, when stimulated by beating, produced endorphins to activate the opiate receptors in the brain.

'My God! What does all that mean?'

'It means that when she's spanked, a girl feels happy.'

'What about men?' she said coyly. 'You said there were switch clubs? I'd like to try one of those, for curiosity. All those flagellation postcards in phone boxes! London must be full of men wanting their bums whacked.'

'A lot of guys like it,' he said, lighting another Gauloise. 'Bitchy women sneer that all males are masochists, but I've always been a whipper. I think the thrill of being beaten is more intense for girls. Girls must have more nerve endings in their buttocks. They're more sensitive.'

'Very PC of you.'

'It's not just beating that thrills, it's the symbolic submission to the whip. A sub wants the security of being helpless, pampered by the lash. No pressures, no decisions to make. All women like to be pampered, don't they? Many male subs are powerful men who want a rest from giving orders, want to be dominated by a woman instead, a sort of nanny figure.'

'Men like you?' she murmured.

'Girls,' he said, 'are natural subs.'

He shut his eyes and drifted into a doze. Nampoong invaded his reverie and, while he feared her whip and her labile lying nature, he was loath to let her depart from his mind. Was he really one of those who craved a woman's oppression? Or was thrashing, as he always insisted, just healthy endorphin fun? He awoke to find his left wrist fastened to the bedstead by steel handcuffs.

'What the hell –'

Zelda stood nude and akimbo in front of him, cradling a fresh bamboo cane.

'Lucky I bought several,' she said, smiling, 'for my bum fairly wasted the first one. Those were Daddy's Met issue handcuffs. I knew I'd find a use for them.'

'Stop fooling. Let me go.'

'Not until you've had a taste of your own medicine,' she said, po-faced. 'I propose to kick your opiate centres into action, Mr Barnett, with a sound thrashing.'

She rolled the words round her tongue, *a signed thrashing*, like a royal. He reached for a cigarette, but her cane whipped it from his fingers.

'Not without permission, slave,' she snapped, then beamed. 'Isn't that what you say? I figure this is the perfect venue for our switch club of two. You won't mind, will you? But if you do, it's more fun.'

Her eyes fastened on his stiffening penis.

'I don't think you mind,' she murmured.

She touched his glans with the splayed tip of her bamboo, making him wince, then stroked the shaft up and down, and tickled his balls. He hardened.

'You will turn over and present your arse for tanning,' she said, licking her teeth, 'until you positively *squirm*. Yum! And call me "mistress". Isn't that what you want, Mitch?'

He twisted to see her body bathed in droplets of sweat; belly, thighs and breasts quivering. Zelda was excited by having him in her power, and that thrilled him. He obeyed, presenting himself for her cane.

'Yes, mistress,' he moaned. 'Yes.'

He gritted his teeth, trying not to groan, as the bamboo lashed him hard. The strokes descended on his clenched buttocks, regular as a metronome, at five-second intervals. Waiting for the next cut was almost as fearful as the cut itself. After an age of trembling and smarting, he once more heard the swish as the cane rose, the whistle as it descended towards him, and her grunt as it struck. Stinging pain spread through him, reducing him to helplessness, yet he did not resist; he felt that the girl's cane and his seared buttocks were joined in an act of worship. *Is this really me? A man who loves to beat girls, and now it's my turn, and I deserve it.*

After eight cuts she paused to light one of his cigarettes, blew smoke over his arse and lodged the cigarette in the corner of her mouth, saying she imagined that was how a real dominatrix behaved, a touch of the sluttish. She sipped a gin and tonic.

'Oh, please, get it over with,' he blurted. 'It hurts like hell.'

'Don't you think *my* bottom hurts like hell? But we've all night for me to skin you. And it's "please get it over with, *mistress*".'

81

She resumed the caning. He strained to wrench the cuffs from the bed, but they would not budge.

'God, I've never been hurt so much!' he groaned. 'Honestly, Zel – *mistress* – I can't take any more.'

'All beatings feel like that,' drawled Zelda, in a trickle of cigarette smoke. 'I've been beaten enough. Every time you feel you've never been hurt so much, and can't take any more. But you haven't, and you can.'

Again her cane tickled his balls and penis.

'See?' she said. 'You're lovely and stiff. Poor Mitch. You just want to be a little boy again, thrashed for being naughty, then hugs and kisses and all forgiven.'

The beating continued past twelve cuts, and gradually he accepted it with a strange determination, almost glad he had no choice: the white-hot pain was a part of him, which he could not imagine ever going away. *I can take it. I can!*

'I know more about this than you think, because I've read about it,' panted Zelda between strokes. 'And Jacqui – well, she's actually in the Scene. She told me so after listening to us in the back room; *she* likes whipping men. She gave me a book to read, *Venus in Furs*, by Leopold Sacher-Masoch. A young fellow falls in love with a cruel woman, and begs to be her slave, but ends up miserable. Most people are masochists, especially men. Why else do they always fall for sluts and bimbos, really unsuitable ones? They like heartaches, and demand whipping for being so stupid. It's easier for girls, for submission comes naturally to us, in everyday things. Dressing to please, making coffee for the boss and that. It's nice to have a little playful revenge.'

'This isn't playful,' he whimpered.

'You whopped *me*.'

'You wanted it.'

'And you don't? Now, where can I stub out my fag? Those pretty balls look tempting.'

'No! Please!'

Laughing, she threw the butt into an ashtray.

'That was fun. I think you're ready to pour your heart

out, Mr Barnett, *boss.* Confess! Why do you let me whop you, when those old handcuffs *aren't even locked*?'

'You bitch!'

'Say you're sorry.'

Her cane lashed him vertically, in his arse cleft, stinging his anus.

'Ahh! I'm sorry, mistress.'

Between strokes, he described his infatuation with Nampoong, about her cruelty, and how he had come to desire it; Shannon's adultery, and his compliant weakness. His confession was punctuated by groans as Zelda beat him. He saw through his blur of tears that her thighs were parted and she was masturbating.

'Yes,' she said. 'I'm as fruity as you, Mitcham. Tell me you like your thrashing.'

'I like it, mistress.'

'Would it be the same if a guy was thrashing you?'

'Of course not. I'm no bertie woofter.'

'But if you couldn't see, what difference would it make? The pain would be the same.'

'I'd know,' he groaned. 'It's not just pain, it's communication. I'd feel it in the cane.'

She dealt a final searing cut, and he shrieked.

'You've taken eighteen, and that's enough for now.'

'Whew!'

She laid aside the cane, shredded beyond usefulness, and clicked the handcuffs open, then ordered him to lie on his back. At once she straddled him, taking his penis in her mouth while crushing his face with her buttocks, and pressing her sex to his lips. A hot hungry animal. He jerked his hips, fucking her throat, as he sucked her wet chatte and she gurgled. After minutes of *soixante-neuf* she rose and slid to his groin, making him enter her.

'I want your sperm inside me,' she panted, beginning a slow writhing of her hips, her pouch milking him as her fingertips masturbated her clito.

In less than a minute he ejaculated, while she cried out in her own climax. Gasping, she rolled off and snuggled beside him, stroking the weals on his arse.

83

'*Now* you may smoke, sir,' she murmured, lighting cigarettes for both of them.

'That was some thrashing,' he gasped. 'I was delirious.'

'I was frightened I might draw blood. I almost wanted to. No, I *did* want to. I've been caned to blood' – she shuddered – 'and it's awful, and scary, but you feel sort of proud afterwards, even though your bum's a mess. Pity it's difficult to grow aloe here, wild aloe vera has a tremendously soothing gel.'

'I wouldn't have minded. I hope I didn't say anything too awful.'

'Nothing I didn't already know,' she purred.

She wouldn't tell him where and how she had taken the awful caning. From Jacqui? Or her mysterious Australian boyfriend? But she knew all about Mitch and Nampoong from Trudi the masseuse, who was the girl that lived downstairs. *And* – coy, regretful – she knew about his wife's toyboy. Gavin Dern brought Shannon into the shop, and they were obviously an item. She tried on corsets and things, and helped herself to loads of free undies – on Mitch's tab – saying Mr Dern would be the new boss. Girl Kit was going to open up next door, to drive Strips out of business, then force Mitch to sell.

'Shit happens,' she said. 'It's all luck, the wheel of fortune spinning. You learn that in Thailand. Meanwhile, here and now, you have the rest of the night to fuck me. Girls always want a man with power, an alpha male, the pack leader, who fucks lots of women. We're like wal-ruses.'

'I think you're like a Thai girl,' he said.

'A trip over there would help you find out,' she said. 'It's not expensive. The proles who used to go to Benidorm now go to Pattaya or Phuket. You'd learn a lot about real life. Of course, there's more to it than those honky-tonk towns. I'm getting quite nostalgic.'

They made love once more, a long *soixante-neuf*, with Zelda gasping and crying in pleasure as he tongued her sopping chatte, then climaxing as she swallowed his ejaculate; and they slept. As dawn washed through the curtains, and the first of the morning trains clattered in the distance, Zelda said she had enjoyed being a mistress, but her true nature was to feel a man in charge. Drowsily, she turned and presented her deliciously wealed buttocks, spreading them with her fingers to show her anus bud. He made a joke about dawn's rosy fingers.

'Ha, ha,' she said. 'Come on, stud. You know where I need you. Have your revenge on faithless women.'

Ready with his waking erection, he penetrated her anus and enculed her with long slow strokes as she whimpered with joy. He marvelled at her beauty, ethereal in the early dawn light, and the capacity of a girl's body for both pain and pleasure; her pride in presenting her fesses for his adoration, her groans of satisfaction as his penis reamed her anal elastic. What was Nampoong's pleasure, except cheating and teasing and getting money from her besotted admirers? He wondered how many men she obsessed, dangling them on her malicious puppet strings. Losers. The broken-hearts club.

Later, they gulped mugs of steaming hot tea and smoked his cigarettes before showering together, while bacon and eggs were sizzling. After shaving with Zelda's razor, he gulped his breakfast.

'You'd make someone a good wife,' he said.

'Wrong thing to say, Mitch,' she replied. 'This isn't the Victorian age. Maybe you *should* go to Thailand. Nothing ever changes there. A Thai girl will suck you off, take it up the bum, or in her left nostril, or whatever you want' – he winced at her sudden coarseness – 'and make your dinner afterwards. Provided you dosh her up properly.'

He said he hadn't time for vacations, with the pressure of business, especially now, with all his problems.

'Like your Thai mistress,' Zelda said. 'Men, always whingeing about their problems!'

She clasped his hand, stroking it.

'Sorry. That was out of order. A naughty girl like me does need thrashing, sometimes,' – her voice suddenly coy – 'and after last night, I could maybe take her place. A bit. Oh, what's any sex, thrashing or whatever, but fear of loneliness? I'm confused, most girls spend their whole lives being confused, you know? Am I a sub, or a dom, or what . . .'

'Zelda, I'd love to . . . I honestly don't know. It was fun last night, and bloody painful, but you *are* really a sub, and I'm really not. The thing with Nampoong is, well, just that, a thing, an obsession, a singularity. You're the sweetest sub I've ever met, but –'

'Then I could be your slave,' she whispered, licking egg yolk from her lips. 'We could even have threesomes, spanking ones, you, me and Jacqui. Wouldn't you like that?'

She wanted so badly to please.

'I'm pretty confused myself right now. Shannon, and Nampoong, and everything . . .'

She sighed, lit a Gauloise, and exhaled noisily, her face sad and grim.

'There's another thing Trudi shared with me. Nampoong doesn't work at Valentino's any more. She caught a flight to Bangkok a couple of days ago, on a one-way ticket.'

11

Sex and Golf

The aircraft broke through the clouds and began its descent to the Bangkok airport. He gazed at the landscape beneath, the bright essence of green shimmering in the morning heat haze, dotted with villages, and water everywhere, in ochre rivers, or glistening in rice paddies. As they approached the Earth, he made out individual houses and golden-spired temples. The dozing man beside him yawned and stretched as the Thai stewardess ordered the passengers to fasten their seat belts, her lilting voice, a mixture of feline authority and sensuous little girl, reminding him of Nampoong.

He half-sought her everywhere, and the lustrous women in the aircraft – round faces, long faces, broad faces – all had her grace and self-assurance. He stirred at the thought of her, patting his wallet where he kept the photos printed from the XXcort website: some decorous and clad, others obscene. His lazy erection didn't seem anything to conceal in the hothouse atmosphere, where every woman dripped sensuality and dreamy fragrance. Concealed in the service galley was a little shrine, with electric candles before a reclining Buddha, to which the stewardesses bowed, hands clasped in obeisance. He was already in Thailand.

He had talked to his neighbour during the eleven-hour flight, mostly pleasantries over copious alcohol, and the meals served by brightly saronged Thai stewardesses of coy sultry beauty. He said he actually liked airline food: a complete meal in miniature, everything organised just so, packed in cute little containers, the dishes devised and prepared just for him, by unseen chefs toiling for their art, with no prospect of applause.

His neighbour shrugged.

'Packaging's the passion of orientals,' he drawled, a languid English voice. 'Women, food, whatever, all gift-wrapped. Appearances are everything, though there's little enough behind them. But try real Thai food, soaked in hot chillis, to blister your mouth off. You can eat or get pissed all day, like the Thais. When they've had one meal, they have another. Cheers.' And he swigged his brandy.

Now, as the plane's undercarriage thudded down, the young man looked at him and smiled.

'First visit?' he asked. 'The excitement's always the same the first time. Wish I still felt it.'

They landed, and Mitch lost sight of his neighbour in the scramble to exit. The airport was big and modern, and seemed to function more smoothly than London's over-crowded hubs. The walk to immigration passed rows of boutiques, a dazzle of soft colours and gracious brown faces. Gaudy posters proclaimed 'Welcome to the Land of Smiles'. He came to a crowded smoking room and dived in – designer-clad girls with pigskin luggage, airline staff, roughneck tourists, besuited euro-businessmen, complicit in their addiction. Amid the fumes, in the glint of gold wristwatches, he found himself sitting next to his neighbour on the plane.

'We meet again,' the young man said, lighting a Dunhill. 'Bloody no-smoking flights, eh? You going far?'

He offered Mitch a cigarette and lit it for him.

'Don't know, really,' he said, wiping the sweat from his brow and shifting in his shirt, already sodden and sticky. 'Bangkok, I suppose. I've heard about Patpong, Nana Plaza, girly bars. My Thai girlfriend, in London, sort of turned me on to the, uh, Asian experience.'

Two months before, he had been crushed by the flight of Nampoong, then confused by Zelda, although she still bewitched him, by the increasingly blatant cheating of his wife, by business worries. Trudi the masseuse confirmed, smirking, that Nampoong had departed for Thailand with no forwarding address, and offered to 'do him the same'. She figured Nampoong would end up in Pattaya, Phuket, or Ko Samui, resorts crowded with sex-starved tourists, where a girl could sell her body. She knew about Mitch and Zelda, too. Females were all in it together. Suddenly, it all seemed so simple. *Walk away. Lose yourself.*

He told his new friend how easy it had been to sell the business, *his* business, discreetly, to the very real, and very rich, Signor Valentino: Strips was now owned by *Divertimento Internazionale S.A.*, Signor Valentino keeping his massage parlour and chip shop in Merton for old times' sake. If Girl Kit wished to play hardball, then he could easily undercut their prices, with suppliers in the Far East. It all went in a whirl, Mitch's fund of cash in an offshore account, and then, sorted for money, he just walked away from house, wife, car, everything. That was the way big-time fraudsters did it, so easy, create a false paper trail, cover your tracks, move. Most people, trapped by the furniture of their lives, didn't have the imagination to up sticks and get *out*. Let Shannon shack up with the odious 'Gav'. He no longer cared. He knew that somewhere in Thailand he would find Nampoong and at last *possess* her: which alone would give his life meaning.

'Pretty smart move,' his companion said. 'Dump the totty, scoop your wad, and off to lotus land, to do some serious poking. But you don't want Bangkok. It's a concrete nightmare, a perpetual traffic jam, air you could cut with a knife. Has like ten million people, and it floods shit all the time because the sewage system is overloaded. I'm Lancelot Delage, by the way.'

'Mitch Barnett.'

Lancelot seemed younger than Mitch, with a thin bony face, weak, rather feminine lips, and longish sandy hair, not very precisely combed. He wore a cream-coloured silk suit, open-necked shirt and sockless loafers.

'I live in Pattaya,' he continued, as though surprised at the novelty. 'It's not far, and I recommend it. Has miles of bars and things. I bet *they're* going to Pattaya.' He airily waved a hand at the thuggish young males with tattoos. 'It's the world sex capital, with girls and ladyboys and massage and anything you fancy. Bungee jumping, golf.' He grimaced. 'Plus, it's by the seaside, and it's *clean*, more or less.'

Mitch wanted his new life to be clean. He couldn't place Lancelot's accent: upper crust, yet in slipped an occasional vowel suggesting it might have started as something else.

'I wouldn't say I'm here *just* for sex,' he said.

'Yes you are. You can't avoid it, old chap. Forget the monks and temples and rubbish. Thai girls are the best shags in the world. BFM, of course.'

'Uh . . .?'

'Brain function minimal. Normal out here. Booze is cheaper in the PI, but Filipinas are noisy, with weird ideas about *romance*. Worse, they speak English. They screw like rabbits, of course, but they want you to marry them in church and take them back to the world, so they can spend all day confessing their stupid sins to Father Flaherty. Thais are Buddhists, and they don't have sin. Mind you, they don't have love either, just crushes. Thai girls are pure honey in a brown jar, and they are *all* available.'

He licked his lips, and his eyelashes fluttered.

'Do you play golf?'

'No.'

'Wise man. You'll just have to fornicate,' said Lancelot. 'Here for long?'

'Hadn't thought. Open-ended, I suppose.'

Lancelot told him the tiresome procedures of leaving the country for a 'check-out, check-in' every three months, and the multiplicity of visas.

'The Thais want our money, but they flush us out of the system, to keep the kingdom pure. Proud of their poxy independence. Queen Vic and the Raj would have done them good. Touch of civilisation.'

He laughed.

'Happily, money can buy everything. Remember that the foreigner is automatically in the wrong. If you're attacked, it's *you* the cops arrest, but juice them up and you're okay.

Some people never leave at all, either they can't go back where they came from, for obvious reasons, or they're just addicted. End up teaching English, or hustling dodgy stocks over the phone in a boiler room. Anything to stay here. Is that you? Changing roles, a new life?'

'I'm not sure. So you live here, then.'

'More or less. Business. A bit of this and that. Keeps the mind active, otherwise every day is the same. Same girls, food, weather. Nothing's changed since the Buddha, who told them not to drink, gamble, fuck, bribe, steal or murder, all the things they do most. It's the Garden of Eden, and *that* was full of snakes. Don't fall in love. Of course, you will.'

Mitch agreed to try Pattaya first – why not? – and split the taxi fare, incredibly cheap. He collected his suitcase, and Lancelot said he wouldn't need half his clothes, few Europeans realising how hot thirty-plus degrees was. At the immigration desk, Lancelot exchanged pleasantries in Thai with the police girl in her smart blue uniform. Smiling, she stamped his passport with a loud flourish, and he disappeared down the moving staircase to the arrival hall. Mitch's passport received the same efficient thumping treatment.

'Transport is excellent here,' Lancelot said, as they passed uninterested customs officers. 'See, they don't want you out of the spending loop. Time in transit is time not buying things.'

They were besieged by girls in blue uniforms, touting for limousine services. He could not take his eyes off them, so winsome and innocent and cute in uniform, with their young bottoms rippling under the cloth. He wanted all of them, then and there. Not just to fuck, but get to know them, make them smile, please them with gifts. *Spank those cute arses.* The girls would point to a printed price, and Lancelot pouted, sighed and clutched his heart, making the girls smile. They clamoured 'special discount for you, sir.' When he had got the price he wanted, they went outside to wait for their car and have a cigarette.

The air-conditioned terminal had been sultry enough, but outside the mid-morning heat hit Mitch like a hammer.

Sweltering, he lit up and blew smoke. He looked back at the limousine girls, by now surrounding another customer, and felt glum that such loveliness had disappeared from his life. It wasn't fair that so many girls should be so desirable, and that he would never know their names, or anything about them, would never slip his hands under those uniform skirts. He had the impulse to fly somewhere, then fly back, just to revisit those adorable touts. Lancelot said the trick of bargaining was *not* to bargain, unlike stupid tourists, or 'grimmies'. You made them bargain with *you*. That way, the Thai didn't lose face.

'Thais will wait an hour for a taxi to go a hundred metres, rather than walk and lose face. Whatever you're up to, as long as it *looks* pretty, it's okay. None of it means anything, it's all face, all packaging.'

Traffic hummed all around them, and the air was hazy with fumes. The terminal was thronged with Bangkok city taxis, the slam of doors and the blast of police whistles. Mitch wiped his forehead while eyeing elegant sweat-free Thai women, posing as their luggage was crammed into a cab. He found that if a beautiful girl met his eye, she did not look away, but smiled softly, with a secret flirting satisfaction, as if to say, I know what you want, and I want it too. And they were all beautiful. Urgent desire flooded his body, pleasantly soporific from heat and travel fatigue.

Lancelot said you had to be careful not to get into an unlicensed taxi, for you would end up floating in some fetid *klong*, with your head and wallet somewhere else. Hence the policemen with guns and whistles. When they had smoked two cigarettes, their car arrived and they piled into the back seat, Mitch sighing in relief at the cool wave of washed air. After piloting the car through the bewildering airport maze of signs and bends and overpasses, the driver slipped on to the thunderous motorway and cruised up to speed. The traffic going into Bangkok was crawling nose to tail, while the route to Pattaya was clear.

They passed trucks, toll gates, advertisement hoardings for familiar European or American products, mostly confectionery or skin creams, ranks of warehouses, factories and freight companies. Behind them, the primordial landscape of trees and hills, unscarred by fields or fences, drenched in green and dotted with wooden shacks, smoke eddying peacefully from their roofs, as though their inhabitants were oblivious of the twenty-first century. They sat oddly with ads for English ice cream or French yoghourt.

He thought of Richmond Park, and the glades of Wimbledon Common, of the grey sea at Calais, and the ferries, like big wading birds, and told himself that it was too soon to be getting homesick. It was a different sun-washed world, and he had plunged into it. He feared, or rejoiced, that he was one of those who came for a week and stayed for years. It was not fair to bombard the new arrival with *so* many luscious girls, when you could go through western airports without looking twice at a woman. He was falling in love with Thailand. It smelled of lust. As they passed through toll booths, towns on the seaward side sprawled in a jumble of shacks, factories, concrete high rise and traffic snarls. Lancelot said that this was the country's biggest industrial development zone, but there was only one industry in Pattaya, and that was sex.

They drew off the motorway and stopped at a strip of shops, filling stations and American fast-food places. The driver needed to piss, so they all did, then went into a Seven-Eleven, where Lancelot bought two six-packs of Singha beer from the cooler. He gave one to the driver, saying 'tip', and the man beamed, cupping his hands and bowing. Lancelot said that was the traditional *wai*, the Thai gesture of thanks and subservience, and a foreigner must never make it. Mitch filed that, along with not pointing your feet at anybody, and not touching anyone's back or head, and the other weird prohibitions he had picked up from Nampoong. Back in the car, the driver stowed his beer for later, and his passengers popped beer cans. Even with air, the car was hot, and Mitch happily let the cold brew sluice down his throat. Lancelot smiled.

'At home, we have a nice cup of tea,' he said. 'Here, you have a nice cup of beer. Plenty of grimmies have beer for breakfast, and carry on through the day. Those are the ones who end up poking the real dogs from the bars, after dark.'

Draining his beer, he sighed.

'But you need something to make it bearable.'

They turned right and at once travelled through open country, and Mitch imagined he was in 'real' Thailand, which was abruptly absurd as they entered an ex-urban landscape of sodium lights, hotels, supermarkets, American fast food, petrol stations and car showrooms. Teenagers buzzed past them on small Japanese motorcycles, their engines farting, usually with one or two mini-skirted girls perched no-hands on the pillion, their bare legs fluttering like silky brown pennants. The girls smiled, seeing him gape at them, with that knowing sultry smile again, signalling they were bent on lechery. Where? With whom?

And all along the humming highway, crouching between innumerable identical shops, there were bars. Pink and blue and red neon, in the shapes of martini glasses, or nude women, or both, winked at them. They were just ordinary pubs, with the doors open, and early afternoon beer-drinkers perched on stools, some staring dully at football on TV, others laughing while feeling up pert young girls, many with tattoos or piercings, in bright skimpy frocks or hot pants. The punters were grey-haired and the girls scarcely out of their teens, yet appearing to find a grope from a wrinkly the most delightful thing on Earth.

He thought he had never seen so many girly bars. Lancelot laughed; they weren't even downtown yet. They were called box bars, or *bar beers*. Thais had everything backwards. As they turned off the main highway and crawled in dense traffic, with the ubiquitous motorcycles weaving through fume-belching trucks and cars, there were shops and more shops, and 'bar beers', a footpath away, most no more than a counter surrounded by stools, draped in coloured lightbulbs, thudding with ancient disco tunes. The throng of pedestrians paid no attention to the bars or the girls within, but he ogled nymphets with their ageing barstool romeos, and the unattached ones, who waved, squawking '*hallooo . . . sexy man!*'

'Now you know why everybody comes here,' Lancelot said.

He nodded, entranced by the spectacle, and the gentle slope of the roadway, towards the sea, the palm trees, the lustrous brown bodies of girls dangerously younger than himself. His life was embarking on a bright new adventure, full of warmth and colour and beauty. He thought of Nampoong, determined to find her in the honky-tonk metropolis, or another, just like it, and for a change his heart was light.

12

The Lucky Strike

The place was a vast bazaar, with neon signs in a dozen
languages, clothing and jewellery and luggage shops (where
was everyone going?), teeth-whitening clinics, 'erectil dys-
functon', 'gent's tailop', 'profectional Thai boxing'. There
was foot massage, oil massage, and physical massage, as
opposed, perhaps, to some other kind. Motorcycles flitted
through the traffic like noisy butterflies, with their cargo of
bare-legged girls. Ugly converted pickup trucks served as
buses, disgorging men in shorts, nervously jocular as they
headed for another bar and its crew of honeys. Polyglot
eateries jostled, advertising smorgasbord, waterzooi, brat-
wurst, bouillabaisse, American prime rib, all-day breakfast; there was even a London eel and pie shop. Glittering
sugarcake palaces boasted transsexual ladyboy shows.

Amid the glitz, the place was *other*. On every a patch of
green there were people sleeping on the grass, under
tree-shade, beside stalls stinking of fried chillies; vendors of
T-shirts, wooden elephants, flick-knives, wristwatches and
sun-dried foreign newspapers; wizened old ladies in pyja-
mas and straw hats, selling deep-fried locusts, spiders and
assorted bugs. Hotels advertised rooms at amazingly low
prices. Lancelot said you took girls back to your hotel with
no fuss. Plenty of married farangs kept a permanent hotel
room in town for wife-free adventures.

'But she always finds out. There are no secrets here.
Everybody knows you, remembers you, and grasses you
up. They are the nosiest people on Earth.'

They turned down a one-way street, with two-way traffic, and there were palm trees and the turquoise sea, bobbing with boats. Another turn brought them to the sea road, a promenade with girls idling on the low wall and calling out 'hello, sexy man!' to the occasional farang who was not too wrinkly or drunk. Passing the ominously-labelled 'Boyz Town', they turned into a street thankfully devoted to girls. The cab stopped before a three-storey hotel called 'Chuck's Lucky Strike', with a neon sign in turquoise lettering. Beside the hotel was a bar, with winking neon, called 'Lucky Strike A Gogo'. Lissome teenage girls outside carried placards announcing cheap beer for happy hour, and giggled invitations 'hello, welcome, come inside, please'.

'This is your best start,' Lancelot said. 'Chuck is a colourful old dude, American, at the sharp end in Nam, but then practically every Yank you meet was at the sharp end in Nam, like every old Brit was in the Falklands. You're not far from Walking Street, where all the grimmies go first, but it's a buyer's market. Just stroll and sample the merchandise. There are plenty of fish in the sea, and they'll be there forever. Remember that these honeypots are penniless, they live day by day, and they all need a new water buffalo for the farm, or money to get their brother out of jail. Don't short-change them because then you're *keeneow*, a cheap charlie, but don't overtip, because then you're the money tree. Remember, nothing's free. Stiff some girl and you'll end up with a broken bottle in your face. You can walk around after dark and not get mugged, but watch out for the *katoeys*, that's ladyboys. They work in pairs and one feels your balls while the other grabs your wallet.'

Mitch wondered how you could tell a katoey from a girl; for by all lipsmacking accounts in the tabloid press, they looked like the real thing.

'Narrow hips, big hands and big feet. Only bits they can't have snipped or siliconed. If a girl's taller than you, or as tall, it's a katoey. In fact, if you have the slightest suspicion it might be a katoey, then it is one. Some of them

97

are quite sweet, and there is always the curiosity how much of their meat they've had snipped. Thais being always broke, they'll have the op as they can afford it, one bollock at a time.'

Mitch got out of the car amid a screech of klaxons from the vehicles behind, and immediately started sweating. Lancelot said he would see him around. Pattaya was quite small, and you saw everybody sooner or later; most nights he looked in at 'Schoolgirls' bar on soi six – sixth street – if Mitch fancied a beer later on.

'Does it ever get cool here?' he asked.

'No,' said Lancelot.

It was blissfully cool, though, inside the air-conditioned lobby of Chuck's Lucky Strike. The place was a museum of Thai curiosities: rugs, tribal masks, statues of girls in the nude, paintings of landscapes, temples and girls fully clad, stone elephants or obscure gods and goddesses, and, in the corner, before the entrance to a cosy-looking bar, a larger version of the shrine he had seen on the plane. It had real candles and fragrant incense sticks burning, with a painted golden Buddha contemplating the offerings of beer, whisky, nuts, fruit and bizarre American snack foods. The room and upward staircase were of glistening dark teak over a parquet floor. It smelled like the house of a grandmother and her curios.

A grey-haired man in T-shirt and shorts clinging to his beer gut collected his room key before steering a giggling teenage girl up the stairs on his liver-spotted hairy legs. Lancelot had talked casually of the price of girls, as though paying for sex was normal. He told Mitch to avoid the 'never paid for it in my life' brigade, for they courted trouble: you always paid, one way or another. So the farangs thronged the bars, flirting and groping, each ready to pay for the privilege of falling in love with his very own honeypot and her mysterious oriental magic.

Back home, there was shame in going to a hooker – *paying* for it! – although massage in a wanky sauna was harmless fun, while for masochists in the Scene a session with a professional dominatrix was acceptable, should no sympathetic girl be at hand. But people would laugh, or spit, if he went with some strung-out junkie up King's Cross, or an old tom in Shepherd's market. Rough trade, yuk. Even high-class *maisons closes* had an air of furtive discretion. Yet here, prostitution was everyday currency, both for sex-starved codgers, and hunky young guys, who surely weren't sex-starved. Were they?

He stepped up to the desk and asked the teenage girl if she had a room. Even the simple request seemed personal, provocative. She smiled – long handsome face, straight nose, perfect conic breasts and ripe buttocks adorning a slim elfin frame, *mouth-watering* – and he took a deep breath. Her name badge said 'Woaw'. She looked lithe, full of gymnastic power, a tigress ready to spring. Was she on the game, too? Would she go upstairs with him? Despite the jet lag and time difference, he felt irresistibly, desperately horny, overwhelmed by the pervasive scent of sex. Hard to see how anyone in Thailand got any work done with so much perfumed half-dressed beauty shimmering around.

Of course we have a room, just for you, sir: de luxe or superior? He felt foolish in demanding the price, a de luxe room costing no more than a few pints in the Rose and Crown. The girl was immaculate in a white blouse with a turquoise bow, a trim linen two-piece suit, also turquoise, and long shiny legs encased in white glassine nylons. Her long silky hair sported a ribbon which also managed to be turquoise. That colour was in delicious counterpoint to the caramel skin; any pastel colour would enthral. She was obviously not on the game, and there was a uniform for respectable business girls, although, according to Lancelot, they were all on it. He felt himself stir at his shock of desire, imagining stripping off those nylons, then her minuscule turquoise panties – they'd have to be turquoise – and caressing her bare brown bottom. Or spanking her. Dizzy with heat and lust, he wanted that girl.

Minutes later, he was showered, and stretched nude on the giant double bed in number twelve, his de luxe room. He closed his eyes, intending to sleep, but in his imagination Woaw was lying equally nude beside him. He drove her image away, and she was replaced by the girl going up the stairs with the beer belly – how could she settle for *that*, and ignore *him*? – then by all the girls he had ogled on the trip into town. He returned to the dream of Woaw and sighed in contented arousal, joyfully feeling his erection. His balls ached with sperm, longing to pour itself into her pouch, soft, wet and warm, between sweet brown thighs. He wanted to fuck her, *now*, wanted to fuck all the girls he had seen. '*I got so much love to give* . . .' Thai heartbreak. After dozing for twenty minutes, he sprang from the bed, still erect, and had another shower, although the air-conditioner in the room was perfect.

No point in sleeping, for he was still full of travel adrenaline, and he wanted every girl in Pattaya, all at once, before they might evaporate. Urgency gripped him: he had to make up for a life of lost time. He felt a universe away from Shannon, from Zelda and all the other girls whose pallid bodies he had slapped and humped like so many cold wet fish on a slab. Thai girls were all brown like Nampoong, hot and earth-sweet, their skins delicious coffee, caramel, brown sugar, promising untold joy as they writhed and sucked and licked with silky tongues, musky bare bodies slippery against his, wrapping dark thighs around him, milking him with soft wet dreams. He shivered at the throat-parching power of his desire.

Like the lobby, room twelve was an Aladdin's cave chock full of artifacts, more explicitly sexual than those on public display: statuettes and paintings of couples copulating in various yogic positions, beside those of the customary elephants and temples. There was not much room for a guest's luggage, as every surface was strewn with merchandise priced for sale: playing cards, chewing gum, dice, condoms in several fruit flavours, lubricating jelly, Japanese pillow books, disposable cameras, rubber clitticklers, butt plugs coyly labelled as babies' dummies, and vibrating dildos in a choice of pink or black, described as muscle massagers. The door was padded and the flock wallpaper thick, so that the room was effectively sound-proofed.

It was a whore's boudoir, but if everyone in Pattaya was a whore, that made him one as well. On the mini-bar lay a handmade book, with pages wrapped in polythene, called 'Chuck's Guide to the Pleasures of Paradise', a manual of erotic etiquette: bargaining, paying, treating, tipping, threesomes, foursomes, what to look for – a teen with no babies, preferably fresh off the bus from the village – or what to avoid, such as a girl with bad breath, which meant she did illegal methamphetamine, called *ya-ba*, crazy pills. Chuck would rather not have such girls in his hotel, for they might go berserk and trash the room. Ladyboys were all right, if well-behaved, and an unwary customer often engaged a ladyboy without realising she was not totally female. If that happened, his advice was just go with the flow, lay back and enjoy the ride. Do not try to welsh on a ladyboy, for they carried knives.

He solemnly informed the reader that butt plugs and dildos were illegal in puritanical Thailand, as was all porno and all gambling. Prostitution, too, was illegal, but a bar girl was a service girl, not a prostitute, and, coincidentally, opening her legs was part of the service. Sex was a transaction, and the customer should not be shy of asking a girl for whatever he wanted, however bizarre. She had heard it all before; he would get an eager yes, or a polite no, and a referral to a lady who could accommodate him. A service girl's job was to please. Get clear whether you have engaged her for a 'short time' or all night. Don't pay until *after* service, but tip extra for an enthusiastic performance. Most girls insist on using a condom, and try not to get upset about this. There was nothing about spanking, but it was undoubtedly acceptable, as everything else seemed to be. ('Girls often agree to BBBJ, a bareback blowjob, but love to give head when you're wearing a banana-flavoured condom . . . Many girls do anal sex. It's up to you, the customer. Just ask.')

He clicked on the TV, which offered three triple-X pay-channels, one Japanese (a bespectacled nerd screwing a sleeping nurse), along with free foreign cable stations. On the Thai stations there was an astrologer reading

101

horoscopes; a gangster movie with blood spurting from a trussed girl's head; various gun battles with slo-mo slaughter; a sequinned ladyman hosting a slapstick game show, with mud and pratfalls. On a local English-language station, a solemn Hindu lady read the news: 'Suicide was the official verdict on a British tourist who fell to his death from his eighth floor hotel room. He had split up from his girlfriend, and had consumed a large quantity of alcohol, and possibly illegal *ya-ba* pills. This brings the total number of suicides in Pattaya this year to . . .'

He switched over to BBC World, with sober tales of bomb attacks and epidemics and disasters, then turned the set off. That stuff seemed so far away, so irrelevant. Below him was a quiet courtyard but, from beyond, he could smell the aroma of sizzling meats, hear the hubbub of the street, the shrill klaxons, the cheers of drunks, and the squawking go-go girls. *That* was his new reality. He dressed in jeans, a short-sleeved shirt and loafers, but no socks, and set off to explore. Descending, he passed another couple going up, hand in hand, the young lad, flushed with drink, perhaps a virgin, going for his first time; she much older, in a tube top and shorts, with her hair dyed in orange and purple stripes, and a garish tattoo on her shoulder. A brass, *moi*? Woaw gave him a smile as he handed her his room key, his fingertips brushing hers.

13

Walking Street

Walking Street, named with unerring Thai simplicity, was a circus, glittering with savage light in the dusk. Girls were everywhere, pacing businesslike to work, or smiling, winking and wiggling, in mocking come-on. Tourists shuffled, their lumpy blonde girlfriends gazing at the whores with bright jealous eyes. The Thai girls *were* whores, and it was strange that such gorgeous creatures, eyes flashing with mischievous fun, were no more than brasses, slappers, tarts. But they weren't jaded. They were girlish, alive, full of fun. They were *different*. He played at counting nationalities – loping American, earnest Swede, diffident Brit, or smug Frenchman, but gave up, as there were so many. The Troika Russian go-go had sluttish blondes touting outside, and only Russians seemed to go in; you could tell them by their spudlike faces and huge bellies. Some foreign girls had their arms round Thai girls, and many stolid foreign men held hands with young mincing males.

'Wel-*come*! Come inside please!'

'Hello, sexy man!'

'Where you come from?'

All the merchandise was on view, with girls touting in front of the raucous box bars. He was surprised to be nervous, smiling shyly, and stepping aside from beseeching fingers, even though some of the girls were fabulous, beyond beautiful; yet he knew that *she* with the bright eyes and smile would not be the drab who grabbed him inside. His lust dimmed, perhaps at the sight of the lesbians and gayboys and perverted old farts strolling so openly in the sight of the occasional bored copper. No one seemed to mind his refusal, or care that the next target was a beer-bellied wrinkly who looked as if he should be tucked up with his TV and evening cocoa.

There was just so *much* of everything. Young girls, pouting and preening, hair shiny, legs and arms bare, in bar upon bar; or street-strutting, for sale, with little-girl hardcore smiles, flowers of the east wanting to be plucked. Where was the thrill of the chase? It was dark, the luminescence of the gaudy street adding enticement to sweet little moon-faces and lustrous brown skins. He told himself that there was all night to party, so he would do it in relaxed fashion: eat first. You could eat on the street, from one of the pavement stalls selling chicken and soup and weird sizzly things, with plastic tables and chairs, occupied by go-go girls in glitzy costumes, absorbed in their guzzling.

He thought of Nampoong, of Zelda, of Woaw, and was suddenly thirsty for beer. He sat down in a box bar beside the street and ordered a Heineken. It came frosted, in a rubber sleeve to keep it cold, but no glass, and his bar receipt in a little wooden pot. Macho, he drank from the neck. When the first one went down, he felt happy, watching the girls and the street action as if his perch on a barstool placed him morally above the strolling frustrates, ogling and sniffing. Pattaya was a good place to be macho; he was king, all those girls there to serve him.

The music, bang boom, was deafening. The bars were filling up, animated by falling dusk. Beside him, a tattooed drunk pinched a giggling honeypot's thighs, then her toes, which made her shriek with laughter. His hand slipped down the front of her tube top and began to fondle her braless breasts, which popped naked from her top, allowing him to bounce them up and down, then squeeze both breasts together in his anthropoid paw. The girl seemed pleased with this attention. He gazed at Mitch with a bleary grin.

'She has the good tits, but it is the feet I like,' he slurred. 'Are you English? I am Olaf, from Norway. The Norway girls are the most beautiful in the world, with the best feet, and best tits, but they are cold as a fockin ice bear. I like to suck the feet. Thai girls have sometimes the good feet, but often they are fockin thick, for pulling the cart like an ox. What is your thing?'

'I . . . panties, I suppose,' Mitch replied, thrilled by such frankness. We pretend to be gents, he thought, with manners and discretion, but we're dirty buggers, really. 'And I like spanking girls.'

'You are a knickers fancier. It is good. The Thai girls love knickers. The English love the spanking. And they want sadic girls to whip them. There is a bar where the girls do spanking shows, Soi six, I think. Near the Big C supermarket. You must be careful, some girls will let you do it, but they are afraid of evil spirits, and pain and fighting. Some girl not use the whip, they think the man will be sadic with her. But she will put a banana up her arse if you pay her enough. They are all fockin whores! If a girl is ugly, I fock her in the arse with a carrot. It is good fun. Carrots are not expensive in the Big C supermarket.'

He patted his girl on the rump and lifted her foot out of its platform shoe, a scary construction of absurd height. He put her toes to his mouth and began to suck, provoking more giggles from the girl and her friends. Mitch said it was called shrimping, and Olaf wheezed with spittle-flecked laughter.

'That is good word!' he cried. 'I am a fisherman, I fish the focking big prawns. Her name is Goong, that means shrimp! So I shrimp the shrimp. I have had Goong many times. And that one, Om' – he pointed – 'and that one, Foon, and that one is Appen. They have no babies, so their pussies are tight, like a ladyboy's arsehole. Appen gives it with the mouth, no condom. I have many girlfriends in Pattaya! They all fock good, but Om is best for *chak wao*, with the hand, if you do not like condom, or you are too drunken to fock. On the fishing boat, everybody makes *chak wao* with a fish, like the ancient Wikkings. We are all Wikkings! So when you English eat your fish and chips, you know where it has been.'

He laughed again, his own best audience.

'I have ten beers, but I am not pissed,' he announced. 'In Norway, we can drink more than the English. They go to the pub and get too drunken to fock, but we are never too drunken to fock. Now I fock Goong.'

Goong helped him from his barstool and he drained his beer, a regal wave of his arm inviting Mitch to sample Om, Foon, or Appen, all girls of guaranteed charm. He shuffled off unsteadily into the street, on his way to fock, while the three Olaf-approved girls draped themselves around Mitch's barstool. Foon and Om had dark-blue butterfly tattoos on their shoulders.

'You buy me one drink?' said Foon, stroking his thigh.

Her fingers slipped to his balls and began to rub. He bought them all drinks and they took turns at rubbing his balls. Smiles from the waitress as the bills piled up in his wooden pot. He had a look, to see how much he was being stung for a glass (he supposed) of coloured water, and found it to be the same as a half of lager in the Rose and Crown. When he asked to taste Foon's drink, he coughed; it was almost neat tequila.

He slid his hand down her mini-skirt and inside her thong panties and began to stroke her bottom. Then he cradled her breasts and squeezed; they were big, jutted rather alarmingly, and felt like tennis balls inside; the fabled silicone implant. He did the same to each girl in turn, eventually sliding his fingers inside her sex. They were hot and honey-moist, and his penis stirred. The drinks kept coming: wonderfully decadent, to snap languid fingers while your hand was pawing a compliant girl's arse or crotch. You couldn't do that in the Rose and Crown, unless you were Swinburne, perhaps. No one knew him here: he could do what he liked. He went to the unisex bathroom, to piss amid gossiping lipsticking girls, and read the graffito: *This is not a dress rehearsal. This is real life.*

They awaited his return, of course, worried he might escape. He felt the same rush of freedom as when Zelda had said yes, as when any girl yielded; at last she fell into your arms, clung to you, sighing, soppy, feeling your godlike male *power*, and unable to resist; the perfume of her hair, of her dress, her magical fabulous girl's body clinging to you, *yours*; the same grateful exaltation, as when a knowing girl bared her bottom for spanks. Here, every girl yielded. His reverie was broken by Foon, clasping his balls as he stroked her buttocks.

'You go with me, sexy man?' she whispered. 'I love you too much.'

The other two edged back; by unspoken etiquette, he was now Foon's. The girl was everything he'd want, firm young breasts, good legs, and – yes – suckable feet, which she had thoughtfully removed from her shoes, to curl her toes around his leg. Even in the smoky cacophonous stink of the bar, her perfume bewitched him. He withdrew his fingers from her moist quim, then sniffed and licked them, saying '*hom*'. Foon, Om, Appen – making a foursome! – all naked together in room twelve, possibly spanking, if he could make it seem light-hearted. Money wasn't a problem, not like London, where a stratospheric bill for drinks and dinner as often as not inspired a headache, or the 'just good friends' routine, and a 'thank you for being understanding'. Damn, these girls understood what their arses were for.

'You want fuck ass?' said Foon, drawing his finger to the cleft of her buttocks. 'You want smoking?'

Vigorously, she mimed fellatio. He recoiled from the crude hooker's come-on. She didn't *really* like him, he was just a bit of meat with money. Hadn't the Norwegian oaf been up her, in every orifice no doubt? All the old excuses of the shy teenager, why he shouldn't approach that inviting girl in pub or party – she was just teasing – then taking sodden refuge in pints. So it was now; pushing a small banknote into each girl's panties, he left, promising to come back later, and saying he needed to eat. The girls smiled, and turned at once to scout for new prospects. No fond farewells. Well, that proves they *really* didn't like me. Almost got caught there.

When he sat down at a street stall, with fiery hot soup and rice, he at once felt a pang of regret for young Foon.

Silicone or no – and her jumbo-sized balcony *did* have a certain ghoulish appeal – she was a goer, would do anything for the right money. He should go back to see her, but no, by now, Murphy's law, she'd probably gone with someone else. She was just a whore, after all. Good riddance. *What a ditherer.* Om and Appen sat down at the same stall and nodded coldly. This was their break; when eating, they were not working.

Fed, he felt filled with new energy. He ducked into a side alley full of go-go bars, all with tuxedoed male touts outside. Selecting one named 'The Warm Pussy', whose neon sign showed a cat in a fur coat, he dived into the plush air-conditioned darkness. A girl in a spangled bikini steered him to a banquette by the wall with a narrow table, where he had a view of the central stage on which a posse of a dozen girls were gyrating.

'You like some drink?' a bikinied lovely chirped.

He got a beer, and sat back to breathe in the perfume of lust in the chill washed air. Around him, the tables were occupied by single men, and there were a few couples, male and female intently studying the anatomy of the nude dancers. The Warm Pussy was not box-bar shabby, but sleazy wannabe glamorous, though with the same universal disco thump-music; he checked his drink tab, and found the price reflected both the ritzy décor and the beauty of the girls, none of them disfigured by tattoos. Their silky caramel flesh writhed, changing colour, under travelling pink, green and yellow spotlights. All were young, with slender graceful faces, flat bellies, firm bums and breasts, and delightful brown nipples, cheekily hard. He allowed himself to lust.

At each break in the music, the dancers shuffled one place forward, a new dancer joining the rear of the conga, and the girl in front, by the door, stepping off. Girls waiting to dance, or having just danced, sat on a banquette at one end of the salon, gossiping in the nude, apart from those who returned to sit on the lap of their previously hooked farang. Curiously, as a girl took up the front spot by the door, she slipped into her bikini. If she rejoined her olaf, she took it off again and let him play with her body. He thought of all beery white men as olafs.

The dancers mimed ecstasy, pouting as they parted their thighs, crouched, or clung to poles, and caressed themselves, pretending to masturbate, with front and rear views. Mirrors on every wall meant that the customers could see all of the girls all the time. Some olafs crooked a finger and a dancer, leaving the line, joined him at his table. This was not like a *bar beer*, where the girls leeched on to their chosen target; here, they awaited the call. Some men pushed a rolled banknote between the girl's thighs, and with a sweet undulation of her hips, her chatte swallowed the money.

He took his time over his beer, then another, until he had selected the one he wanted, a slender succulent teenager with perfect firm skin and buttocks, pert breasts, and an outie belly-button, giving her flat tummy a beguiling innocence. Her hillock was completely shaven, unlike most of the other girls who had trimmed to a moustache. When she faced his table he smiled and mimed kisses. She smiled back. Her bumps and grinds seemed pleasantly decorous, even tasteful, hinting at a sensuality in reserve, which she was keeping for the right man. *Not your average hooker. She's different.*

He pointed to her, then back to him, and patted the seat beside him. Her smile grew to a beam, she nodded, and turned to spread her cheeks at him, treating him (and everybody else) to a vision of her sex and anus. She smiled for him and with finger and thumb pulled her lips apart, letting him see the pinkness of her pouch. He stiffened, thinking that he would soon be enjoying penetration. Mouth-watering – yes, definitely. As she progressed up the line, she gazed at him in the mirror, occasionally baring her teeth and licking them in promise of the delights to come. She donned her bikini for the final tune, but as soon as she came off the stage, so did her garment and, swathed in pastel light, the tender young beauty walked sure-footed on her high heels to sit naked beside him.

14

Cradle Snatcher

Her name was O. She spoke some English, apart from the usual whore's catcalls and, when he had ordered her a lady drink, ritually asked his name and origin. England and Mitch established, he learned that she came from Udon Thani, and he feigned understanding, saying that girls in Udon Thani were the most beautiful in Thailand. She smiled, showing dainty pure-white teeth, and cupped her hands, bowing her head in a *wai*, with a submissive 'thank you'. She was eighteen years old, new to the game; she had been in Pattaya a month. His penis was hard, for she wasn't really a whore, she was different, she was his beauty. It was crazy, he was scarcely off the plane, and a nude perfect girl whose body shamed the word 'luscious' was bowing to him. How could so much beauty be packed into such a neat parcel? Every cliché – poetry in motion, magic moments, you were made for me – suddenly seemed right. This was not his gut-wrenching obsession with Nampoong; O's body was a pool of pleasure into which he longed to plunge. All those years of lusting after girls, as he mentally undressed them! Here was the real naked thing. He rested his palm on the silk of her buttocks, and she smiled coyly. He stroked her bottom, letting his finger brush her cleft, not too far inside, but enough to make her tense and quiver, with a little 'ooh'. Honey filled his balls. If she even touched him there, like the other girls, he felt he would ejaculate in his pants, and it seemed a wonderful liberation, a delicious feeling he had not had since he was a horny teen. He had never come in his pants, except with Sylvie. He should now. O wouldn't mind, she would take it as a compliment.

She informed him, with hand gestures (but he was watching the quiver of her breasts), that her name meant 'cradle'. It was not her real name, which ran to six or seven syllables. Thais used nicknames. He asked her what others meant: Lek meant small; Foon, dust; Appen, curiously, apple; Om, 'save money'. Other names were animals, plants, or descriptive: 'fat' or 'stupid'. He didn't see the attraction of calling yourself dust, or fat, or stupid. Perhaps that was why, as Nampoong said, Thai girls swapped names a lot.

'You have many ladies,' she said solemnly. 'You butterfly. Butterfly hop-hop, one lady, two lady, three lady.'

He said he had only just arrived.

'No have other lady? Speak sure?'

'Scout's honour,' he nodded earnestly, then joked 'Story of O', reflecting she had probably heard that before; although the average olaf looked far from literary.

She smiled, not understanding, and sipped her lady drink. Abruptly, the lights in the bar went out, save for the spotlight over the bikini-clad dancer next to the door. The door opened and a Thai male put his face through the curtain. Mitch had seen no Thai males prowling Walking Street; all the questers were foreign. The man peered briefly at the bikini girl, then withdrew, and the lights went back on.

'Police,' she explained. 'Must check girl have shirt.'

He stroked her tender breasts, soft, but firm, no silicone here, and she pouted, closing her eyes, with a little 'mm . . .'

'You have no shirt,' he said.

'Just for you.'

They had more drinks and she sat on his lap, allowing him to caress her breasts and bottom; her thighs were closed, although he could have felt her sex, but he wished to keep that treasure sacred. He played with her belly-button until she said it tickled, and looked at her softly

111

swelling hillock, pretended to seize it like a falcon its prey, but did not touch her. He stroked her hair, silky smooth like her skin and dancing on her shoulders, then thrust his nose and lips into it, saying '*hom*', and she giggled, crying '*bagwan!*'

'What does that mean?'

'Bagwan, have black heart, say same to all ladies.'

She whispered that she had to dance.

'You come home with me?'

She nodded again, blowing him a kiss, and ascended the stage. Mitch leaned back and lit a cigarette, relief, excitement and glory washing over him. *Sorted!* So easy! The agonies of courtship back home, some neurotic bitch with her precious armour-plated quim, scoffing your vittles and whining about commitment, don't want a purely physical relationship, I've been hurt before. God, you could write the script. Of course, with her skull full of that crap, you only *did* want her for her fucking quim. Zelda, she was so weird she was okay. Nampoong . . . well, she was *different*. Christ, maybe they were all different.

She danced just for him, her sex pointing always at his face, and her movements more lascivious than before, now that she was booked. It seemed an age before she advanced doorside, popped into her bikini, completed her turn, then rejoined him, bare-breasted, and sat on his lap. In the crotch of her bikini nestled a banknote.

'Farang tip,' she said, bashfully.

Some fat shit had slipped her a note when he wasn't looking! He felt a stab of jealous rage. Didn't they know she was with him? He had probably stuffed it in her cunt . . . *his* cunt.

'Who was it?' he snarled, intending to throw the money in the bastard's face.

She put her arms round him.

'I forget,' she said. 'All farangs look same.'

'Let's go. I want you now,' he said.

The serving girl came back with an amended bar tab. He settled his bill, frowning at charges that seemed to have come from nowhere. O explained that he had to pay a bar fine to the owner, for depriving him of her services. It was the way.

'You mean I'm subsidising some pimp? I'd rather give you the money.'

She scampered off, to return bare-legged but demure in a short red shirt-dress and sensible elegant shoes. The skirt was pleated, swirling and bobbing around her fabulous legs, which were long and softly curved, rippling with dancer's muscle. She took his hand and they went out into the street, to smiles and good lucks and farewells from her colleagues, for she had scored early. On the way back to the Lucky Strike, he took her to a restaurant and fed her, wanting to be seen squiring her, his property. A pleasant feeling of guilt and naughtiness filled him, for he was cheating on Nampoong. Other girls smiled: *When you're finished with her, come back and do me.* There were so many willing eyes. Perhaps that was why she wolfed her food, seeming anxious to hurry to his hotel, asserting *her* possession.

Woaw was off duty, her place taken by an epicene male night clerk, tall and slender, who handed over the key to room twelve with a flutter of his long eyelashes; the name badge announced him as 'On', and, in shadow, he could have passed for a girl. He smiled a friendly smile. O went before him up the stairs and he peeped at her scarlet thong panties revealed by the swirl of her skirt. He looked back to see a faint grin on the night clerk's lips. O inspected the room with interest, thumped the bed, and began pawing the gewgaws on sale. She embraced him, her lips blowing into his ear. He felt for his wallet and, making sure she saw, took out large banknotes and tucked them into her purse.

'Tip,' he said, ignoring Chuck's instructions, and thinking that he should establish his good heart right from the start. 'I want you to stay all night.'

She nodded yes, hugging him fiercely, then disengaged and bowed, cupping her hands.

'*Kop kon kaa* . . .' she murmured, thanking him. 'We shower?'

He threw off his clothes; his erection throbbed. She let him slowly strip her, tickling her to make her laugh, and kneeling, reverently to unroll her panties, which he thrust to his nose and lips, breathing deeply, and intoning '*hom*.' She blushed and laughed more, pulling him to his feet and into the shower. Before joining him, she squatted on the loo, tinkled discreetly, and squirted between her legs with the rubber irrigation tube. Revelation: in Thailand or France, you have a dump, you clean yourself, but in bidet-less Britain, all those smug sloaney girls walk around with shitty arseholes! Beneath the designer frocks and knickers, a slithering channel of yuk. It was both repellent and thrilling. Under the hot spray, she soaped him, although he would not let her spend too long caressing his penis.

'I'll go off like a rocket,' he said.

She stroked his shaven pubes, scratching him with her long fingernails, and saying it was sexy. Most farangs were covered in hair, which she did not like. Thai men were smooth, but she did not like Thai men – few Thai girls did – because they were cruel and lazy, beat their women, and drank whisky while the women worked. When it was his turn to soap her, he knelt, and after washing and rinsing her toes, and kissing her sex, he took each foot into his mouth and sucked. His fingers penetrated her anus, and she cried that it tickled.

'You want fuck little hole?' she asked.

'I want fuck everywhere,' he replied.

'Up to you.'

She had to towel herself completely before stretching on the bed; then apply talc and scent (on his room bill); again, he kissed and licked her feet, his erection aching. Turning her over, he licked her bottom, his nose in her cleft, breathing in her scent, then chewed her belly-button. She pushed him back, to kneel and suck his penis; after a short delicate fellatio, she parted his arse cheeks and penetrated his anus with her tongue. He could not wait; roughly spreading her thighs, he entered her, gasping with glee at the tightness of her pouch, and managed only a few strokes before he did, indeed, go off like a rocket.

She nuzzled him.

'You have big power,' she whispered.

She hadn't demanded a condom. Better and better. Then, in post-coital ennui, he thought that if she didn't use one with him, how about the others? All those horror stories about the dread disease. Nampoong never used a condom either. What the hell? Like taking a bath with your boots on. *Qué sera, sera.* O took beers, one each, from the fridge, and lit a cigarette for him. Still griping, he quizzed her about the extortionate bar fine. It seemed crazy, when there were willing girls everywhere. She said the Warm Pussy looked after its girls, paying them a salary, for which they had to chalk up ten bar fines every month. She had been an infant school teacher, in Udon Thani, but it did not pay well, and she needed more money for her family. He gulped beer and sucked on his cigarette. At least ten olafs had fucked her. What number was *he*?

'But I have no boyfriend,' she said, stroking him.

'I don't believe you. You are so beautiful, you must have a boyfriend.'

'No!' she said fiercely.

It seemed a point of honour, and she wasn't going to tell the truth, anyway. However delicious, she was a whore. And his penis was stirring again. He descended to her quim and tongued her, then made her sit on his face where her buttocks writhed prettily, crushing him in their perfume, and he bathed in her juice. His mouth glazed with her moisture, he asked her to spank him.

'You want sadic?' she said, surprisingly unsurprised.

She held him on her thighs, with his face at her feet, and gave him an expert, quite painful spanking while he shrimped her toes. More beers, and she asked if he wanted to spank *her*, 'but not big hurt.' He took her over his knee and gave a light spanking, until her delicately wriggling bottom blushed, and she gasped with sweet little moans. Without asking, he made her crouch, parted her buttocks, and penetrated her anus. She moaned and gasped 'up to you.'

Her anal elastic gripped his penis like a marrow. Her head was pressed to the pillow, her spine twisting. She

115

panted, moaning shrilly at each thrust. A primal scene, the male dominant, shaming the helpless female, giving his seed not to the cunt, the place of life, but pouring it in the place of sterility, pain and waste, in denial of her very womanhood. *We fuck women because we are jealous of their beauty, which we can never possess. We punish them for having cunts.* He wanted to possess the girl wholly, hurt her with love, and, in her shame and pain, to *be* her, to taste her young body as she tasted it; to change identities so that she, miraculously possessed of her own penis, was fucking *his* anus. Then he would know her. *But you can never truly know a woman, only her movements, her act.*

He slid his hand between her thighs, to find her oily wet, and, rubbing her clito, he spermed at the root of her anus. When he withdrew his softened penis, she asked him submissively if she could make *chak wao* and, approved, she masturbated, coolly and clinically, until she orgasmed. *Chak wao*, having a wank, poetically meant flying a kite; even verbal packaging was cute. Afterwards, she sprang up and kissed him on the cheek, then, when she had visited the bathroom – he lay back, relishing the gurgle of water on her private places – she retrieved a dildo from the basket of Chuck's sale goodies.

'You want me make for you?' she asked mischievously. 'Fuck you behind?'

He said no, for she was not really serious.

'Up to you. Many farang like.'

The thought intrigued him, but made him queasy. Imagine fucking Olaf's hairy arse. He lay, contentedly smoking, on the bed, with O curled in his arms, planning their next coupling after he had rested. By his body clock, it was late afternoon back in London. He was entitled to a little siesta. He dozed off, to awake with the lights still on.

When he awoke, she was gone, and so – on hurried inspection – was a few thousand baht from his wallet: not all the cash, but, puzzlingly, an odd amount. Also gone were the banana-flavoured condoms and the dildo. She must have seen the photos of Nampoong in his wallet and been jealous, and, although she shouldn't have been there in the first place, female logic would find him guilty of cheating on her. One photo had Nampoong's face scratched out. Room twelve was beginning to cost a lot more than room twelve.

He cracked another beer and lit a cigarette, smoking until his initial rage had passed, to be replaced by uncertainty. Rolled by a cheap hooker! All alone in a foreign land, not knowing what the police might say if he complained. In this cockeyed honky-tonk town, they might sling *him* in jail for immorality. Then he laughed. He'd had his money's worth – God, that luscious brown body! – and she'd taken only the cost of a West End taxi. In fact, these girls were like taxis, you rode them as far as you wanted to go. A diamond jest. Anyway, he knew where to find her. What superb one-upmanship, to corner the bitch, and smile, and say he understood, was not angry, and still wanted to know her. Now he had reason to give her a real spanking.

15

Greenhorn

He awoke to sunlight streaming into his room. Fuelled by
dreams of Nampoong and O, he touched himself, pleased.
The heat, the flowers, the smell of girls – Thailand was
superbly erectile. The defacement of Nampoong's photo
did not distress him as much as he feared. It showed she
cared for him, in some perverse way, and had provided him
with an adventure, so soon. There remained the question
of Nampoong, whether he had come here to find her, or
forget her. He groped for his watch, found it was a quarter
to nine, and felt that joy, upon early awakening, of three
extra hours added to one's life. He stretched, lit a cigarette,
and tumbled out of bed, his eye caught by a flash of scarlet
underneath his tousled coverlet. O had left her thong,
perhaps a bizarre forget-me-not, or perhaps her bottom
hurt too much to wear it in her thief's urgency. It was a
prize. He had something of hers. He pressed it to his face,
breathing deeply of her fragrance, then pressed it to his
balls.

After showering, he shaved his whole body, relishing the
sexual power of smoothness. Body hair seemed an encum-
brance, a cover-up. There was sensual pleasure in the act,
lathering and scraping legs, pubis, belly. Millions of men
shaved their chins every day, with scented foam and lotion,
luxurious self-mutilation, a triumph of marketing. Why
not the rest? What you see is what you get. Pleasant, to
matter-of-factly touch your penis and balls, as a nurse
would, free of wanky inhibition. How little we know our

bodies, so many people unacquainted with their all-important anus. Doctor finds a fucking polyp up your arsehole, you admit you never checked in there. Nampoong had turned him on to a smooth body; hell, he *must* look for her. On impulse, he put on O's panties. They hugged, tickling, as he pulled them tight. He felt a tingle in his balls, sheathed in *her* wondrous cache-sexe.

Hungry, he descended to the lobby, where the uniformed Woaw was on duty. Her smile seemed a little forced. Did she know about his adventure last night? He assumed the epicene On, seeing his girl flee in the small hours, would have told her, and she might be dreading an irate farang complaining about his missing cash. But he could prove nothing. Why stir?

'Wonderful night's sleep,' he murmured – her smile brightened – then, brazen, 'I am happy to see you again, for you are so beautiful.' *Try saying that to some bird on the nineteen bus.*

She looked down.

'You enjoyed your evening, sir?' she murmured.

Her smile said 'I know what smutty boys are like, why you all come here, and I tolerate, but disapprove'. Her mien was steely, I'm not for sale, irresistible.

'Yes. Fascinating. I'd love you to show me around.'

'You are on holiday, but I must work.'

Looking him reproachfully in the eye. A little pout of her lips: don't try it, back off. He felt the string of O's panties nestling sharply in his cleft, and imagined Woaw taking a whip to him for impudence. Electrified, he stiffened against the flimsy cloth pouch: partly from the voluptuous fantasy, of course – Woaw stripped to her imagined turquoise skimpies, breasts bobbing, scarcely contained by their cups, and powerful young thighs rippling as she thrashed him – but also shocked, because suddenly he really *did* want a whipping from this girl, wanted to see her cruel smile as she made him smart. Anything seemed possible here, and such freedom made him shiver. He took a giveaway city map from the desk, his hand passing close to her breast, and wondered if she saw his erection – hoped she did, and sensed her authorship.

In the coffee shop, a dark-eyed teenage waitress in a pleated turquoise skirt served him breakfast. He said her waist-length hair was pretty, and *she* smiled, with a submissive blush. She had pert breasts under her crisp white blouse, and fine legs, sheathed in sheer white nylons, acceptable in the air-conditioning but quite unsuitable for the heat outside. He sipped coffee and wolfed bacon and eggs while scanning her rounded buttocks, with just a hint of high bikini line, and wondered what colour *her* panties were. *No, idiot! This is breakfast!*

Chuck, no doubt a horny old devil, probably supervised their costuming, making sure that panties were pulled up tight. He would himself, with such a hareem. He imagined spanking the juicy waitress, but wanted Woaw to thrash *him*. So what if he was on the cusp of masochism? Like the time of day, it didn't matter, for Thailand released you from the bonds of meaning. The Scene seemed a bit self-important with all its solemn categories. Here, you could be anything, reinvent yourself, like that Welsh bint in *The King and I*, a mere servant, claimed the king of Siam fell in love with her. In Asia, nothing real, except tits and arse.

The street was quiet, with most of the shops closed, or just opening. Pattaya was not a morning town. He crossed the sea road and began to stroll away from Walking Street, along the promenade, looking at the boats bobbing offshore. The crashing Channel or Atlantic beckoned, promised, inspired voyages of discovery, but this complacent turquoise pond was a sea for staying put. No Thai Columbus ever sailed forth. There were a few huffing joggers, elderly farangs, arms and chests dismally wobbling. Thai girls passed him, crisp and clean and bright in office suits or dresses, and he smiled at every one, receiving smiles in return. The breeze was fresh and warm, the sky azure, the scents of trees and flowers and females intoxicating. If Pattaya wasn't paradise, it would do. In Europe, it was coming on winter. Grey skies, rain, cold, damp smells, and no smiles.

The sun was rising high, the city gradually stirring to life. Overdressed and sweating in his long trousers, he came to a shopping mall, and wanted to buy light clothes, but the place did not open till eleven a.m. To blend in, he needed shorts, a singlet, rubber flip-flops, a baseball cap. No, not a bloody baseball cap. Surely there must be non-ghastly headgear somewhere. *There* was a mission for the day. He saw the same shops, repeated indefinitely, and wherever it was possible to squeeze a box bar between a Seven-Eleven and a T-shirt emporium, there it was, draped with girls. Stalls were laden with shiny fruits and vegetables, bigger and more luminous than their drab European cousins. Like the bars and their human blossoms, strange flowers sprouted in any roadside nook. Nature rioted, rampant, and for sale. Everything was for sale. In leafy side streets he found several cheap-and-cheerful hotels with monthly rates. Most guests at the Lucky Strike no doubt appreciated the sex toys in the rooms, all that pervy kit and caboodle, and they would be Chuck's age, like attracting like. But he didn't need equipment.

He stopped for coffee and a smoke, and watched the world go by while examining his street map in between eyeing the young bare-legged waitress. More smiles, more arse-wiggling. She doesn't even know how powerful her beauty is, her adorable slut's innocence. He debated a hotel move, and, although Woaw's presence was an argument to stay where he was, it was a bit tacky, trying to pull a hotel receptionist, like a sleazy businessman chatting up an air hostess. He walked on, past the Tourist Police building (for tourists, or against?) and the further he went, the more bar beers and strip joints he passed, their denizens cooing at him, even at this hour. All the bars had Buddha shrines where arriving girls performed rapid prayers before starting work.

Some still harboured drinkers from the night before. One of the rumpled boozers – beer-gutted, stained T-shirt – was arguing with a girl in hot pants and a spangled top, something to do with her mobile phone, which she kept withdrawing from her hip pocket to make seductive noises in broken English to some third party. She shrilled at the boozer who kept trying to interrupt her chat or grab her phone, and he jabbered in German; both were angry. Cops lounging outside the Tourist Police, a few doors up, paid no attention. They were slim, with sullen pouting lips, wearing tight brown uniforms, and of indeterminate sex.

A second, then a third girl joined the argument, gesturing wildly and shrieking, first at him, then at each other, while the German bellowed. The word 'money' in English floated across the road, then 'no have boyfriend!' Not having a boyfriend seemed a point of honour with Thai *filles publiques*, no matter that their declarations of chastity defied logic. Suddenly, he patted his money-belt, and her bottom, then embraced her. She shrieked with laughter, crying *'Mein Liebchen!'* and they lurched on to the pillion of a motorcycle taxi which putt-putted away. The cops gazed after them with lizard's eyes.

Though he was pleasantly dazed from jet lag, and the draining of his balls by the vulpine O, Pattaya was beginning to sink in. He could have a beer right now, pick up a girl with a wave of his fingers and the rustle of a banknote. *I wandered lonely as a cloud* . . . nobody knew where he was, or cared. Wonderful solitude, wonderful freedom. Like a kid loosed in a toyshop, he could do anything he pleased in this playground of the senses. Perceptions were heightened, every flower, or smell, or colour seemed beautiful. Trudging through cold London, you saw grey people hurrying, turned in on themselves. Here it was all smiles, unless you were a cop, preening sullenly in his bumboy's uniform. What to do today? Explore. Shop. Drink. Fuck everything in sight. What to do any day?

After shopping for clothes unthinkable at home, he returned to the hotel for an afternoon nap, and, first, a cold beer. Having retrieved his room key from the curtly smiling Woaw, who was helping dim tourists, he entered into the dark air-conditioned bar 'Up Chuck' (lugubrious American joke?) beside the coffee shop. He slid on to a stool and ordered a Heineken from the burly jocund

122

bartender, who he assumed was Chuck himself. He was the only customer. Chuck's own beer stood by his loaded ashtray, beside a shot glass and a tequila bottle. After wiping sweat from his head with a newly acquired kerchief, Mitch lit a Gauloise.

'Tourists,' he sighed, wishing to establish that he was not one. 'Are they trained to ask stupid questions?'

Chuck laughed.

'Everybody is someone else's tourist,' he said. 'T.I.T. This is Thailand. You get here, you leave your brains at the customs. Or else, adapt and survive. It's all *sanook*. Have fun or die. You're Mr Barnett, in room twelve, right?'

'Right. Mitch. You must be Chuck.'

'Sure. Welcome to paradise. Any trouble last night?'

His accent had a pleasant western American burr.

'No. Why do you ask?'

Chuck stroked his cropped grey beard.

'You took that O, from the Warm Pussy. She's a regular. Great piece of ass, but light-fingered.'

'I . . . yes.'

Foolish to assume he was invisible.

'Nothing in this town is unnoticed,' Chuck said.

'Well, there was no trouble. Sweet as a nut.'

His magnificent tryst, his holy communion with O's tight sex and anus, his worship of her fragrant bottom – no more than a great piece of ass. A regular! How could she be, when she had only been in Pattaya a month?

'So you're not a tourist,' said Chuck, polishing a glass. 'You came at a good time, just before the place fills up for the winter season. You here for long?'

He confessed it was his first visit and that he had some business which might take a while. Chuck sipped beer and lit a fresh Marlboro.

'You mean, chasing up some chick that ran out on you,' he said. 'Shit, man, you'll forget her. Look at all the pussy for sale. Don't tell me O wasn't good. She took a dildo away with her, right? She always does that.'

Mitch blushed.

123

'She was very good,' he replied, cool, man of the world; guy talk.

'Go-go dancers usually are. They keep in shape. So now you've two chicks to chase after,' Chuck said helpfully. 'And by tomorrow, you'll probably have three. Way it is. See, back home, you try and explain this place, they don't believe you. They can't understand, or won't understand. All their lives they're starved for pussy, when here you can have anything you want, and they freak out. But treat the girls right, or the boys, up to you, and they'll treat you right. Just don't fall in love. *Again*,' he added. 'Watch out for O's boyfriend.'

'She told me she didn't have one.'

'They all do.'

'Say that, or have one?'

'Both. Thai hookers think you get upset if some Thai beefcake is porking them. We're all brainwashed back in the world, you're mine, jealousy, owning the bitch, all that down stuff. Here, it's just meat and money. More of a pisser that your money is feeding the Thai asshole his booze and pills. And they always tell you they've only been here a month, or a week. Then a greenhorn thinks he's getting a near-virgin. Some girls are professional virgins. They fuck during their monthly, which most girls won't, and charge the dude five hundred bucks for taking her phony virginity. Japs like that. And US Navy officers.'

'I suppose I'm a greenhorn. What about O's beefcake?'

He drained his beer and ordered another, while Chuck refilled his own glass. He figured Chuck was one of those who was never quite sober, and never quite drunk. He seemed moulded to his array of bottles and beer taps and the dark wood bar, like a dusty American far west saloon. Chuck's nostalgia. The home continent he would never taste again. Up Chuck was an oasis; beyond a partition the Lucky Strike A Gogo thumped and squawked.

'You'll find out, if you see her again. If you don't, then it doesn't matter. No way am I going to give advice, I learned that a long time ago. You only get blamed when the dude ignores it. First, I made all the mistakes. Came here, went apeshit, bought a bar, fucked all my bar girls, breaking them in. It was fun. Used to go up to the village, get them green, at the bus station. But you don't shit on your own doorstep. Thai hookers are the most jealous creatures. Specially the katoeys. Knives, broken bottles. It was chaos. Know the strongest cable in the world? It can pull any weight up a mountain, or over a cliff. It could drag down the moon, if you had one long enough. A girl's pussy hair. Guy gets tied up with that, his brain turns to jell-o, there's no talking to him. Who cares, this is the finest place in the world to be young again. The years roll off you, and you're free to be a knave or a fool. But these gorgeous girls I have working for me here, *especially* the front office staff, would I touch one of their ever-loving pussy hairs? No way.'

'What if a girl shaves her pussy?' Mitch said.

'Then, my friend, you're *really* in trouble.'

16

Schoolgirls

He awoke at twilight, lunchtime in Europe, but he enjoyed the disorientation: he was living someone else's time, not really here at all. All his life, he had felt he was somewhere else, observing himself from a distance, no more so than when a performer in the Scene. Even at the sex act, he imagined his coupling from above: *what do I look like*? Pattaya was the first place he didn't feel somewhere else. Everyone was a performer. All the familiar brand names were just imported glitter to cover this bare theatre of lust: mocking reassurance of the self, lonely for home. *But that's all they are, anywhere*.

Already he felt an old hand, with a routine: shower, shave, coffee, then out to the bright lights. Sundown, pink and orange and purple and turquoise spread across the ocean, silhouetted the palm trees. Lights of shops and bars aglare, everything sparkling, cajoling, wanting your money. No money, no honey. He wandered the streets, wearing shorts and rubber sandals this time, for the heat was still clammy. The olive-green shorts were pseudo-military, the kind favoured by fatties with Rambo fantasies, and had zippered pockets, to stow his wallet, or hand grenades. O's panties were snug against his balls.

There were some European girls on the street, ambling with a languid hooker's dawdle. They looked Slavic, with sulky lips, bleached hair and high cheekbones, and congregated where the restaurants served couscous, or borscht. He thought of Zelda, with a *frisson* of desire, but he hadn't come here for pallid European girls. Should he beard O in her den? Given her shaven sex, that was funny, and he laughed aloud, congratulating himself on another witticism, what a diamond jester. Plenty of time for her, for everything. The night is young. Later, drop in to see Lancelot, now that he had something to laugh about.

'Hello, boss?' chirped an Indian tailor, perched outside his shop. 'You like nice gent's suit? Best quality. Hundred euro only.'

'Do I look like I need a suit?'

'For when you go back home.'

'This is home.'

His words made him shiver. Perhaps he wanted them to be true. Pattaya, home. *Nomen omen.*

At a street stall he ate soup to the rhythmic tap-tap of pestle and mortar, grinding vegetables for *pok-pok*. Sated, he selected a bar at random. Australian rules football glared from the TV screen before rapt middle-aged skinheads. There was a girl there, doe-eyed, young, shyly demure in a black dress that covered her except for bare calves and shoulders. Porn (pronounced 'Pon') was her name, surely just off the bus. He bought her a lady drink, and discreetly stroked her firm cart-pulling thigh. Beside him, an olaf was feeling his girl's belly and sex, her dress pushed up, panties stretched by his paw.

'No baby?' the oaf slurred.

'Speak sure, no baby. Good fucky-fuck.'

'You go with me,' Mitch said to Porn. 'Bouncing.'

She nodded. Easy as that. He took her. Hand in hand, like soppy young lovers, they walked back to the hotel, and he got a rude look from Woaw as she handed over his room key.

It was a disaster. Porn draped herself in a towel to strip, and turned her back to him. Her discarded underthings were a drab beige. She locked the bathroom while she showered alone. On the bed, she covered herself with a sheet, and looked away, grimacing, as he sucked her toes. She insisted on a condom. Thus encumbered, yet erect, he prepared to penetrate her sex, dutifully revealed, but with her head turned, not acknowledging that part of her. Gently, he took the sheet from her so that he could kiss her nipples. Her breasts were lovely soft brown domes. *No*, she cried, and pulled the sheet back. *I shy.* Her legs were dutifully spread, but that seemed the extent of the transaction from her viewpoint. She exuded sadness, *hurry and get it over with.* His penis wilted.

'If you're shy, why are you working as a hooker?' he growled, but she didn't speak much English; luckily, for he sensed a tale of abandonment, poverty, sickness.

He tried again, but failed to be excited by the unhappy farm girl. He gave up; paid her the least he could get away with, and told her to go. She accepted the money and bowed before scuttling out the door; evidently, non-penetration meant no transaction. Now he did want a transaction! He descended the stairs, with balls aching. Woaw smirked. On the walk to soi six, he drank beer in a couple of seafront bars, allowing the novelty of teenage girls, feigning interest in who he was and where he came from, to wear off. The shopping mall, closed earlier, was now open, and enticingly air-conditioned.

Venturing inside, he saw acres of lingerie, bras, bikini panties, thongs and threads: mouth-watering, seductive, in every imaginable colour, from blood-bright red to lemon yellow, lime green, sea blue and coffee. You imagined girls inside them, row upon row, like fruit hanging on trees. He fingered the garments, admiring the workmanship; he should have imported some of this stuff for Strips. The girls in the mall stood gossiping and looking bored. Any girl in a workplace was young and glamorous, no older than thirty. The oldies packed off to the village, the package no longer tempting.

As he passed the whores on the seafront, two stunning young streetwalkers in garish spangled dresses rose from the shadows to pursue him. Why sit there, in obscurity, not under the street light? They were teenagers, and beautiful.

'Hello, sexy man.'

'You want two ladies?'

Their faces and figures were perfect, at odds with the scruffy beach road, its sleeping vendors, Buddha shrines and cracked pavement. He was tempted, but they were too blatant. Smiling, he tried to sidestep them. One of them grabbed his balls while the other mimed fellatio.

'Smoking?' she cooed, with a throaty giggle.

He winced, and removed the hand from his crotch, murmuring 'no, no, not tonight,' and shaking his head. Both girls were tall and slim, strongly perfumed, shiny black hair luxuriant, their breasts full, their long legs stockinged under taut buttocks. They wore deep *décolletages*, and one grasped his hand to place it inside her bra. He felt warm soft flesh – the girl giggled as he squeezed her tiny nipple button – and was tempted to take them both, until he felt fingers glide across the secure hip pocket holding his wallet. It was delicately done, but it was done. Angrily, he brushed them aside – 'No!' – and pushed past them.

He looked back, saw the large hands and feet, heard the gravelly undertone to their hoots of derision. Ladyboys! Yet they seemed feminine, and the breasts he had squeezed were real breasts, even if enhanced by silicone. They were squeezed into corsetry, giving them traditional hourglass figures, and squeezing the paltry most out of their male buttocks. Their smell gave them away, if nothing else, like the scent of a hospital room, trying to cover the odour of sickness, or an old lady, scent ducts withered, over-dousing herself in lavender to hide the decay of age. Yet in appearance they were sensuous, and he had been tempted. They needed a lesson in marketing, though. *Do they think I came down with the morning dew? Stupid cunts!*

He crossed a T junction with a large Buddha shrine, and the beach road became a series of expensive hotels, shrouded in foliage, with yet more restaurants in between, and an occasional bar of *Mittel Europa* pretensions. They had few customers; in the high season, they would no doubt be packed. Had to be, to make any money. But then, the simple structures could not cost much, and the girls essentially worked for free, with the system of bar fines for the pimp. Perhaps you could, after all, make a nice relaxing profit, owning a whore bar in Pattaya.

Soi six was dim and in shadow, with no lights but the moon and the neon of the scattered bars. The girls sat outside, chatting and smoking, more relaxed than in the frenetic downtown. They cooed invitations, with lazy good humour, not taking their task, or him, too seriously.

'See you tomorrow!' they sang, mockingly, as he walked past.

He saw 'Schoolgirls'. Its neon sign showed a nude girl in high black boots and black gloves flexing a cane between her hands. The girls outside wore mini-skirts of pleated red tartan, cheap white plastic belts, white blouses and red neckties dangling with pleasant sluttishness from an elastic loop. They did look like tousled schoolgirls, some with their hair in plaits, or pony-tails; their legs shone in real black nylons, with sensible leather shoes. They beckoned him, opened the door, to release a rush of cold washed air, and cheered as he went in. It was the same as the other places: a bar, plush seats at the walls, stools for oglers around a stage, with girls in bikinis dancing listlessly to the same tunes heard everywhere.

He sat down and ordered a beer, peering in the gloom to see if Lancelot was present, and the waitress, in school uniform, told him that the show was about to start. The place was full, Germans and British mostly, with several couples, and all gaping at the stage, not at the straggle of dancers, but in anticipation of what was to come.

A gong sounded, and the dancers scampered away, unapplauded. The lights dimmed and a snake of girls in school uniform mounted the platform to stand in formation as a slow sinuous music began, with an insistent drum rhythm. The girls began to gyrate, fingering their blouses and ties. In unison, they unfastened the first buttons of their blouses, then the second, showing breast and bra; then the third, the blouses open to the ribcage. Pouting, they slipped off their ties, and pinged the elastic, before discarding them on the corner of the stage.

The audience cheered the traditional striptease, female customers seeming more excited than their male companions. The girls swayed, fully unbuttoning their blouses, and flapping the shirt tails like butterflies. They slipped the garments low on their shoulders, wrapping them tightly, to imprison their breasts, thrusting up the bra cups, while tongues licked pouting lips in fake excitement. In a flourish, the blouses simultaneously came off. Schoolgirls in skirt and bra and nylons; he felt himself enjoyably stiffen.

Bare brown skin was a cheeky comment on the school uniform; the girls smiled as they stripped, making sly fun of their rapt audience. Holding their belts in their teeth, they played with the zippers of their skirts, rubbing their thighs together with a shimmer of sheer nylon as the fasteners opened and closed. Finally, the skirts slithered down silky nyloned thighs revealing thong panties, worn over the garter straps, and an array of suspender belts, fluffy, frilly and lacy, each girl in a different pastel colour. They stepped out of their skirts and one girl, in pink knickers, stooped to pick them up, folding them neatly in a pile, with her large breasts wobbling deliciously. Each put her fingers to the tiny cache-sexe covering her mound, and rubbed herself. The mimed masturbation was convincing and, in the spotlight, the panties blushed with faint moisture. She was the creature of male fantasy, a girl pleasuring herself, mouthing, *if only you were here, doing it to me*.

They danced, teasing, their fingers trying to unhook bra straps, pretending they would not loosen. The audience cheered encouragement; encouraged by her girl companion, a blonde drinker stood, lifted her T-shirt, and unhooked her own bra, to show how it was done, while urging them on in an Australian accent. Her bare breasts gleamed in the spotlight, and she got cheers too. In the flickering light, her snub nose reminded him of Zelda. Suddenly, onstage, half-a-dozen pairs of brown breasts sprang naked into view. The audience whooped.

Banknotes were stuffed into crotches; when each girl carried a bulging purse, the waistbands began to slide down over the undulating thighs. They made a show of difficulty, that the panties were reluctant to come loose, for their gussets were stuck to the quim lips. At last, the thongs were at their ankles, the shaven mounds gleaming in the spotlight. Nude but for stockings and suspenders and shoes, the girls parted their thighs and prised open their chattes. He was throbbing. What a great country. They *wanted* you to have a stonker.

The girl in pink assumed centre stage and took a fluorescent turquoise ribbon from her sex, handing it to her comrades who pulled several metres of the twine from the girl's body. When the ribbon was extruded, Pink put her thighs around the central pole and held her arms up for the others to bind her in the ribbon. The girl in lemon suspenders tied her in a knot, and all the others picked up their belts. They mimed a flogging on her bottom, while the tethered girl writhed. Perhaps it was not all mime, for the belts snapped realistically, but the light plastic could not hurt much. She took just a few lashes from each girl, after which she was released, theatrically grimacing and rubbing her slightly reddened buttocks. She fetched a stool upon which she perched, and pointed at her friends.

They lined up, still jiggling to the music, each obediently bending over Pink's thighs to receive a dozen spanks. The crack of her palm on bare skin rang out over the music. This was not a mime; Pink really was spanking them, proven by each girl bending over to touch her toes, displaying her buttocks blushing a delicate rose. Pink slid off the stool, and knelt; Lemon was held upside down, and the girls embraced, tonguing quims. The others paired off, until three couples gamahuched on stage. Their moans, belly-heaves, and, eventually, climax, seemed genuine.

– *They really are lezzies, they mean it.*
– *Das ist echter Orgasmus!*

Act followed act: a girl was covered in scalding hot wax, cleverly not spoiling her nylons; balloons floated at the ceiling, and a girl crouched, thighs spread, to burst them with darts fired from her vulva; a girl squatted to pick coins from the stage floor with her quim lips; another cracked raw eggs in her sex, and sucked the contents into

132

her pouch, spitting out the shell fragments; another squashed a banana and squirted mush into the faces of the oglers by the stage; another writhed to the music, drawing from her sex a long string of razor blades. The techniques were interesting in themselves. Already sated with sex, one did not pant impatiently for a girl's kit to come off.

– *Wouldn't see this back home for the price of a pint.*
– *You're not wrong.*

A German heated a coin with his cigarette lighter and tossed it onstage. When a girl stooped to pick it up in her sex, she shrieked, and dropped it. She yelled curses, but since the joker's table was loaded with lady drinks, no one was going to expel a big spender. Besides, all the Thai girls laughed at her. All part of the fun. *Sanook*. He caught Pink's eye, briefly mimed spanks, which made her laugh, then gestured for her to join him, and she happily nodded yes. A hand clapped his shoulder, and he turned.

'*There* you are,' said Lancelot Delage.

17

Pink and Lemon

He told Lancelot about O and his run-in with the katoeys, then about the hopeless Porn, and Lancelot replied that you occasionally got a dud, shy, straight from the village.

'You tipped her. If you'd fucked her, she'd have had a week's wages. Never feel sorry for one of these fucking lazy whores. Anyway, there's plenty of squirt here.'

He had Pink, in only panties, nylons and suspenders, on his lap. Lady drinks clustered on the table; one for the waitress, for another girl, and for Lemon, too. Buying a girl a drink meant she had to give you some time, talk to you, let you grope her like a gauche teenager, a retro pleasure, while you held court. They saw he was a spender, first assuming he was German, though he corrected them, explaining, with finger stabs on an imaginary map, where England and Germany were.

'They don't know the difference,' said Lancelot. 'They can't read maps, half of them can't read at all, and don't know the world is round. Or if it is, we live on the inside.'

Regally, he stroked Pink's bare breasts. Lemon crouched opposite, and he squashed her nipples playfully to the table top. The girls giggled, not caring about England or Germany; he didn't, either. The Australian girl who had lifted her T-shirt was exploring the girl sitting on her knee. The mama-san, a strikingly tall woman in a sequinned purple evening gown and high heels, hovered, affectedly stroking her long shiny hair, to make sure everyone was happy, so Mitch bought her a drink, too, and one for

Lancelot. They all seemed to know Lancelot, who drank 'jack-coke', Jack Daniels and cola, and treated him with playful deference, but did not flirt.

'If you're a regular here, I suppose you've had most of these ones.'

Lancelot smiled, and shrugged, but did not answer. Mitch's penis bulged in his shorts, but he didn't try to hide it from their eyes. Being aroused was approved, you were a good spending customer. Pink's fingers began a groin massage. She was very good, knew where to touch.

'Big power,' she whispered, licking his ear, then blowing in it. 'We go upstairs?'

'Maybe.'

The mama-san cooed in a smoky contralto that there were 'very nice rooms' upstairs. 'What you like, what you want. Two lady, three lady, up to you.' Power indeed, pick and choose. What *did* he want? Order up some sex, like ordering toppings on a pizza. Sit and drink, not hungry to get into her panties, for she was hungry to get into yours. Why did anybody bother to stay in England? He cupped his hands around Pink's bare bottom, feeling very faint skin swellings where she had been mock-whipped, and put his fingers into her cleft, tickling her.

'Oh, *chakachee*,' she squealed.

He put his fingertip inside her anus a little, and she squirmed, licking her lips and breathing hard.

'*Chep*,' she gasped. 'Hurt me.'

'Didn't it hurt when you were whipped?'

She smiled, and nodded.

'Not same. Play game.'

'I want more than a game,' he said.

Lemon thrust her breasts in his face and made him suck her nipples. The breasts were big firm and bouncy to his fingers.

'Silicone,' hissed Pink.

'Not silicone,' cried Lemon. 'Hundred per cent lady. You silicone.'

They pretended to box. Pink retrieved his hands, and made him knead her own breasts, then her rival's.

135

'Both lady,' he declared solemnly. 'No silicone.'

They howled with laughter. God, it took so little to amuse them. Lancelot said Bangkok was the world capital for cosmetic surgery, filling tits, snipping off cocks, or refastening those chopped by a jealous wife. Guys flocked there to be made into ladymen. No questions, Thai doctors understood that a fellow might want his tackle removed, or a girl her breasts pumped, for glamour. We're just parcels of meat, not selves, for Buddhists have no souls, they only have spirits.

He picked up Pink's dainty feet, and began to suck her toes. All the girls, including the demure mama-san, shrieked in delight and made faces. Then Lemon demanded the same and, hands cupping their bottoms, he complied, licking each in turn. He said he would take a room and two ladies, settled his enormous bill, then allowed Pink and Lemon to lead him upstairs. The room, three flights up, was more or less clean, obviously lived in, with dresses hanging in an open wardrobe and shoes piled beneath. It smelled pleasantly musty and intimate, of food and girls' bodies. The noise of the bar downstairs was reduced to a muffled thud. Beside the rumbling fan, a gecko scampered across the ceiling, its tongue darting, to snap up bugs.

He watched them peel off their nylons and panties, willing them to tease him, take longer. He relished every move and gesture, the coquetry of stripping naked; far from the fumbled urgency of western courtship. The second skin revealing the first, brown and tender and succulent. You wanted to peel the skin from them, expose the meat beneath, the essence. Briskly nude – part of *work* – they fetched towels and smoothed the double bed while he made himself naked, looking at their three bodies in the wall-to-wall mirrors surrounding them: the thrill of the act needing the reassurance of watching it. All sex was voyeurism, the body an erotic spectacle, another *you*, outside you.

The girls were superb: sleek, muscled, smooth-shaven and gleaming brown, his body pallid beside them. There was a bathroom next door and, in the shower, they played with the irrigation squirter and soaped him, then each other, with amusement at his shaven pubes. They assured him it was delightful, that he was 'handsome man, big power', as, under their deft caresses, his penis rose. They pawed him, murmuring that they too wanted white skin. There were jars of whitening cream on the bathroom shelf. He said that Europeans liked brown skin, 'very sexy lady' – for it was dark, mysterious, untouchable, a promise of wild sensuality. Both girls had beautiful skin. They thanked him for the compliment, but insisted that brown skin was for poor people.

The sheets on the bed were clean, but not fresh, smelling of girl, and a long black hair was draped across the pillow. It was exciting to soil a girl's bed. He knelt to kiss each girl's sex, savouring her juice; then lay back and made each straddle him, rubbing his penis between her breasts. They were expert, of course. With a stab of jealousy, he imagined Nampoong enjoying a threesome, perhaps on this very bed, and longed to find her. What, though, was there to find? The surface package of skin, brown or white: what you see is what you get.

'I want sadic,' he said; it felt naughty to be cheating on Woaw.

Gestures conveyed that they were to whip him, not the other way round.

'You want stick?'

'Yes, yes.'

They seemed to know about 'sadic'. Pink delved in the wardrobe and produced two broomsticks, bamboo poles, with wide sheaves of bristles attached. He nodded, and they giggled. Flogging someone with a broom! A knife was produced, and the sheaves cut off, leaving a stub of bristles as a grip; now, the heavy sticks looked menacingly painful. He shivered, turned, and presented his arse. First with the hand, he explained, to warm up. *You want pok-pok!* They were all smiles. He lay over Pink's thighs, with Lemon squatting on his head, her chatte hot and warm against his neck. Pink hand-spanked him twenty or so slaps, then changed places with Lemon, who gave the same. *Hurt*, they said, waggling their spanking hands. *Me hurt*, he laughed, rubbing his arse, and they laughed too. Pink stretched the elastic of her panties thong and quickly knotted it round his head, with the gusset at his lips, and he breathed in her rich aroma. She was practised, knew *his* sort. He could see through the stretched translucent nylon, as through misty pink goggles underwater.

They stood one on each side, and the flogging was savage: thud, not sting. He gripped the bed, writhing under the lashes while, in the mirror, the girls' lithe bodies whirled, a ballet of dominance. Their teeth were bared in a rictus of cruel pleasure. *That* was what he wanted. They enjoyed their work, their eyes narrowed on his flesh as their bare young breasts bounced, thighs and bellies rippled. Efficient, as if they were threshing wheat, or pounding millet. Making *pok-pok*, the antique female task, grinding, smashing, crushing. He looked at their eyes, hoping to perceive the girl within; the eyes glinted, alive, like the cut of the rods.

As his arse smarted, his penis was rigid. Life and power seemed to flow from his beaten buttocks, filling him with love as he inhaled the perfume of Pink's sex. Lemon added her own panties, so that his face was sheathed in the musky exudations of their two groins: a gaudy surgical mask, heaving like a bellows with his gasping breath. He took the lashes in sets of half a dozen, with intervals for him to crouch and kiss their feet through the panties while they admired their work. They beat him for half an hour, until his skin was leathery, and his welts dark.

Pain throbbed through his body, yet he had never felt so alive. He shucked the panties from his face, and licked the toes of each girl, then made Lemon sit on his face while Pink, on top, fucked him. He scarcely noticed her fingers unrolling the rubber (unidentified fruit flavour) over his penis. Tongue in Lemon, penis in Pink: a pleasing symmetry. Beyond the rim of Lemon's thighs, he glimpsed their tableau in the mirror, a curiosity. *Look at that, a bloke and two bare-arse tarts.* He came in only a few strokes, the orgasm satisfying though perfunctory, even unneeded, a polite formality after his beating.

He tipped them what he figured, correctly, was over the odds, for they both made *wais*, with sing-song thank-yous. He danced down the stairs, his arse stinging and cleansed. Back in the bar, he started a new bill, and bought drinks for them both, and for the mama-san, who smiled knowingly, and for a couple of the uniformed schoolgirls. Pink mimed flogging and, entering into the spirit, he rose and rubbed his arse with a grimace. They howled with laughter. He sat between schoolgirls, crowding round him, and jostling for place; he pushed his hand under two bottoms, and stroked. They smiled brightly. His fingers slid under their panties while the girls took turns rubbing his groin, crying *no power*. His erstwhile paramours thought this was funny.

'You must have tipped them well,' said Lancelot, sitting down beside Lemon. 'Had fun?'

He said it was great. Lancelot bought him a beer, and another stiff jack-coke for himself.

'They're real schoolgirls, you know,' he said distractedly, 'senior students, from St Bernard's International School in Bangkok, although this uniform is one I made up. Lots of girls need pocket money. They don't see themselves as whores, they're a cut above, young enough to like their work. Fresh, in love with themselves, hoping some rich foreign arsehole will marry them and whisk them away to his gingerbread castle.'

He said this in a listless, cynical drawl; then explained the hierarchy of bar girls, streetwalkers and go-go dancers, each class despising the other. Dancers were despised because they immodestly showed their underwear; bar girls, because they had to take anyone; streetwalkers, because they were not pretty enough to work bar. Discos contained streetwalkers with the price of a drink.

'But they're all the same sluts,' he said.

'Don't you . . .?'

'Not here. You don't shit in your own back yard.'

The mama-san smiled at them, like a beautiful snake.

139

'I own part of this place, you see,' said Lancelot, apologetically. 'And I own part of St Bernard's. I'm sort of the fixer. That's why Goong puts up with me. Here, if you need a job, there's always work teaching English. It's a boom industry.'

'Me, a teacher? Hardly.'

'You can read and write, can't you?'

Lancelot raised his glass to the mama-san.

'I'd rather like to have my own bar,' Mitch said suddenly.

'For free poking, I suppose. You could buy this one.'

'It's for sale?'

'Most bars are. People get fed up with them.'

He named a figure – 'just ballpark, you understand' – and it sounded cheap.

'Of course, there's the rent, and wages, you have to feed the girls, and juice the cops. Have to sell a lot of beer, or get a lot of bar fines.'

Mitch asked him how he got into this.

'Me and Goong. It's her bar, technically. I like to have a few bits of business going on. And she's good in the sack, for a katoey.'

'Oh? Sorry, I didn't realise . . .'

'No problem. She looks real, doesn't she? Takes all the hormones.'

'Well! I mean, I wonder . . . what it's like?'

'Pretty good, actually. Ladymen know the tricks. I'd invite you to bar-fine her, but she'd cut my dick off. Thai women do that, and katoeys are twice as jealous. But we could both have her in a spitroast, she likes that.'

He mashed out his cigarette and gulped his jack-coke.

'God, sometimes you get so tired of it all,' he whispered.

Mitch extracted his fingers from the schoolgirls, sniffed them, with a sigh of *hom*, then licked them. Pink put her lips to his ear and blew. He offered to buy her panties. The deal was done; Pink stripped off her panties, and he handed over the money, then kissed the cache-sexe – more whoops – before stuffing the garment in his pocket. He bought Lemon's, too. While Pink looked the other way, he got out his photos of Nampoong, the polite ones, including the one where O had scratched Nampoong's face.

Lancelot studied them and said she looked familiar, though they all looked the same after a while. He advised Mitch to let it be, for these things usually ended in tears, *mucho grief, my friend.* Goong said it might be a girl called Lek, who used to work down the street. But she went to England. Another girl said she was sure she had seen her, sitting on the sea wall at Beach Road, a few days, or maybe weeks, before, holding hands with a farang. Mitch bit his lip.

'Sure?'

'Sure, hundred per cent. By her body.'

She was looking at the photo with Nampoong's face scratched out. As good a likeness as any.

18

Black Heart

Day slouched into lazy day; his arse hurt from his tanning by Pink and Lemon, but pleasantly: a mild warming throb. Wearing O's thong, or Pink's, or Lemon's, made him tingle, his naughty secret. He bought a pair of black split-crotch panties, for curiosity. He looked ridiculous, his penis flopping out and the balls sheathed. But it was weird fun, invading female territory. He added to his collection, returning to the hotel, and Woaw's keen glance, with a gift-wrapped package tied with a red ribbon. It contained thong panties, lyrical with frills and tassels, yellow, blue, green, red, black and pink. The salesgirl helped him with the size; he needed the largest.

'Madame big lady?' she said, smiling sweetly.

'Same as me,' he said.

She nodded.

'Panties for you, very beautiful,' she said impishly; *they always knew*.

You never really got used to the heat, the sweat, the humidity. Quickly, you learned where the malls and bars were that had blessed air-con. He browsed in the art shops, watching painters producing fake Dalis or Matisses. Paperbacks recounted relentlessly cheery misadventures of old farts with cheating girlfriends – still, you have to love them, don't you? The local paper headlined charity dos by some foreign chamber of commerce, the women glittering, the men lupine, great investment potential here. *Sure, pal.* Did their starchy wives know the truth? The suicides were tucked away in the inside pages. Only the lonely. In one seaside bar, he got to know a genial Irish fellow, insofar as you could know anybody out here. Declan worked in a boiler room, hustling investments over the phone.

'Sure it's fucking money for old rope. Americans west of the Mississippi are the biggest suckers, then New Zealanders and the fucking Irish. People who have money, but it's from inherited land, or dosh from Brussels, and they dream of being off the farm, but they haven't a clue how things work in the real world. Ask some fucking Paddy to invest in a uranium mine in County Galway, and he'll spit, but tell him they've struck gold in the sea off Phuket, and his cheque's in the post. They all want to live the dream, see, think their phony share certificate comes with cunt attached. That's what keeps me here, fuck'em. But where else can I go?'

He flirted with Woaw, who turned deliciously hot or cold, then listened to Chuck's stories of bankruptcy, heartbreak and deceit, with rueful hints of his own history, the whores in Saigon with razor blades in their pussies, the dope, the murders. Did some black market stuff, cigarettes and army issue condoms stolen from the PX. He had kept watch, as his buddies fragged an unpopular gung-ho lieutenant, diving for cover as his tent exploded. It was no different than they did to prisoners, he had seen women's cunts ripped open with bayonets, babies stomped to mush. But the fragged lieutenant liked interrogating girl VC. He would strip them, hogtie them, and whip them bloody with bamboo rods. A pervert, he deserved to die. Mitch thought the American lexicon curious: a girl's sex ripped apart was a cunt, but one open for business was a pussy.

Pattaya, then a fishing village full of cheap brothels, near the U Tapao military airport, was where the troops went for R&R. The sex-hungry soldiers did not corrupt the Thai culture, as there was no culture to corrupt, except whoring. Chuck came back after the war, dealt in used cars, motorcycles, army surplus, had to carry a gun. Like many, he opened his girly bar, got stung. Married a hooker, took her back to the States, but after a month she ran away. He followed her back to Thailand, but other girls helped him forget her. Had children, some with a junkie whore later murdered for a twenty buck debt by a dope dealer, who was executed. He looked after his children he knew about, the rest got lost in the net of family, or were sold into quasi-slavery, to settle distant and obscure debts. He thought them Americans, but they were Thais, just paler than the rest, and you could teach them nothing, their progenitor a mere farang.

Some black girls, selling their pussies on the streets of Pattaya, were granddaughters of his buddy Jeremiah, killed in the war. He would never knowingly let that happen to his own kin. It was quieter now, with the European tourists, and no memory of war, but the Russian mafia stirred things up, and Pattaya's numerous shootings and dismemberings went unpublicised, lest they scare tourists off. Best concentrate on selling sex, or a hotel to have it in. Nobody got hurt that way, except a little bit. Sure, Thailand sucked, but where else could you go? There were worse places to await death.

Mitch visited 'Schoolgirls' again, and Goong greeted him warmly, but Lancelot was absent, and Pink and Lemon were taken. In truth, he did not want them to whip him again. For a whipping to satisfy, it must be from an enemy, a vicious sullen girl who liked giving pain, not a friendly one, eager to please: real fear and loathing, the complicated chemistry of submission. That was what all those heartbroken boozy slobs really wanted, a kick up the arse. Masochists all. A Thai wife, said Chuck, would tongue-lash and physically beat you, if allowed the upper hand. Her notion of fair play was, what's mine is mine, and what's yours is mine too. Guys liked that, liked suffering.

He saw the Australian girl in another bar, where there was a dance routine by bejewelled katoeys in sumptuous frocks. You could see the show streetside, no false mystery, just girls doing their work. She was accompanied by a stunning katoey, while efficiently groping a real girl's bottom, and returned his conspiratorial smile. Sometimes he picked up a girl in a box bar or disco, avoiding the ones with dope breath, and took her back to the hotel for a night, or else a short time. He liked intercrural sex, she leaning back, rubbing his penis between her thighs, his shaft pressing her hillock and sex lips while he sucked her toes, then ejaculated over her belly: the pleasure of lordly disdain.

He took a couple from Chuck's A Gogo, although he tried not to think of Chuck 'breaking them in'. A girl had had a thousand cocks inside her, but if you couldn't put a face to them, it was all right. Most were cheerful polite peasant girls who had come to the big city rather than grow old picking rice. All admired his pale skin, and pooh-poohed their own luscious coffee colour. Ads urged Thais to buy skin-lightening cream and look like a farang. How stupid! Yet perhaps the farangs were stupid, with their myth of dark girls: Africa and the orient, sultry pools of sensuality; sex without sin; bare-breasted negresses; Haggard's Ayesha, *She*.

The girls were plentiful, willing and greedy. The Thai base line was being broke, and the whores were so grasping, because every day they had no money, meaning *no* money. Sex was an addictive commodity, whatever deviance you cared to pay for; even masturbation was no shame but an amusing curiosity, and often he would have a short-time girl masturbate for him. Woaw said frostily *you have many lady*, and he was unsure if she disapproved, like one of the Thai dragon-women with a farang husband, sperm donor for her pale-skinned designer babies, and forbidden to scan the public merchandise.

His collection of colourful fruit-flavoured rubbers perversely grew, although a girl for all night, who 'liked' him, would take the second and subsequent couplings unprotected, as if she had already done her Buddhist condom duty. 'I miss you too much,' she panted, getting ready for another bout. The photo of Nampoong elicited different responses, or any, to keep the paymaster happy. She worked in a bar, in a go-go club, as a streetwalker, had gone to Phuket, to Germany, to her home village in the south, or the north. All agreed that she was called Lek, or perhaps Foon, or Porn.

He checked out the vague tips, but they only led to more tips, equally vague. Meanwhile he was in second youth, inexhaustible, with an endless supply of fuck-beasts, no chatting-up, no dithering, no bullshit. Just the primordial scene: command, banknote, fuck. *Sanook*. He bought their panties and wore them unwashed, fragrant with girl. He was becoming an olaf. Surfeited by girlflesh, he relished the vouchsafed moments of genuine desire, an unintended vision of breast from a girl bending over, or a skirt riding up to show the mystery of a smooth bare thigh straddling a motorbike: girls fleeting, never to be seen again, leaving you to wonder, who is she, what is she like?

He conjured up English girls glimpsed at dusk, huddled in raincoats; girls with their hair blown in the wind, seen on the deck rail of a Channel ferry, or from afar, walking on a fog-shrouded beach; girls alighting from buses to scamper into a crowd, or vanishing into taxi cabs, growling to unknowable destinations. Girls covered, withdrawn, private: the erotic power of the elusive. So it was with girls in the Scene; nude, they wore invisible robes of whipped pain, their energetic wriggles, their gasps and shrieks, their goshes and ouches and oohs, middle-class-polite veils of concealment. There were no dreams in Pattaya, crass earthly paradise, unless everything was.

One morning, after a good night with a juicy teenage waif picked up in a Seven-Eleven – gagging for it, liked it up the bum! – he sat down after breakfast with a calculator. Over a large espresso, he worked out his worth in cash, and what he would be worth, after monthly expenditure x, in ten years, accounting for cautious investments, bank interest and so on, and cautious indulgence in whores, no splashing on boat, car, or house for some cutie; in twenty years; thirty, forty, fifty years. He was staggered to find that he had enough money to keep him here for the rest of his life.

There, under a harsh mocking sun glaring from a pure blue sky, the story of his remaining youth, his decadent middle age, his crusty declining years, numbers doodled on a paper napkin. He felt giddy, looking at the map of his existence. *Is that it?* Thailand swallowing him up. He would be broke when he got to eighty, but he could get there. Far from *what do you do, what line are you in, what's your career curve*, mortgages and double glazing and the best route to work: instead, the land of lotus-eaters. How long could you live on lotus and maintain a passion for *bonks de politesse*? He needed an occupation: perhaps his own bar. Like Schoolgirls, only better, a real spanking bar.

That night, he returned to the Warm Pussy, and O was there. She wasn't dancing but sitting with a gaggle of girls in thongs, and he walked straight into their midst, sitting beside her. He relished the fear and embarrassment in her eyes. Straight away, he pushed a large banknote into the gusset of her black thong panties, relishing her confusion.

'Remember me?'

She nodded.

'I miss you too much,' he said gaily.

A smile, doubtful.

'Sure?'

'Sure. I want go with you one more.'

Her friends, by unspoken etiquette, melted into the shadows. She babbled, sorry she had taken money, it was only a loan, her friend needed it for the doctor, she would pay it back; sorry she had taken the dildo, she was a naughty girl, *jai dam*, black heart. He told her he had not reported her theft, but wanted his dildo back. His tone tolerant, amused; she giggled.

'No have. Give to my sister.'

'Sister', in Thaispeak, meant anybody female.

'I must punish you.'

He mimed thrashing, and her eyes widened.

'You want pok-pok me?'

He nodded.

'Same you give me. Sadic. Big *sanook*.'

She made a moue.

'Then you don't need to give back the money.'

'Sure?'

'Sure.'

She licked her lips.

'Up to you,' she said, with a shiver.

On the way to his room he bought a broom, getting the vendor to wrap it in a newspaper. Woaw at reception gave him a stony look, but glittering with curiosity. Once in his room, he picked up a dildo from the helpfully replenished stock, and waved it at her, pursing his lips in mock anger, and with a reproving waggle of his finger, which made her laugh. He said he had spanked many girls and wouldn't hurt her much, just a little. It was like the pepper with which Thais doused their food.

'I not believe you.'

'You do like pepper, don't you?'

'Yes.'

'Well, then.'

They stripped; she looked at his lemon thong, and demanded to know where he got it. I bought it in the shopping mall. *I think you have other lady*. Pouting. This is Pattaya, what do you think I do here? There's nothing but ladies. He raided the fridge for drinks and gave her one – to his delight, she opened the bottles with her sex – then sat back, smoking and sipping beer. She wanted to shower, but he said she could shower later. His nostrils drank in her musky bar scent, of smoke and sweat and perfume, as he watched her working with his fake Swiss Army knife, whittling the broomstick down to a rod. Her fingers stroked the shiny wood. *I think chep mak mak, big hurt*, she murmured. *Speak English, big thud*, he replied, rubbing his arse and miming comic distress. She laughed again. *Sanook*, he said, and she shook her head, bowing, as she handed him the shorn bamboo stick. She had even sliced the end into a snake's tongue. No *sanook*, she whispered. *Big thud*.

She stretched on the bed, fingers and toes clutching the sides. O's dark bottom shimmered, trembling, as if all the fruits of Earth were ripening in her bare young body. How could such beauty exist? Crouching, she thrust her buttocks up to him.

'I bad girl, have black heart,' she whispered. 'I want you sadic. I want you beat me.'

He began to cane her bare bottom. Her body wriggled, the buttocks jerking and clenching as stripes appeared on the smooth brown skin. The croup seemed to jolt upwards, greeting each stroke as the bamboo fell. She discreetly gasped and whimpered, *Ahh . . . ahh . . . hurt too much*. At first, he lashed gently, but as the beating went on, the strokes became harder. Writhing, she chewed the pillow. He gave her a dozen, then stopped. *More . . .* she whimpered. *Want more. O bad girl.* He gave her a half dozen, then another; every time, she wanted more. *Not stop. Not stop.* He paused, to stoop and kiss her bottom, running his finger up and down the downy cleft, the cheeks spread and glowing from his beating. Smelling her crevice, the musky acrid scent of her intimate *self*. The magic of a girl's bare arse, the only part of her she can't inspect. Her true secret place.

He gave her a dildo; she took it from the crinkly wrapping, without looking at him, or changing position, then raised her hips and pushed it into herself. As he beat her, she masturbated with the rubber cylinder, filling her sex. She shut her eyes, moaning *yes, yes*. When her bottom was darkly glowing, he grasped her by the hips and penetrated her anus, sans condom. The real thing, intoxicating scent of danger, commitment. Shortly after he commenced her buggery, she came, noisily, her sex wet, both crevices impaled. *Good,* she moaned. *You do it good.*

This time, O did stay all night. She confided that she liked a man to beat her. She did not know why, but whops on her bottom made her come. She liked to feel a man's power and cruelty, punishing her for everything she had done wrong in her life. She had stolen from him, half wanting him to take her again, and punish her. Other men were too meek to complain. Were there other girls like O? Yes, she knew some. Would they work in a bar where the customers wanted to pok-pok them? Of course. She gave him her black thread, and he put it on.

'Black panties, black heart,' he said.

She smiled, prodding his chest.

'Now you black heart.'

In the morning, Woaw smiled coyly.

'I listened to you,' she whispered. 'Lady O speak me. Pok! Pok!' – she mimed beating – 'You sadic.'

She wagged a playful finger.

'I like sadic, same you. I like to make pok-pok.'

I think she fancies me! I'm in with a chance here.

19

Visa Run

He moved out of the Lucky Strike, taking a monthly room in the Lotus Court a few blocks away, and echoing to the same conveyor belt of couples clacking urgently up the stone stairs. No longer a greenhorn, he was tired of the elaborate room stuffed with erotic gewgaws. He continued to drop in to talk with Chuck, and chatted up Woaw, now he was not a guest. It was fun, to pursue courtship rather than transaction. He brought up 'sadic' and 'pok-pok', and she thawed, her smiles less coy, seeing he was serious, as he eyed and complimented her glassine nylons, now white, now turquoise. One day, he said he was going to tell her a secret – she was agog – he whispered that he liked spanking girls, and collected girls' panties.

'I know! You very bad man.'

He would like to buy the turquoise ones she was wearing. Wanted to smell her beautiful bottom. Gales of laughter.

'Oh! Panties, big money. One million baht.'

'I am scared your boyfriend will be angry.'

'I have no boyfriend.'

Once a girl lied that she had no boyfriend, she was hot. But Woaw was a cut above, not really a whore. She frowned, pointed a finger upstairs.

'I am not same other ladies. I not have sex for money.'

That usually meant she had sex for money. He looked astonished, hurt, anxious, reassuring.

'Of *course* not. Just your panties.'

'You want to put them on?' she murmured, fingers on lips, stifling a giggle. 'I think yes.'

'Yes.'

'Then I must watch. Funny!'

'Okay' – shrugging, with what was meant as a nonchalant smile – 'you sadic, I think you want to pok-pok me. I think I'd like that.'

'Up to you.'

First, he explained, he had to fly to Malaysia. The stamp in his passport told him it was time to do a visa run. Get a double-entry tourist visa, Chuck said, that'll do you for six months, with extensions. Woaw asked if Malaysia was in Australia and he said no, it was not far. In Europe? No. America? Not that either.

'Many ladies Malaysia,' she pouted. 'Big bouncing.'

'I don't think so. They are Muslims.'

'Up to you.'

He had *her*, now. The thrill of a hidden asset. Taxi to the airport, brand new, seamless, efficient: smiling brown faces, get you where you want to go, to start spending money again. The lunchtime flight was full, noisy with squealing kids. Boarding, he caught sight of the Australian girl; their eyes met, a brief exchange of complicit smiles, then she was gone, into the back of the plane. He had drinks with his neighbour, Jeffrey Farthing, who was English, combining a visa run with business, a glamour photographer, sold pictures to all the men's magazines. Chubby, estuary accent, staying in Pattaya for a while, he was out here to build a photo archive, just the right side of legal. He said you met some colourful characters.

'Back home, they call me Jeff, but abroad I use Jeffrey. Classier, see? And the Thai wenches, they call me *Farting*. Bit of a giggle.'

'You do porno, then.'

'If you like.' – smiles, men of the world – 'Don't they have funny names? Porn, that's a laugh for starters. And Phuket, depending how you pronounce it.'

'I shagged a girl called Porn.'

'Haven't we all.'

152

Jeffrey got a girl, or girls, twosomes, even foursomes, and shot photo sets for England, the US, Germany. The French were pretty filthy, but liked it soft-focus and romantic; Italians and Spanish wanted mostly sharp-focus anal. Yes, he worked with *Chance* magazine, paid well, his biggest client, and authentic, the readers really did wife-swapping, chutney-chasing, all that crap. For white models, Latvia and Lithuania were it – do anything for a bottle of vodka. Thai girls were lovely jubbly, reeking of sex, though shy at first. Katoeys were uninhibited but greedy: chicks with dicks, for Brazil and Italy, where guys liked it up the arse. Made videos, too, you had to think of the internet, but there was still the lure of glossy paper, something you bought and owned. You could take your time with a mag, it didn't rush away with you.

Some of the Arabs in Pattaya wanted you to film them knobbing some Russian slag, to show to their mates back home, wanking in the fucking desert. And Aussie couples wanted a souvenir of their threesome with a Thai bitch. Had one, they got a ladyman to fist the bloke while his bird sucked him off. Christ on a bike! Those Aussies, think they're all Crocodile Dundee, but you wonder. Cambodian girls would do anything for a bowl of rice. Malaysia was puritanical Muslim, but you went for Chinese and Hindu girls. Tight little slits, and I don't mean their eyes. If they drop a kid, they have a caesarean, so as not to stretch the doorway. Lovely jubbly. Mitch asked about fetishes, without saying he wore O's black thread.

'Spanking and that? I do some, mostly videos, but these days the mags get away with hard-ons and penetration, even spanking. Those kinky types are fussy, it all has to be just right. Most Asian girls don't understand. Too thick for play-acting, and shy. They've got a thing about pain.'

'Haven't we all?' Mitch said.

Jeffrey said he used to sympathise with girls but now thought them all selfish sluts, just commodities. If you could have them for free, good luck, but usually you were kidding yourself. There was always a price, whether your money or your freedom or your sanity. That's why he liked southeast Asia. The girls knew they were commodities, you paid cash, and were quits. Girls were okay to have around, if you tipped them right, let them know their place. They needed rules, needed to know you were the boss. Guys got grief when they expected too much, fell in love and that. It wasn't love, it was blue balls, and *she* was calling the shots. A smart bloke avoided romance, no bullshit, no headaches from tarts with ideas in their heads. And you could have as many as you liked; change her for a younger model before she got dodgy innards.

Was life just a random series of encounters with myriad girls? Brown, black, white, pink, all deliciously different: all the same, when the panties came off. Another wet little entrance, another jerking of the loins, another squirt. Fire of lust dimmed by satiety. Need spanking to make the embers glow.

KL international, a mammoth steel and glass affair, modules and satellites, like spidery grey Lego, the ego trip of some politico who wanted the world's biggest airport, like every other Asian country. Designer shops, a huge shopping mall; you couldn't buy a toothbrush, but you could kit yourself in brand names, or spring two thousand dollars for a bottle of antique French brandy. A little train whisked you to immigration, and he found himself straphanging beside the Australian girl.

'We can't go on meeting like this,' he said, and she smiled above the whooshing of the train.

'You're the man from Schoolgirls,' she said. 'The one that likes being whipped.'

She knew, too. Jeffrey, pinioned further along the carriage, seemed to overhear, for he grinned at him.

'Yah,' he said, shrugging. 'And you like girls.'

'Touché,' she drawled, in her smoky melodic voice. 'I like men too. I'm not lesbian. I *hate* lesbians. Bloody *tom dees*, ratshit old dykes.'

Her eyes wide, daring him to be shocked. But he met her gaze, and they both smiled. She was tall, with a lilt to her accent that wasn't pure nasal Australian. They jostled out and got to the immigration line where, lone woman in a

154

male world, she seemed happy to cling to him. Jeffrey was in another queue, and nodded, making a *phwoarr* face. *You've pulled, you lucky sod*, he mouthed. Mitch introduced himself, and the girl said her name was Leda, and she, too, was going to the Thai Embassy for a visa. They emerged into the concourse, and Jeffrey bustled in with an expert's eye on Leda, as possible photo material.

They agreed to share a taxi, cheaper than separate train tickets. Jeffrey was going to some four-star hotel up by the Petronas Towers, but Leda knew a nice place in China-town, three stars, cheap and clean, in the middle of all the good restaurants and shops, fake designer shoes, American shirts and Swiss watches. That suited Mitch fine. Malaysia looked rich, factories amid lush greenery, scrubbed housing estates and shiny new cars, as they sped down the freeway. It was sweltering hot, even with the cab's air-conditioning. Kuala Lumpur seemed pleasant, low-key, not too big, smoggy or crowded, but the air was baking, and when they stopped at the hotel, the few steps from cab to lobby had him in a sweat. Jeffrey invited them for dinner, later, at his hotel.

Mitch and Leda took adjoining double-bedded rooms in the Zurich Inn in Chinatown, a fake Swiss place with wooden panelling and pictures of cows and lakes. He showered and put on fresh shorts, shirt and Pink's thong, the tight thread giving a thrill of his own sexual power. *Like a girl wearing ben-wa balls up her cooze.* They had tea in the hotel, Leda wearing a simple white voile dress, bare legs, a red bra and panties faintly visible through the cotton. She had an artful flower in her hair and a simple gold neck chain. She looked delicious.

They made small talk about Pattaya, skirting the subject of bars, each complicit in the other's secret. Both knew sex was why they were in Pattaya, but it was refreshing to chat up a girl that you didn't want to fuck. Well, he didn't *not* want to fuck her, but she was more lesbian than straight, not some drabbo, but svelte and beautiful in a *jolie-laide* way. He couldn't place her accent, and asked. Ukrainian, she said smugly, married to an Aussie, domiciled in Perth.

155

Australian passport, of course. She waved her hand to show her expensive wedding ring.

'He's my sugar daddy, rather *mature*, but I love him. Perth is so lovely, have you been? Very British. Danny lets me do what I want, like coming to Pattaya on my own. And I have to tell him all about my adventures. He gets off on that.'

Unspoken, that she'd been a hooker. That's how you got a sugar daddy, a rich old fart.

'He lets you pick up girls?'

She shrugged.

'Yes. In fact' – a sly giggle – 'he likes me to go with girls. Don't men find that exciting? He says he'll buy me my own bar in Thailand if I want, and I'm thinking about it. All those girls, mine! Well, *you* come to be whipped.'

'Not entirely.'

'I've often wondered what sort of girl likes to whip men. Australia is like England, men think it's fun to be beaten.'

He gave her the comparison with pepper and mustard.

'Any sort of girl likes it. Believe me.'

'Why should I not?' she said, rolling her tongue around her lips and making wide mocking eyes.

He spoke of his marriage, about the Scene, his affair with Nampoong, and his quest for her.

'Perhaps you deserve beating,' she said, 'for cheating on your wife, only you'd enjoy the pain. Men are wicked, like women, except that men know it. You come for brown girls, and so do I, so we're the same, really.'

When he confessed he was wearing Pink's panties, she laughed, tapped his nose with a fingertip, and said he was a naughty boy.

'But you look a bit like a girl, I mean your lips do. That's a compliment.'

He said his French aunts fussed over him when he was little, and said the same thing.

'Well, there you are, then.'

In the hours before dinner, they strolled through late afternoon throngs: Australian backpackers, serene Malay girls in headscarves, long-legged Chinese and Hindu girls

156

with short skirts and juicy tight bottoms. *All spankable.*
Like Thailand, you could buy anything, and cheaply. They
stopped for Tiger beer and fish soup; he bought a genuine
fake Rolex for a tenner, at which Leda wrinkled her pretty
snub nose. He did not compliment her on it, for she would
interpret that as coming on – always praise something silly
she hasn't thought of – so he told her she had lovely
elbows, and she laughed. She knew it was her bottom and
breasts that demanded compliments.

They drank several ice-cold beers. The city, so unlike
Pattaya, was a place of business, where people caught
buses and taxis, shopped and ate and clutched schoolbags
and briefcases, normal people, scurrying through the
baked air, pungent with odorous steam from woks and
food stalls. Chinese men in shorts sat smoking over tea or
beer or bowls of soup, with gaudy Chinese newspapers,
and gazing dimly into the crowded space, creating their
own small hermitages. Yet Pattaya, its liturgy of sex, was
burned into them.

In England, it would be cold and rainy, sleet sluicing the
London streets, girls with their hair tucked inside damp
overcoats fragrant with their bodies, holding a boy's hand,
both laughing, warmed by love, a brave huddle against the
wind. In Calais and Dunkirk, seagulls swooping and
cawing from the Channel, ferries hooting, cleaving the
dark waters, cranes gaunt against grey skies, the clatter of
fairground carousels as girls and boys giggled over their
cornets of *pommes frites.* But in this cauldron, he did not
care about the cold northern lands. Humankind was born
and nurtured in heat, should live in heat.

They drifted, two fetishists, shrewdly scanning the
crowds in the markets, each wondering how the other
would react. He eyed succulent strutting Hindu or Chinese
girls, or modestly elegant Malays, and smiled at Leda,
knowing she found them as tasty; she would finger a
studded leather belt, and pout in mockery. He eyed her
trim bottom, her gently trembling breasts, her hair fluttering in the smoky stifling breeze, the elegant fingers posing
the cigarettes he lit for her. Their shared fetish secrets gave

them the complicity of lovers. All those busy humdrum people, if only they *knew*. To tell her she reminded him of Zelda would be an obvious come-on, sure to backfire, for all women think they are unique.

'Like all foreigners, you come to Pattaya for sex,' she said. 'For you, the erotic power of whipping.'

She rolled the words round her tongue, savouring the last.

'It's not purely sexual. Erotic, yes, if you take eros to mean the life force. It's *cathartic*. The eighteenth century philosopher, Rousseau –'

'I have read Rousseau,' she said drily.

'– in the *Confessions*, as a boy, his tutor was the beautiful Mlle Lambercier? He makes it clear she thrashes him, and he craves it, and for many years whipping is his only conception of eros. But you come for sex too. What else is there in Thailand? Apart from golf.'

'I come to explore my nature. There is poetry in a girl loving another girl. Here, in this heat, the barriers dissolve. Your soul is freed, flying up like a bird, to see what is truly inside you. It doesn't matter whether the beautiful brown flesh is boy or girl, and sometimes you can't tell the difference, nor want to. You can look at an attractive man, and see the girl hidden inside. Nothing to do with queer, it's all good. So many men go with katoeys! By the way, are you planning to fuck me?'

'Plan! No, I . . . of course not . . .'

'Why not?' she pouted.

'We scarcely know each other.'

'Feeble! Did that stop you and Nampoong? Or the bar girls?'

'Well, I . . . of course I'd . . . I mean, if . . .'

She put a finger to his lips.

'You poor boy, you couldn't afford me. I might beat you, though. A little catharsis. Then we can be good friends.'

158

20

Sinner Dinner

Leda looked at her real Rolex.

'Hungry?'

'Not really.'

'We've time to kill before dinner. Shall I beat you?'

Casual, businesslike, friendly. Just like the Scene. His heart leapt.

'You're a quick worker.'

'No longer a worker. You'll get a beating, nothing else. A girl must satisfy her curiosity. Yes or no?'

'Yes. But with what?'

'We'd better buy something,' she said vaguely, gesturing at racks of belts.

She selected the heaviest man's belt with the hardest studs, and he paid. They passed through the hotel and he was shy, certain everyone guessed their purpose.

'Your place or mine?' he said.

'Mine, I suppose.'

He felt as nervous as his first time in a French whore's bedroom, but tried to be nonchalant. This is something I do every day in the amiable London suburbs.

'I'm new to this,' she said. 'I suppose you'd better take your clothes off. You know, I like you. You are more thoughtful than the usual lowlifes in Pattaya. Fancy knowing Rousseau.'

He stripped, and she ordered him to leave his thread on.

'That way, I'll pretend you're a girl. You don't mind?'

'Not at all.'

'Nice thong. Doesn't hide much. I suppose you shave your balls, or have a girl do it. Mm, nice and exotic.'

They agreed he would take twenty lashes with the belt. He did not expect her to remove her dress, nor did she. He enjoyed playing a sub, instructing her to fold the belt double, studs out, and lay it on hard. He relished her look of fear as she swished the air.

'It looks painful,' she murmured.

'That's the idea. Don't chicken out. I need it brisk, refreshing.'

He lay on the bed, face down, wondering what the Commoners would say if they saw him in sub's posture. Leda made him shift to face the mirror, and watch her at work lest he fantasise someone else was thrashing him. He had no erection, and she asked if that was normal; he replied that with a real sex partner, he would be stiff.

'I don't excite you?'

'We're just good friends, remember?'

'Not till I say so. Now you've been cheeky, so it's good for me to feel annoyed, isn't it?'

She hitched up his thread, tight in his arse crack, saying his buttocks were pretty. Then she whipped him quite vigorously, laying the strap on his bared rump with pauses of several seconds, as if she knew what she was doing. He gasped, dutifully clenching, and she said again that he looked very pretty, or his arse did. In the mirror, her face frowned in concentration. After his twenty strokes, he inspected himself in the mirror, proud of his blush, while she poured tequila from her duty-free bottle. He gave her a few ceremonial gasps and groans while rubbing his sore arse, which seemed to please her. She brushed his weals, very briefly, with her fingertips, and declared she didn't realise the belt would cut so deep, that it must have hurt terribly. He said it did. They sat, smoking and drinking, Mitch still half-naked.

'*Now* we're friends,' she said.

He gave her a hug, and kissed her cheek, before she waved a reproving finger.

'I could get used to it,' she said, then blushed. 'Maybe Danny, my husband, would like me to do that. Not as hard, though.' She sighed. 'I don't know when I'll be back in Perth. He really wants me to buy a bar, as much for him as me. He fucks around, you see.'

'In Perth? Shouldn't shit in your own back yard.'

'You're joking. Goes down to Fremantle, to the sailor bars. Fremo's only a few clicks away. Sometimes I go with him.' She shrugged. 'Hell, that's the way it is. But a bar here, a woman on her own . . . I don't suppose you'd be interested in a partnership? Like Lance and Goong? Don't tell me you wouldn't like your own stable of cuties.'

'You tempt me. It's just that . . .'

'I know. This Nampoong creature. I'll have to meet her one day.'

He dressed while she took a shower, stripping off before him with studied casualness. She knew he was watching, of course, and pirouetted her bottom just the tiniest bit. He told her she had a good body, and she thanked him for the compliment, saying it was very civil of him. She left the bathroom door open as she squatted on the lavatory, then showered while they continued to chat. He said Jeffrey seemed okay, colourful character, liked a drink.

'If I had a dollar for every colourful character! Most of them are bloody alcoholics. It's one of the perils of travel. Nobody cares if you have booze for breakfast.'

She emerged, nude and dripping, her hair wrapped in a towel in a delicate cornet, folded with a woman's artless grace. He glimpsed her bare mound, with a pretty red butterfly tattooed just above her quim lips. She dressed rapidly: red underthings and shoes, bare legs, a demure black dress with a high neckline that clung to her jutting breasts. In the taxi, Leda said she had never met a pornographer before.

'You've led a sheltered life, then.'

She lit a cigarette and blew smoke.

'I've always had somebody to shelter me.'

They met Jeffrey in the hotel bar, where he had in tow a ravishing Hindu girl in a slinky blue cocktail dress and

161

white shoes. Her name was Cheetah, or sounded like it, and she said she was a masseuse. She had a long straight nose, big brown eyes and slightly mocking rosebud lips, immaculate brown skin, a figure that made Leda's nose wrinkle in envy, or desire. Mitch wondered at the man's skill in equipping himself with a female so soon, or maybe she was already in his address book; he assumed she was a *fille publique*. After a lot of scotch, they taxied to an Indian restaurant and washed the searing food down with cold beer.

Leda was coming on to the Hindu girl, quite blatantly, as the meal and drinking progressed. Often, they whispered to each other and went to the loo together, while Mitch and Jeffrey made lad's talk. Cheetah said mischievously that foreigners drank a lot; Jeffrey said you needed it in this heat, and you sweated it out. Leda wanted to know all about Jeffrey's work, and he said it was humdrum really, no hanky-panky. She didn't believe him, for a good-looking man like him must have all the girls he wanted, do them before he photographed them so they would look sexy and dreamy and aroused, like this. She mimed.

He smiled with false modesty, not about to disagree, and said girls were natural exhibitionists, or else why did they queue up for glamour modelling jobs? They liked flashing their boobs, their bums, their legs, teasing, see? And having sex in public. In England they had 'dogging', where couples would park their car on a country road, turn the lights on, and hump for the watchers, with lots of grunts and groans. A girl wanted to shock, express her freedom, but always within a framework of rules, she had to feel safe, a rebel without rebellion.

'She wants to be off the leash, act the slut, go crazy in Ibiza or Greece, shag her brains out, but it's planned craziness, and it ends. She has her air ticket home. Out here, the craziness never ends.'

The sex event, or modelling session, was special, a time out of time, like the hookers in Thailand, for whom the most lubricious stunts were just part of work. It was her body doing the thing, not *her*. The readers of *Chance* sent

162

in their stories and pics of some holiday beach, with the wife shafted by local hunks, while hubby took photos. Or his wife with a girl, him getting his rocks off on the lesbo stuff. On holiday, another world. Then, back to life as usual in Guildford or Solihull, with their happy souvenir snaps.

Leda's hands were often under the tablecloth, fiddling at her lap, and Mitch suspected a game of footsie, or more, subsumed in the bustle of the restaurant. His arse still smarted pleasantly from her strapping, and her moves on Cheetah excited him. Jeffrey grinned regally, confiding that *Chance* was picking up his entertainment tab on this trip, so he could stick everything on expenses. An implied nudge-nudge, know what I mean.

'You have to lob in some hefty exes, to show you're a player. Course, they expect some product in return, silly sods.'

Whatever was going on between the girls, Leda was the dominant partner. She was cool, while Cheetah grew more and more excited, with narrow eyes and glistening lips. Jeffrey obviously approved. Mitch could see, or hope, where this was heading. He wondered if Shannon still read *Chance* mag, perhaps together with the noxious Gav. They went back to Jeffrey's hotel for a nightcap, and had several.

'Go on, have another Chivas, it's on the mag.'

'Won't they want some product?'

'Ooh! Naughty!' – Jeffrey, eyes wide, as if astonished.

The conversation was daring, Cheetah pretending shock at their tales of Pattaya as they skirted the question that was in their eyes, but not on their lips, until Jeffrey broke the ice.

'I could set up a scene, with you guys, *if* you wanted me to,' he drawled. 'Might be fun.'

'Doing what?' said Leda.

'Whatever comes to mind. Mitch likes a bit of spanky-panky, eh? Cheetah, well, she's up for anything, a right disgrace, she is' – Cheetah giggled – 'in fact, *she* could do with a spanking, couldn't you, Cheet?'

She giggled again.

163

'You, Leda, well, we don't know . . .'

'Let's find out, then,' said Leda. 'I'm tired now. Tomorrow evening? Dinner, then . . .?'

He nodded.

'Okay, yeah. A sinner dinner.'

They all laughed at that. Cheetah's consent seemed taken for granted, and they said their farewells, sultry with the hint of excitements to come. Back at the Zurich Inn, they went to their separate rooms, and Mitch went to bed, to be awakened half an hour later by Leda's rap on the door. He opened, and she asked if he would mind terribly sharing his bed? Not for sex, it was just that she hated to sleep alone. He agreed. *Toujours le galant.* She doffed her robe, nude underneath, and they stretched out naked between cool sheets, ruffled by the humming air-conditioner. He was flattered by her trust, but she said it was normal in Pattaya, no one was frustrated, you could be grown-up about things.

'Am I not supposed to put my arm round you?' he asked. 'Just good friends.'

'You can do that. Nothing else.'

He did so, and asked if she fancied Cheetah.

'Of course. Don't you?'

'Not so blatantly.'

'Right. Did you know I had my toes in her vagina?'

They talked idly of the bar they might open, perhaps calling it 'Smackers'. He cuddled her, until they drifted to sleep, her hair on his shoulder. His penis remained magnificently limp, and when he awoke in the morning, he felt exhilarated. To have slept naked with a beautiful woman, and not taken her, seemed the height of achievement, even though she *was* some kind of lesbian, despite her protests. Why so coy? Flaming benders always insisted they were 'bisexual'. But her gratitude put her in his power; he was one up.

'But what would you have done if I'd tried anything? Sentence me to whipping?'

'Oh, no, I'd have *refused* to whip you. Really, if you'd moved on me, I wouldn't have objected. It's only a fuck, after all. On the other hand, I wouldn't have encouraged it. You're too nice.'

One down again.

They taxied through the city, sunny and laid-back, the traffic not oppressive. At the Thai embassy, in a leafy suburb, they took numbers, and sat, waiting for their turn at a window. An Englishman had grief over a work visa. You must go to Bangkok, they said. But I did, and they sent me here, he wailed. Various Africans and Asians were bemused by the application form in English. Mitch and Leda had no problems, paid their money, and were told to return at the same time tomorrow. They spent the rest of the day in more shopping, Leda buying clothes, while he bought admittedly senseless electronic toys. They talked, less idly, of Smackers: now it was 'our bar'. Since she had thrashed him, and slept chastely with him, their intimacy had blossomed; they *were* good friends. In a restaurant, he picked up a Malaysian English-language newspaper.

'My God!'

'What are you my-godding about?'

There was a photograph of a group of schoolchildren watching in disgust and fear as a burly Sikh policeman administered a judicial caning, not to a man, but to a dummy. It was designed to deter the children from crime. Beside it was a photo of a real judicial caning, the victim naked, strapped to a vertical frame, and covered with padding for kidneys and thighs, like an obscene robot. He had been convicted of rape, and his face was contorted in agony.

'I didn't know they did that here,' he said. 'It's barbaric.'

Leda licked her lips.

'I don't know,' she said. 'Rape is a serious crime.'

'It says they cane people for overstaying their visas, for heaven's sake.'

'They must think that's a serious crime, too.'

At dinner the mood was subdued, but they were all tense and eager at the prospect of the scene to follow. Leda openly held Cheetah's hand and rubbed her thigh, bare under a skimpy sequinned blue frock held by spaghetti

165

straps, with a strapless scalloped blue bra beneath. Jeffrey assured them it would be a doddle, nice and easy, plenty of liquor and some good blow for those who wanted to smoke. Just go where the flow takes us, okay? When the girls visited the loo, the males had a conversation in ladspeak, consisting mostly of gestures, raised eyebrows, jerked thumbs, knowing grins, and sage nods, to preserve masculine dignity. Wouldn't dream of asking in so many words, but. It was established that no, Mitch was not stuffing her, that Jeffrey had made her for a dyke straight away, that Cheetah swung both ways and more, that Mitch wasn't averse to a spanking from a tasty girl. Jeffrey was hot to see them get it on with Cheetah. He mimed spanks, then snapshots, and Mitch pursed his lips.

'Caning's not so funny,' he said. 'It seems frightening, but you get to know your limits, how to manage pain, sort of like jogging. Whether you're top or bottom, it's about control.'

'Jogging! Fucking handsome.'

21

At the End of the Day

Jeffrey had a penthouse suite, with a balcony overlooking the twinkling city. He had rented small studio lights, all that his Nikon and vidcam needed. Course, back home he couldn't do this, staying in some damp B and B. Cheetah didn't know what a B and B was, and Leda said it meant breasts and bottoms, touching her, as if to instruct. Cheetah retorted she knew what breasts and bottoms were. They laughed, Jeffrey rolled joints, and they smoked happily; Mitch rarely did, but this stuff was good.

Scotch glowed golden in crystal glasses, sparkling like the city. He felt dreamy, on top of the shabby scurrying dirty world far below, the bodies of the two girls shimmering with beauty. Princesses from heaven. A gobbet of ash fell from his cigarette on to the carpet, and Cheetah said it looked like a monkey turd, and everybody found that hilarious. Jeffrey was telling risqué modelling stories: jealous husbands, nude photo sessions, wet T-shirt sessions, girls who proved to be blokes, blokes who proved to be girls. No, really! the girls cooed. Mitch took off his shirt.

'Somebody's got to start,' he said, and the girls went 'ooh'.

Jeffrey said he should keep his togs on, to show he was the director. The girls booed, so he stripped to his bikini briefs, fake leopardskin (*oh, do me a favour*), which made them laugh. They wolf-whistled Mitch, posing and simpering in his thong, then slid their dresses up. Now it was the

167

boys' turn to whistle. Tits out for the lads, Jeffrey crowed, not unpredictably. Leda unhooked Cheetah's bra, letting her breasts spring out, and, before Cheetah could respond, she freed her own breasts, squashing them against the Hindu girl's while kissing her on the mouth. There was a little slapping of bottoms as the girls French-kissed, with Leda pushing Cheetah's panties down over her thighs.

'That's the ticket,' said Jeffrey.

He closed the drapes and flicked on spotlights, casting harsh shadows. Cheetah pulled at Leda's string until both girls stood naked in the pool of light. Leda reached forward and ripped down Mitch's thong.

'Careful . . .!'

His penis was erect. Jeffrey lifted his Nikon and began to take pictures, 'to get things going'. The girls posed and pouted, pawing each other in slippery embraces. As he snapped, the girls' poses grew more lickerish, with open-crotch shots, masturbation shots, and toe-licking shots when Leda took Cheetah's slender feet in her mouth. She put a finger in the brown girl's anus, and another in her vulva, while Cheetah stroked her hair and fingered her breasts. It was all casual, friendly, as it should be. *Readers' wives. Suburbia.*

'Diamond,' Jeffrey enthused, and started his vidcam.

With some contortion, the girls tongued each other, quivering bodies entwined. The strong light gave their skins the creamy texture of soft animal hides. They ended in *soixante-neuf*, caressing on the bed, until they moaned and gasped climactically, the coverlet damp. Mitch sipped and smoked on the sideline. Unlike Jeffrey, who was working, he was erect. Crushing his duty-free Dunhill, he knelt and sucked Cheetah's toes, hoping to make Leda jealous.

'Now we're in the mood, right? I got sound, you just ad lib the script, say whatever's cool.'

The girls sat on the sofa, smoking, with Cheetah on Leda's knee, while Jeffrey explained the scenario. A video had to have some kind of story line, see? Now, for this one, they would have to get their kit on again. Lazily caressing Cheetah's breasts, Leda made a moue.

'Only for a while, darling. You don't think I'd waste that fabulous bod.'

'*Bagwan.*'

Mitch is a salesman, of, let's see, shower attachments. He's giving her the verbals, then starts groping, and they get their kit off, and go at it hammer and tongs. Bit of spanking, oral, water sports, stuff in the shower, whatever takes their fancy. Then they're on the bed, and Mitch is giving Cheet a right seeing-to. Regular, up the bum, whatever. Suddenly Leda comes in. What's this! You filthy pigs, and so on. She grabs a whip, going to give them both a hiding. She whips Cheetah, lots of wailing, then Cheetah sits on Mitch, while Leda whips him. Then the three of them get it on. Mitch holds it in as long as he can, no come shots, too gross and American.

'You won't beat me *very* hard?' Cheetah asked Leda.

'Wait and see. It depends how angry I am.'

Jeffrey took him aside.

'Sure you're cool about the whipping part?' he asked.

'Yah. I'm a natural, aren't I? Mummy spanked me with a cucumber on the bare arse. Makes a man of you. She caught me wanking with this girl's panties, once.'

'Naughty. A cucumber, fuck me, that's good. Pity we don't have one. There's that fancy fruit bowl, but nothing there would do. I bought a nice whip today, though. Leda can find it in the wardrobe. Did you like your mum?'

'Of course.' *I did, didn't I?*

'I hated mine. Psychopathic old bag. Oh well.'

Barefoot, in his absurd leopardskin knickers, Jeffrey lifted the camera. Leda crouched by the door, which she would bang, pretending to enter, as Mitch and Cheetah positioned themselves on the sofa.

'Roll'em!'

Mitch's twinge of doubt, that his penis would wilt before an intrusive lens, vanished when he smelled Cheetah's musky body pressed against his. Her fingers touched his groin. He slipped off her shoulder strap, and Cheetah obligingly let both breasts tumble from her dress top. As she unbuttoned his shirt, exaggeratedly moaning and sighing, he groped her, licked her earlobes, and crushed her nipples against her ribs, making her squeak. Bit of rough trade. Mitch the dom.

'Oh! You're very persuasive, but I'm not sure I need another shower attachment,' she chirped; drama school diction. 'I'm very clean! My feet are clean, my breasts are clean, my *pussy*'s clean. And my mouth is *so* clean.'

Her fingers clasped his balls. He French-kissed her, and imagined he could taste Leda's juice on her lips.

'Oof! Didn't that taste nice?' she gasped.

'Yes, you're very clean,' he said inanely.

'Wouldn't you like to check the rest of me?' – her hand stroking his penis – 'Ooh! What's this?'

'I think you know,' he said. 'You're a very naughty girl.'

'I'd so hate to be spanked for being naughty. Please, sir, please, not a spanking on my poor naked bottom!'

He pushed her dress up and his fingers, under her panties, found her smooth sex, which made delicate little sucking sounds at his caress. Soon they were nude, Cheetah subtly positioning him so that their bodies were best exposed to the camera; she was aware of the lens. Thighs wide as he frotted her, she bent to lick her nipples, groaning in surprise, as if discovering a new thrill. He swooped, and began to suck her wet quim petals.

'Yes . . . ooh . . . don't stop . . . ahh . . . yes! Oh!'

To his amazement, she convulsed in a breathless, apparently genuine climax. So soon!

'Whew!' she gasped, clutching him. 'Now, why don't you demonstrate your appliance?'

It was so corny, he had to suppress a grin. Leda's face, watching from the shadows, was stony. Jeffrey followed them into the bathroom, incongruously stocked with his male toiletries, and she turned on the shower. She grabbed the tubing from him and deftly attached it, to spray her vulva held open by finger and thumb. He joined her in the shower and wrestled her for the squirting tube, inserted it into her quim, anus and mouth, then slapped her breasts and belly with it. Cheetah squealed in delight.

170

'You deserve spanking, you naughty girl,' he barked, real Hollywood stuff.

'Oh, no!' she cried. 'A bare-bottom spanking! I *knew* you were cruel, and I'm so helpless.'

He dragged her, dripping, to the bed, put her across his thighs, and spanked her buttocks a couple of dozen. Then she leaned back, legs spread and back arched in a yoga contortion, babbling dirty talk: take me, take me, I can't resist, you've got me all wet, you filthy brute, fuck me, fuck me hard with that big cock, fuck my wet pussy. He penetrated her sex, finding that the yoga position deliciously tightened her, and she gasped, you're so big, fuck me, it hurts, don't stop; hogging the script. He withdrew, and wrenched her hair, and she fellated him, deep-throat, lips at his balls with her fingers busy at her clito. This lasted a long time until she released him, and crouched face down, to display her buttocks. His penis, oiled by her saliva, penetrated her anus from behind.

'No, please don't bugger me, not that!' she wailed. 'My bottom can't stand a big stiff cock inside! You'll split me open! Ooh!'

'It's what you deserve, slut!' – worthy of an oscar.

He enculed her briskly until the door banged; quick footsteps, and they were in Leda's shadow. You filthy pigs, the moment my back's turned! The wardrobe opened, and out came a vicious little leather whip, adorned with red tassels. Slut! Beast! This deserves whipping. Both of you. His penis plopped from Cheetah's clinging anus and he whined, please, no, I can't stand pain.

'You can take my punishment, you monster, or I'll call the police.'

'I'll take your punishment,' he stammered; acting was fun.

Pouting to the camera, Leda stripped to bra and panties.

'I'm going to enjoy this,' she said.

He didn't need to act, for it wasn't friendly; the whip stung hard. As the pain of her lashes streaked across his arse, his whimpers were muffled by the pillow he chewed. Cheetah sat on his head, and he supposed she was frigging (*a right disgrace!*), for he felt her juice moistening his hair.

171

'Mm! Mm!' he squealed.

Nampoong had never whipped him this hard, but he remembered Zelda: *Every time, you feel you've never been hurt so much, and can't take any more. But you haven't, and you can.* He wondered what his arse would look like in the pages of *Chance* magazine. Cheetah gasping, yes, yes, ahh! Coming *again*? Leda snarling, I hope you've learned your lesson, sir (nice quaint touch), and it was Cheetah's turn. The Hindu girl resumed her crouch, bottom up and face in the pillow, as Leda whipped her. The bare fesses squirming beautifully, hectic cries of pain.

He pulled her hair, and she took him once more in her mouth while Leda striped her. Tears in Cheetah's eyes as she fellated him, fingers masturbating her slopped pouch. Mm! Mm! He had been worried about coming too soon, but in the drifting dream of the whisky and smoke, he could control it, floating above his body, observing himself. Look, some bloke getting sucked off by a whipped Indian girl. Every sense heightened, the colours of the room and the bare bodies vivid, Cheetah's dance of pain in slo-mo.

Leda's intent face was creased with fury as she stroked. She reached behind her and unsnapped her bra, letting it fall, her breasts quivering like white jellies. Leda's panties off, she picked a banana from the bowl and thrust it into her sex, masturbating as she flogged. Then, the whipping over, he was sandwiched between two slippery nude bodies. Writhing, nibbling, sucking, stroking, all in hazy slo-mo, Cheetah eating the banana, skin and all, glazed with Leda's fluid. The whip thrust into his hand, Leda pleading, unscripted: 'Whip me, I want to know what it's like.'

Leda crouching, arse up, her face gripped between Cheetah's thighs as his whip lashed her. Squirming, she did not cry out. Tough girl from the steppe. Cheetah tweaking her nipples, bending to lick them, always acting, a real trouper. After a half-dozen whipstrokes, he penetrated Leda's sex, fucked her brutally and, figuring enough screen time had elapsed, spurted inside her. Hm, no banana-

172

flavoured condom. But the silky wet warmth of the naked chatte, so welcoming. Cosy up inside the womb. Cheetah groaning in orgasm as Leda's mouth sucked the Hindu girl's clito, and Leda crying out in her own spasm as his seed washed her. He withdrew and kissed the butterfly tattooed on her hillock. *Well, that's that, then.*

But Jeffrey was there, nude and chubby. He leered, eyebrows raised, you don't mind, do you, as Leda lay on her back, thighs apart, primal female submission, and his penis entered her. She looked at Mitch, her eyes glistening in triumph, as she was fucked in front of him, until Jeffrey grunted, ejaculating. *My woman fucked by another male, his sperm in my womb.* But she wasn't his woman, hell, she was a Ukrainian whore, and they were just good friends.

'Lovely jubbly. Now you know my kink,' Jeffrey panted, with a wink. 'I like a buttered bun, me.'

'Well,' said Mitch. 'I thought that sort of thing only happened in movies.'

'That *was* the movies. But hey, at the end of the day, it's all just a glorified wank, innit?'

Leda did not sleep with him that night, but went to her own room after blowing him an air-kiss. He dreamt of Cheetah as Kali, the four-armed Hindu goddess of time. One of her hands masturbated her chatte, which dripped blood, while the others waved knives and cut his penis off in gruesome cinematic slo-mo. A little hungover at breakfast from all that good scotch, and unsettled by his dream, he didn't know whether to be jealous, or annoyed, or what, at Leda's coupling with Jeffrey. It was his fault for initiating the scene, but anyway, he had done her *first*.

'You raped me,' she drawled lazily.

'I'm sorry.'

She laughed.

'Don't apologise. It was nice.'

'Only nice?'

'You made me come, didn't you? Jeffrey didn't. I don't know if I want to be beaten again, though. It's scary. I wonder if your whipping brought me off. My bottom's still sore. I looked at it in the mirror.' She shivered. 'Anyway, it's all fun, but there's more to life than sex. I can't stand these losers in Pattaya, who are obsessed with nothing else. They should get a life.'

'Maybe Pattaya is their life.'

'My God. Can't you tell the difference between life and fun? Fun doesn't make you happy. All these girls served up on a plate! Guys should stay at home and enjoy being frustrated.'

'That's a bit too deep for me.'

'I suppose so. You're nice, for a chump.'

They picked up their passports, enriched by gaudy visas, without trouble. The aggrieved Englishman was still there, saying he had *phoned* Bangkok, and they said he must get it done in Malaysia. No, you must go there. But they said I had to stay here. Desperately, he flourished documents, a life contained in bits of paper. We know nothing about this. Go to the Thai embassy in England. But I've just *come* from England! That is not our problem. A European raising his voice to the orient, and the orient inscrutable, mocking, hating. For once, we are not begging you to buy.

Same trip back to Pattaya, in reverse: taxi, airport, taxi, climbing stairs, waiting in line, security, or not much of. The netherworld of grey plastic, rubber, metal, tinted glass. Seeking out the meagre accommodations where they let you smoke. They talked of Smackers, their bar, as if it already existed. Money, partnership: he was being drawn in, selling it to himself. Was Leda more, or less desirable, now that he had ejaculated in her, established her cunt as his territory? She seemed friendlier, even tender, towards him. Fucking a woman changed your friendship, surely. But what was it? A hygienic exercise, a *bonk de politesse*, a game of ping-pong? Their coupling had cemented mateship, just as with Wendy and the girls at the Commoners. Nothing meant anything. No relationships and all that mushy women's magazine crap. If the Scene was anywhere, it was here.

On impulse, he showed Leda the photos of Nampoong. She scanned them, said she was tasty.

'I think I had her once. A dancer, did all the pussy tricks. Lovely body, and hot. Wanted too much money. Called herself Lek. But I can't be sure. They all look so much alike, don't they?'

22

The Bounty

'An orgy in Malaysia! No way, buddy,' Chuck chortled.

'Yah, diamond, it was,' said Mitch. 'Birds all over the place, gagging for it' – putting on the estuary English – 'Here, wouldn't it be great to pick girls off the branch, hanging there like fruits? Or phone for delivery, like a pizza, extra topping. How about delivery *with* a pizza?'

'You British,' sighed Chuck. 'What about the thrill of the chase?'

He was waiting for Woaw to get off work, after her shift. He felt jubilant, for he'd *pulled*. A quick approach, routine casual. Meet for dinner? In one of the plush hotels. Not a word to her boss. A fleeting smile, and silent nod, yes. The magical yes. It was going to happen. Not, um, yes, a quick drink (but I must get home to shampoo my hair, or collect my laundry). *Yes*.

He looked at his watch, drained his beer, and rose.

'Time to go. Those whores won't fuck themselves. Somebody's got to do it.' Arf. A bloke's bloke.

He watched her leave the Lucky Strike, not in her turquoise uniform. She wore a short black skirt and breast-hugging white blouse, like a schoolgirl, though still in turquoise nylons and high heels. He realised just how young she was, dainty and serene, picking her way through the squawking hookers. He was pleased at stirring in desire, just by looking at her. Girls never understood that you ogled them to feel that one-in-a-million spark, to rekindle your own virility. How much more so, here, with hectares of brown flesh on view, and the palate swiftly jaded. Woaw was truly sexy, because unavailable, hard to get, mysterious. Leda was right, guys doted on Thai girls simply because they were available, no messing around. The great horizontals of history, Cleopatra, Mme du Barry, Nell Gwynne, were frumps. To score, they just had to smile, advertising that they *did it* a lot.

He was at the hotel before her, settled in the restaurant. She arrived as he was working on his second beer. She smiled briefly and picked up the menu, then had a long jabber in Thai with the waiter. Heaped platefuls of shrimp and pork and rice and leaves arrived, and she attacked them, just like Nampoong: first stuff, then talk. Frightened her food would melt, or be stolen by some other peasant.

'Full?'

'Full.' Beaming happily; God, they're like children.

She had a large bag, and he wondered what was in it, so asked. She smiled, a ravishing smile, with the promise of all female mysteries, and said he would find out soon when they went upstairs. She thought he was staying here! He went to book a room – happily they had one, at an outrageous price – and he came back with the key fastened to an enormous hunk of unstealable plastic, placing it on the table with the smugness of some suburban arsehole dropping his Benz keys on a bartop.

Nice, that once a girl had agreed to eat with you she was inevitably going with you. She knew what her honeypot was for, to earn a feed, and a tip. Scene girls, too, knew what they wanted, and didn't play mind games. Just *gimme*. Woaw's fetish was whipping, not improbable in a country with no hangups about corporal punishment, where the TV actually showed schoolkids being beaten with sticks, or farm girls lashing pigs and water buffaloes. She murmured that she was sure of his good heart, and O had said he wouldn't turn angry. He said she was more beautiful than O, unsure if he meant it, and she simpered. They took the lift upstairs and when he opened the door, she knew at once he wasn't staying there, for his things weren't in the room. Thai girls didn't miss a trick. In every sense.

She seemed pleased that he had paid just for her. No aroma of whores on the pristine bedspread, as she would expect. Back home, erotic encounters were the spice of life, but here they were taken for granted, they *were* life. Nothing else to do. You ignored the stories of war and butchery in the south, war and butchery in the north, the corrupt arseholes who ran the place, the beggars, the homeless, the imprisoned, people dying without money for a doctor, and, next door, cowboy Cambodia, the mother of all fuckups, whose only apparent purpose on Earth was to make Thailand look good. Pattaya was little Las Vegas, its slots ever-open. *Everything you want, you got it right here in Patt-a-yaaa.*

The room was standard soulless de luxe, with a balcony and sea view. There was a mini-bar, and he poured drinks, Woaw taking only fizzy water imported from Canada, with a price to match. He put some of it in his scotch, and lit up, but she didn't smoke either. They sat on the balcony and watched the boats twinkling on the ocean. She wasn't in a hurry, like a whore, eager for her next trick, and not nervous, except that she made him promise not to tell her boss. Chuck did not know she was 'sadic'. Why, he was the sadic one, for making his girls wear hot nylons, suspender belts, farang things.

Should he fuck her or not? Would she be annoyed if he did, or hurt if he didn't? What a delightful puzzle. Back home, inane showing off, buying drinks for some tease who knows you're gasping to get into her panties. Here, the liberty of a baron with his maid. You may have it tomorrow, m'dear, I prefer to read a book tonight. He asked Woaw if it was time for her to open her bag; coyly, she did so, and removed a coiled leather whip. She said it was for driving water buffalo.

'So I'm to be a water buffalo?'

'Yes.'

He let his penis harden. She asked him what he had done in Malaysia. Had he gone with many ladies?

'Only two.'

She pouted.

178

'Lady pok-pok you?'

'Yes.'

She picked up the whip and stroked the heavy leather thong, slowly uncoiling it.

'Not many farangs like lady sadic. I must be careful, so they not think I am bad girl, mafia, take drugs. I am angry you go with other lady, and I want to pok-pok you very hard, but only if you like. Up to you.'

He gazed at her serious young face, dappled by starlight, at the soft-swelling breasts, the firm thighs, the glaze of parted lips, so kissable, yet Thai girls didn't kiss on the lips, you kissed them elsewhere.

'Yes, I like,' he murmured. 'Shall we ...?' *Toujours galant*.

All business, she made him strip completely, removing his girly thread (giggles), then teased him about it: *you ladyman*. She directed him to stand naked against the wall with his legs splayed, arms stretched, and his fingers clutching the lintel. She kept her clothing, but shucked off her shoes and stood in her turquoise nylons. Her feet were sweaty; he breathed deeply of their scent.

'I wasn't sure if you liked me when I was staying at the Lucky Strike,' he said. 'I like you, number one.'

She smiled, and whispered that she liked him, too. She was *heung*, jealous of his other ladies, and wanted to punish him.

'Yes! Yes, go ahead.'

Her whip whistled, striking him on the shoulders with a searing crack that made him shudder, then lashed his arse. He gritted his teeth, for it hurt abominably, yet his penis was stiff, slammed against the wallpaper by the force of her strokes. His gorge rose, and he could not help gasping. Mostly, she flogged his buttocks; his body glowed with pain, every welt pulsing. He twisted his head, to relish her pert conic breasts quivering, her arms and thighs rippling with muscle. Mutiny on the Bounty stuff. *God, it hurts. Whipped by a fit young girl in a schoolgirl's uniform. What a perve I am.* After every second stroke, she panted her mantra, that he was naughty.

She went past ten strokes, and when she finally put the whip down, he was cleansed, smarting, alive. Her slave. He crouched at her feet, clasped her dainty ankles, and began to lick the nyloned toes, savouring the taste of her sweat. His fingers stroked her calves, knees, then thighs; still, she did not object. Should he . . .? With her toes in his mouth, he reached under her skirt, over the stocking tops and garter straps, to bare thighs, moist with sweat-dew. Breathing heavily, she began to caress his shoulders, and did not protest as he rose to push his head under the skirt and press his nose and lips to her panties. They were moist; he kissed the tiny wet cache-sexe. Her hillock was shaved and, filling his lungs with her perfume, he licked its bared skin, outside the tiny triangle of cloth.

'You're so beautiful.'

'Oh! Thank you. Have black skin, not beautiful.'

'Yes, beautiful. Nescafé.'

She laughed – it took so little – said thank you again, and drew him up to crouch with his face at her breasts. The turquoise bra swelled with her soft flesh, and he took each cup in his mouth, sucking the nipples under the fabric. She clasped his head to her breasts and unfastened her bra. In grateful adoration, he kissed the large soft nipples crowning her firm cones, quivering to his caress: sacred form of cone, pyramid, tower, extrusions from the Earth, thrusting to heaven. He embraced her, kissing her hair, and rubbing her nipples with his, then drew her to the bed.

Her skirt and panties slipped down, and she opened her thighs, most magic of surrenders. Framed by frilly turquoise suspender belt and nylons, her shaven hillock gleamed, so pure and innocent. He kissed her buttocks, tongue in her cleft, then her thighs clamped his head as his lips fastened, sucking, on her quim, and she moaned, *ah, ah, yes*. Parting her thighs, he mounted her, missionary position, and, after only a few strokes, ejaculated at her wombneck. He lay on top of her, still inside, and nuzzled her hair with his nose, marvelling how her prim beauty turned animal, once naked. No use wondering who had pierced her hymen: some smooth Thai boy in a rice-paddy rut, before he was taken away to the army, leaving her thankfully unfertilised, unlike so many abandoned girls who ended up working bar.

'*Hom*,' he gasped, sniffing her hair.

'Thank you. Sexy man.'

'I'm sorry you didn't come.'

'Yes, I come. When I whip you, I make *chak wao*.' She giggled.

'Why are you sadic?'

She shrugged. 'It doesn't matter. Up to you.'

'Perhaps when you were little, whipping the water buffalo . . .?'

She nodded; sometimes she was charged with punishing her unruly little brothers, thrashing their bare bottoms.

'Why do you like whip?' she asked. 'Good for heart?'

She meant the affective heart, not the pump.

'Yes. It makes you feel young and clean. Full of love.'

She gazed into his eyes, blushing a little, then took a carton of soya milk out of the mini-bar, poured it into a dish, and squatted, bathing her sex, *sabai dee*, good health. She could suck the milk inside her pouch and squirt it out, making bubbles in the dish, entrancing him. The king encouraged people to drink milk – it had iodine, or something. He watched her play with her sex lips while he smoked and sipped scotch. Her mundane hygiene seemed to free her tongue, she was just a girl cleaning herself after work. Yes, she had whipped farangs, not many, for she made it clear she would not have sex with them, though she discreetly masturbated as she flogged. He was the first she had bounced, since she liked him. The others, she simply wanted to hurt, to make them bleed. She had not whipped him hard, for she wanted him to like her. He was pleased she took the trouble to lie, or bend the truth, so sweetly.

He seized her smelly discarded nylons and held them to his nose, kissing and sniffing them. She wagged her finger, saying, *naughty boy, you need more pok-pok*, and spanked him over her thighs. After a few dozen spanks, he clasped her buttocks and kissed her hillock, her sex, her anus. He

181

took her feet in his mouth and licked her soles, to her squeals of pleasure. He wanted to kiss all of her at once, eat her up. She crouched to engorge his penis with her lips while she inserted a finger into his anus and reamed him, then her bare fesses crushed his face, wreathing him in her odour of sweetmeats. You could sneer at a girl, break her trembling little heart for a moment or two, but when her buttocks smothered you, smelling her, with your lips drinking from her sex, you were her slave.

'The perfect bottom,' he murmured into her anus bud.

She rose, then let her jaw drop as he stuffed her discarded panties into his mouth and began to eat them. *No, no*, she cried, laughing. Her panties in his mouth, he oiled his penis with her quim juice, parted her buttocks, and penetrated her anus. He enculed her for over two minutes while she whined, with soft little squeaks, like a mouse. *Oh, oh, good*, she whimpered, when he finally ejaculated. As she rubbed her bottom, making pained faces, he told her his plans for a spanking bar, and offered her a job. She wasn't sure, had never worked bar, that was only for the desperate. What would her family say? He tried to persuade her she would not have to go with customers, just whip them. Big *sanook*! The tips would be good. Her eyes sparkled, and she promised to think about it.

'Up to you,' he replied; but everyone liked a job offer, and everyone in Thailand was mad for money.

She thanked him for buggering her, said she loved it, despite the *chep*, for that way (forgetting his sperm already in her sex) she wouldn't have a baby. They went to sleep till dawn. She lay on her belly, bottom sweetly up, and he gently raised her, to slide his face under her naked sex. They lay for a long time, with his mouth her sleeping quim's pillow, as he breathed the wondrous innocence of her young body. Like that, he drifted into dreams, awaking briefly to push a banknote into her bag, wrapping it around her whip. Always tip, pay your debt, never owe them anything.

And in the morning, she slipped away, after pressing her nose to his hair, and murmuring *hom*. No see-you-agains, no mumbled farewells and, on his part, no acting the ubersexual, metrosexual, neo-lad, all that sad phony shit back home. In this town, you were maybe just a fat fuck with a beergut, but you always saw them again. He wondered if he would find Nampoong, and supposed he would; what goes around comes around. He wondered if he really wanted to. Showered but not shaved, he walked out into the fresh sea air, birds and lizards and crickets chirping, and a magnificently striped turquoise butterfly collided with his face. He thought, neither happy nor sad, *That's that, then.*

23

Treasure

It took time to set up a bar, and he left things in Leda's hands. She knew a good lawyer who spoke English and had a posse of girlfriends to scout for premises. The winter tourist season would be over, and they could be up and running before the next influx of tattooed euro-hordes. He moved out of his hotel into a bungalow a few metres from the beach, a way out of the town centre, but a short walk from bar glitter. Leda had found it for him. He had a large garden with flowers, mint, aloe vera, mango and papaya trees, and when neighbouring Thai matrons walked past to eye him he would offer the fruits, establishing himself as 'good heart', his thong exciting no comment since a farang was weird by definition. Leda did not mention their Malaysian adventure, nor suggest a reprise. They sat in the garden, drinking and smoking, she demure in short denim skirt, tan bare legs, a clinging sleeveless T-shirt with no bra, and wraparound sunshades. He told her she looked very tasty, very Cannes film festival.

'Thank you. You look nice in that thong. You'd look sexy dressed up. You're so slim, despite all that beer! Must be your metabolism. I could see you as a girl, and that's a compliment. I do prefer girls.'

'Mummy used to joke that she wanted a girl instead of me,' he said. 'Perhaps my metabolism strives to oblige her.'

'Well, it overlooks your rather menacing penis.'

Once, after a couple of tequila and lime juices, she abruptly, coyly, demanded a spanking. She didn't know

184

why, her bottom just felt tingly. He obliged, putting her over his knee on the sofa for a few dozen smacks on the bare. She squirmed enthusiastically.

'That's better,' she said, rubbing her bottom. 'It really is sort of cleansing. I could get hooked on this, you beast.'

'The price is your panties.'

'Then what am I going to wear?'

'Nothing.'

'You really are a beast,' she said, but handed over her fetching frilly white string.

It was nice to be friends with a woman, having got the tupping part out of the way. She had heard a rumour that Lancelot and Goong were in a hurry to sell Schoolgirls. A bar she had her eye on, 'Wet T-shirts', run by a biker from Berlin, well, he had been shot dead by his dope-dealing partner, who was in jail, and the police chief was running the bar for himself; perhaps he had ordered the hit. They shrugged. *T.I.T.* What a same story. Gradually he constructed an expat identity: bank account, rented motorcycle, post office box, cable TV, mobile phone, and a pleasant married lady as maid. Some nights he would stay in and read, watch the BBC or French television, or the Italian, for vast omnipresent bosoms; the American channel, braying propaganda, was useful for the weather reports, and the smug satisfaction of sitting naked with an ice-cold beer while reading the minus temperatures back home.

There were English bookshops, including a musty second-hand place run by an ex-seaman from Grimsby, where he loved to browse; he bought a tattered French book, the lubricious memoirs of a Rousseauesque eighteenth-century rake, one Marc Delatour, who had been guillotined in the Terror. A baron, he had fled Montpellier after various erotic scandals, including the near-mortal whipping of a prostitute, taking refuge in Calais, where he became a sea captain. It was about as far away as you could get, where no one would think of looking for you, but Robespierre's Jacobins in Arras uncovered his true identity and sent him to the Bastille. An engaging old perve.

He strolled the seafront strip near his home, amid beach-tat shops, the stink of fried food, the placid gurgle of sewage into the sea. The occasional crunch of metal, usually a motorcyclist bowling up the wrong side of the road, did not turn his head. He bought a funny wooden snake from a wandering vendor. The roads were clogged with towed boats and jet-skis, middle-aged arseholes on big bikes, and buses full of Japanese who never walked and never mingled. They had their own unspeakable girly bars, no Europeans allowed. He was soon on friendly garden-fence terms with Anglo neighbours, and they discussed girls, sex, why they stayed here, justifying themselves for choosing lotus land. *I stuck a banana up her cunt, and it broke, and I sucked it out. – She jerked me off over her tits, then licked up my jism – I like them to piss on me. – No shit! – Yeah, sometimes, ha ha. – She got her clit pierced, comes if you shake her.* Frankness was all, confessions at dusk, slapping away the mosquitoes. Soon he brought girls home, like his neighbours. Midnight orgasmic cries, the owl hoots of suburbia.

Some girls called or texted incessantly, why you no come see me, I love you too much: business girls checking their client base. Then, you butterfly, fuck you (they all knew that phrase), I go with other men. Whores pretended they weren't whores, and cunnilingus made them cling-ons. Thai girls loved it when he tongued them off. Thai men wouldn't do that, beneath their dignity, just wham bam, and back to the whisky bottle. But there was a grotto of wonders down there, clams, oysters, roses, orchids, a fleshy terrarium.

He continued to visit Chuck for guy talk over beer, which Chuck chased with double tequilas, and Woaw greeted him with a serene smile. They exchanged pouts and nods; she was cool, not threatening to become a cling-on, while he suspected that O might, or else he was afraid to find her paired off. You always think a girl will wait. An olaf would weep into his beer about his honey, who, in his cash-sending absence, was not, as promised, in her village, but selling her arse on Walking Street. Why does she do this to me? All the love stories were the same, stripped down: money, fuck me, feed me, buy me water buffalo. Perhaps all stories everywhere were the same: Tristan and Isolde, the Holy Grail, the Iliad, just glorified water buffalo sagas.

Frequently he saw Jeffrey, who gave him a DVD of their home movie, and now he would have to buy a computer to look at it. He also received a set of glossy prints, and they chuckled together, phwoarr, like old soldiers over a distant campaign. Jeffrey was cheerful company. He always photographed the 'wenches' he bedded. Flap shots, split beaver, anal, dildos, the fucking works, mate. He and Mitch would take a girl back to Jeffrey's hotel, and Mitch would fuck her while Jeffrey photographed, before taking his turn at the buttered bun. There was no problem getting the photos developed by a friendly photo shop; like prostitution, and everything else illegal, pornography was universal. Sometimes they did a 'spitroast', one male in a girl's mouth, the other in her sex. Girls who did this thought it funny, and rewarding. Australians were very fond of spitroasts, according to Jeffrey, those Crocodile Dundees, know what I mean. Where did that leave *them*? In a haze of tequila, it didn't seem to matter.

'Make a wench laugh, and she'll do anything,' was Jeffrey's street wisdom.

He prowled the back streets in the small hours, with ramshackle bars and girls just off the bus from the village, selling their arses for rice before they got it into their heads that they were beauty queens. He adopted an alter ego, Marc from Calais, speaking only French (also useful for repelling over-friendly drunks). No squawking in fractured English, no names: truly, a zipless fuck. But what did a fuck mean? More interesting to see how she swept the floor, did her hair, or made a cup of tea. Eventually, even the raunchiest, laddiest lads saddled themselves with a dragon missus, then boasted about her jealousy, if she caught me fucking around, she'd cut my dick off. Proud of being wanted.

At last, he went back to the Warm Pussy. O was seated on a groper's lap, but, seeing Mitch, joined him at once.

She greeted him with delight, and he bought her a lady drink while they held hands, watching the other dancers, jabbering merrily to each other. A punter occasionally prodded a banknote into a girl's boot or vulva, where it disappeared, deftly trapped. It was understood O would go home with him, her eyes lighting up when he told her he had a bungalow by the sea. She wanted to know what he ate, and he said, usually in restaurants. She frowned and said she must cook for him. He told her he had a housekeeper, and she declared that Thai ladies were lazy.

'You pok-pok she?'

'No.'

'I think you have many ladies. I speak lady Woaw. She pok-pok you' – she mimed whipping, and giggled – 'you butterfly. But you not fuck her, I not broken heart.'

So Woaw had been economical with the truth.

'Well, you have many men.' *Ten cocks a month . . .*

'Working! Use condom!'

'You whip them?'

'No!' – feigning shock – 'Only you.'

Back at the bungalow, with a pale moon overhead, she promptly seized a broom and started sweeping, saying that it was dirty, establishing her territory. He sat with drink and cigarette, watching the supple movements of her body while the ceiling fan whirled lazily. He told her to take off her dress and undergarments, and she did, beaming, as she did her dusting, washing, and wiping in the nude. She crouched on all fours to scrub the floor. When she approached his chair, he swung his bare feet on to her back and rested them there. She stayed still, panting like a dog, his footstool.

After she had cleaned to her satisfaction, they showered together and she fellated him, rubbing her clito while she sucked, and bringing herself off, or pretending, at the moment of his ejaculation, as she swallowed his sperm. He was not allowed to wash himself for she must do that, and she scrubbed him, a nanny with a little boy: two jobs done. Afterwards, she poured him a fresh drink and lit a fresh cigarette in her quim, sucking the smoke in, before solemnly handing it to him. The end tasted moist with her fragrance.

'You eat, then pok-pok me,' she ordered, settling the question.

He planned to keep Woaw for sadic, and O for submission. He knew her too well to take pleasure in her beating him, whereas he could never really know Woaw, his dark mistress. O cooked prawns, mussels, fish, pork, rice, and stewed unnamed vegetables, which he wolfed, washing it down with beer. She remained nude, serving him, and opening beer bottles with her sex, the go-go trick. She ate, too, after serving him, but crouching on the floor by his feet, and using a newspaper as tablecloth. She joined him in a tequila while he smoked his after-dinner cigarette. The TV bleated some news about rail disasters, floods, snow, back in Europe, and he told her to turn it off.

He pointed a finger; without speaking, she went to the bedroom. He brandished his wooden snake, which slinked in the air, and she started in terror, not at the beating to come, but because she thought it was a real snake. Naked, she lay on his bed, and he whipped her buttocks twelve strokes – tail for sting, head for thud – until they were bruised purple; she moaned and shrieked, writhing prettily, her bottom a beautiful battlefield. Why twelve? Ancient system of counting in dozens. Atavistic. He thrust his fingers between her legs, found her wet, then mounted her, and fucked her quim from behind. She proudly thrust up her wealed and wiggling bottom, masturbated as he fucked, and, as he ejaculated, signalled her own climax with gasps and squeals. Afterwards, he rubbed her bottom with soothing gel scooped from spiny aloe vera fronds.

'What about your boyfriend?'

'No have boyfriend,' she said, aggrieved.

'Chuck says you do.'

'Have girlfriend ladyboy. Not same boyfriend. But I finish her. You big power, now I stay with you.'

He learned that she stole from her customers for her katoey paramour, who needed money for the snip operation in Bangkok, and also liked dildos and other toys.

189

Now her katoey had enough money for the snip (*Kerrist!*) and had vanished to the clinic. They drifted to sleep in each other's arms, until she woke him at four in the morning, saying she wanted to swim in the sea. She made him put on a thread, her black one, and shorts over it, while she wore her bra and panties with a towel at her armpits. In rubber sandals, they padded to the ocean front, silent, under a pale moon. Nobody around, no food stalls, just velvet sky, ocean, and palm trees.

The tide was in; she jettisoned her clothing and he took off his shorts. They waded in and began to splash, O swimming like a fish, naked, unlike most Thais, who could not swim at all, and went into the sea fully dressed. He felt her attack him, ripping off his thread, and toppling him. He came up, spluttering, and swam after her, far out into the sea. She wriggled and splashed and squealed with delight as they grappled, then, gasping, they splashed back to the shore, crawled under the promenade deck, and fucked amid bones and shells, with the sea frothing around them.

How many times out here did fellows say, *if only the folks back home could see me*. Afterwards, she hugged him and said thank you. She had always wanted to do it on the beach, having seen it in an American movie. Sand everywhere, bits of crustacean and seaweed all over them. Love in the bloody sewage, O delighting in slapping him, to kill the pouncing mosquitoes. Wrapped in her towel, she dug for clams, just under the surface of the sand; a couple of bicycles wobbled past, their beery riders peeking. She filled his shorts with the clams, so that he went home in just the thong. One of the ladies from up the street saw him, and waved politely.

He awoke to bright sunlight and the aroma of cooking, then lurched from the bed, making waking-up farts and groans. Nude, she had a cigarette already lit, and handed it to him, then served him a hot perfect cup of tea, following it with a clam omelette. As she passed back and forth to the kitchen, bearing toast, butter and jam, her lovely bottom waggled, a patchwork of dark weals. He ate with the sounds of cleaning in the background, and then she swept the floor again, lighting another cigarette for him with her sex, casually, as a humorous duty, not a show. *I could get used to this.* As he smoked and drank tea, she carefully wiped the wooden snake with cooking oil. And she hadn't asked for any money, an ominous sign. Neither had her mobile phone warbled, for she had turned it off. She had made no departure noises. Nor did she.

Thereafter, he slept well, despite dogs screaming in the night, the croak of lizards, the encroachment of the dark countryside, for O lay beside him. At the thump of a falling coconut, she would shiver, and say they could kill you, landing on your head; one of her sisters had been killed by a coconut in Udon Thani. Another sister, her twin, had her kidneys 'explode', her limbs swell up, and she couldn't walk, or, obviously, work. With no money for hospital, she died. There was no rage in her voice, just curiosity at Fate. Perhaps that was her black heart, a survivor's guilt.

They were, he supposed, an item, without pleas and promises, but simply because she chose not to leave. Most days, she expected a beating – 'up to you' – though he was careful not to scar her unduly. She remained nude indoors, and in the garden wore only a towel, or bra and cache-sexe. In the house, he went nude, like her, and when her girlfriends came to visit, they took him for granted. Her nudity was normal, for she was his slave. There was an exhibitionist thrill in being casually naked amid females, strutting his stuff, allowing his penis to stir. She said she needed punishment for unspecified misdeeds, but he believed she was that rarity, a genuine submissive.

When the monsoon rain bucketed, she dug a trench, let it fill with water, then splashed in it, in her bra and thong, until she was dripping with mud. He had to beat her then, for being dirty, and did it in an outhouse with a concrete floor, where the muddy water drained. After a beating, she would masturbate for him, sometimes with a peeled papaya as *godemiché*, writhing, a go-go dancer, knowing that men enjoyed watching a girl pleasure herself. He

191

would eat the papaya, lathered in her juice. She was happy to have a home, and asked for no money, although he gave it. He taught her to make chips, and she fried them in the nude, not wincing at the hot oil splattering her breasts. A treasure.

24

Tightfisted

O got rid of his maid, who departed (along with his fake Rolex). *She* was his maid. Every day, she swept and cleaned and dusted, in the nude, but draped in a towel to place beer and joss sticks for Buddha and king. She took perverse pride in sitting outside, nonchalant in cache-sexe and skimpy bra, for this was how her master liked her. Neither did she conceal the faint bruises on her buttocks, shiny with application of aloe vera. She cooked breakfast omelettes, and knelt before him as he slid the scalding food straight from the pan on to her spread buttocks, eating off her as from a plate, while she trembled, with a little gasp, whenever the prong of his fork stabbed her bottom. He said he would like to eat her. Make O soup.

'Thank you,' she said, pleased, and they laughed, for he was thinking like a Thai, that sex was funny, as when he pushed a flower in her chatte and ate it.

Content to watch TV, she did not want to go out for entertainment, and asked no questions when he did. She did venture to a tattoo shop, on her way home from the Big C supermarket, and had her outie navel pierced, with a little ring through it. She was overjoyed when it pleased him, and added nipple-piercings, for which he bought her a pair of gold rings. When she wore them, he loved to embrace her and feel the gold scratch his chest. He fashioned a leash, with cords to pass through her three rings, and would lead her around on all fours, like a pet. He liked to shave her pubes, parting her thighs to make sure every bit of down was denuded from her anus and perineum, then scrubbing her lathered anus with a toothbrush, 'for clean'. She said it tickled. She would cling to him in the middle of the night, when ghosts invaded her dreams.

He met Leda in restaurants, lest O suspect she was more than a friend. She assured him that Smackers would be there, in good time, and, when there was a suitable location, he would be drawn into the arrangements. Not yet having parted with cash, he was content to put things off. He continued his visits to whores – addictive, like tea or booze or smokes – choosing bars far away, or a deafening disco, full of freelancers jiggling under strobe lights, a sea wall of sound. There, 'Marc' was unknown, taking a teenage honey for 'short time' to an upstairs room, reeking of past sweat and sperming. The rougher the trade, the better: his unease punishing him for his addiction. Getting the thing over with seemed important, another score. Funny how, after doing it, you thought of all the other ways you could have done it.

Bars opened and closed with dizzying frequency, Croatian one day and Belgian the next, endless fools seeking the elusive pot of gold. One afternoon, he found a new go-go bar, the 'Sexy Girls', in a side street, not far from home. He watched two door girls chanting and bowing in the doorway, for Buddhist good luck, to start the working day. They were dressed in schoolgirl kit, short tartan skirts, white socks and blouses, and looked deliciously young, with the standard long dark tresses, although real schoolgirls had to have hair cut decently short. It was windy, and gusts blew their little skirts up, showing they had no panties. At each exposure of their bottoms, they charmingly struggled to subdue their skirts, while continuing to pray. He stirred at this voyeuristic treat.

He entered the dark cool bar, sat on a banquette and ordered a beer. It was the usual stage, air-con, and *Sultan of Swing* blasting away, while some bare-breasted dancers twirled, their bras dangling, in case a cop looked in. The ambiance was not city centre hustle, but indolent, suburban. Before one of the hovering tarts could annex him, he crooked a finger at the little door girl, who joined him, looking deliciously flustered. He bought her a lady drink, establishing good heart.

She bowed, thanking Marc. Her name was Nit, from Udon Thani (of course), she had been working in Pattaya only three weeks (*possibly* true), and said she was eighteen years old. She was tiny, a slip of a girl, her elfin body firm and ripe under the incongruous costume. Did she know how she aroused a European male, schooled in illicit fantasy? Her face was slender, with straight nose and wide lips, girlish but knowing, the mysterious charm of some brown, painted queen from ancient Egypt. They clinked glasses and he put his arm around her tiny waist. She did not resist. Why should she, when her colleagues laughed under boozy groping?

It was her seeming innocence that drew him to her, the vision of her schoolgirl's bare bottom, her unsuccessful combat with the exposing breeze: a vision, a moment of pure beauty. He began to caress her thigh, and she smiled shyly. He was stiff; *this* was the thrill of the chase. He slid his hand under her buttocks. She rocked back and forward, and the other door girl smiled. He stroked her breasts through her blouse, and she accepted the caress; then put his fingers under her bra and cupped her tender young cones, the nipples hard. While her buttocks trembled, sweetly crushing his palm, he touched her pubes. It was firm, a young fruit, not shaven because she had hardly anything to shave, only a silky layer of down. And her sex was genuinely slippery. He listened politely to the usual life story, working in a factory, injured, boss bad heart, no money, come Pattaya, live four to a room with other bar girls, send money home . . .

'We go upstairs?' he said, and she nodded, with a private smile.

Her friend smiled congratulations, and he bought her a drink as well. They went upstairs, same old room above the same old honky-tonk, and stripped off, Nit quite shy as she bared her top, the breasts quivering, hard and small.

Before she removed her skirt, he knelt and put his head under it, to tongue her, parting the lips, and taking her little clito in his mouth. He performed a tender cunnilingus while she moaned softly, and her sex became very wet. He breathed deeply of her fragrance, the shadow of her skirt making the act secret and daring: he was stealing a kiss, a naughty thing.

Then they were naked on the bed, her legs stretched wide, and he gazed at her sex, deciding whether it resembled more a mussel, an oyster, an orchid. He sucked the lips, and her thighs clasped his head. Turning her over, he kissed her buttocks, but she was timid, for she had a jagged pink scar there, and said that it was her work injury, a piece of steel had cut her so that she wasn't beautiful enough to be a dancer. He said it was beautiful, all of her was, and licked the scar. She said her quim was *mai hom*, not fragrant, as he smelled her deeply, lifting her thighs to expose her anus. He insisted she smelled beautiful, and put his tongue into her anal crevice, then gave her long cunnilingus, until she shuddered in climax, her sex soaking. He produced a strawberry-flavour from his collection, but she made a hash of rolling it on, so, as she giggled, he showed her how.

He made her put her skirt back on, then lifted it and penetrated her, marvelling at the virginal tightness of her pouch. He wondered what she had been like as a little girl, what she would be like in twenty years, wanting to chart every stage of her sweet life. But it was hopeless, you could never know them. Rutting came first. After only a few strokes, her slim body writhing under him in her schoolgirl skirtlet, he ejaculated into the rubber. That was that, then. Dirty old man fantasy realised. He gave her an extra-generous tip and she bowed, gratefully astonished. Now he must remember that in the Sexy Girls, Marc was good heart. Perhaps he would one day thrash or encule her. *I think she fancies me, I'm in with a chance, I'm working on her*, the eternal delusion. He emerged into bright sunlight; ho hum, just another afternoon. Yet the memory of her skirt fluttering in the wind, and the peek at her bare bottom, a glimpse of half-remembered, perhaps never experienced innocence, would stay with him always.

His love-making with O was in stark contrast, with frequent beating, and anal penetration. When tonguing her clito, he stabbed his fingers into her rectum until he stretched her tiny channel with all five balled into a fist. Fisting was a gay thing, but submissive girls liked it too. It could not fail to hurt, and the humiliating pain made her passionate, as he punished her for his own straying. Their coupling a savage fight. He insisted on taking her in the vulva during her monthlies ('Aunt Rose has arrived,' as Sylvie said), despite her embarrassment, for she was a heavy bleeder; this mortification added to her submissive pleasure. He loved the squelching of his penis in her gushing red chatte, as though her sex had turned into some wild wounded beast, her true self. In this ultimate intimacy, he thought he truly loved her.

He continued to chat with Chuck, for now the news meant something, though it was always the same. A teen singing idol got fifty years in jail for pushing ya-ba and ketamine. A prostitute was found cut up, her parts stashed in plastic bin bags, dumped separately in Bangkok, in punishment for a thirty-dollar gambling debt. In Pattaya, a man sitting in a bar, in broad daylight, had his head lopped off by a machete, his assailant placing it in the carrier basket of his moped before escaping. The venerable abbot of a monastery was on the run, charged with buggering twelve-year-old novices. A police general, caught with underage girls and a bag of heroin in his Benz, was promoted to an 'inactive post'. A dozen people witnessed the son of a cabinet minister shoot a man dead in a nightclub for stepping on his designer shoes, but no charges were brought, for lack of evidence. 'Sometimes I wonder if this place really exists, if I exist, if anything exists,' a drunk in a bar slurred (Swedish, suicidal).

The epicene On had disappeared from the Lucky Strike and, seeing Woaw alone, at work in turquoise, giving him a complicit smile, or icy pout, made him stir, and proposition her again. The meeting was as before, this time with a room secured in advance. She whipped him, wearing only her turquoise skimpies and nylons, and chiding him for not coming through with a firm job offer, as she had decided she would like to try. She locked his new wristwatch around his balls, and called him her tick-tock man. She taunted him that she had been seeing another man, a nice American, stripping naked for him, and letting him fuck her after his whipping. Up to you, he groaned, as she lashed his bare. He abased himself before his vengeful goddess.

After his whipping, he spent a long time sucking her stockinged toes, but she did not take the hose off as she lowered her panties. She climbed on to him and sat with her bare bottom on his face, crushing him, her croup gloriously heavy, then leaned forward to remove his watch. She thrust two fingers into his anus as she expertly fellated him, three fingers, finally her whole fist. So young, her expertise horrified and thrilled him. He spread his thighs, in submissive missionary position, his mouth busy at her sex, as her anus and thighs filled him with intoxicating acrid scent. *Fuck me*, he moaned, *yes, fuck me.* Her dainty fist stabbed his rectum, the pain awful, as she sucked him to orgasm, and swallowed his sperm. *Yes, yes*, he whimpered. *Ahh . . .*

She pushed his watch into her pouch, and wriggled, laughing, then removed it and handed it back. It glistened with her moisture, and he sucked it before putting it on. She would not stay the night but scooped her banknote, all businesslike. She said the American wanted to marry her, take her back to America, but her grandfather would be angry if she left her employment. But she was free, and would please herself. They agreed on another rendezvous, in a week's time, and that night he whipped O with the wooden snake to punish her for his sin. His arse still smarted the next day, at another meeting with Leda, about the bar; he met the lawyer, the banker, the real estate man.

On his subsequent date with Woaw, she brought a friend, a slinky, sultry girl, tall, with big brown eyes, long legs and long glossy hair. She said that Ouan would like to watch, and he didn't mind, surely, for she might be suitable to work at Smackers. Other farangs liked to be watched, showing off as she whipped them, even her mysterious American. Ouan meant fat, but she was delightfully slim, and simpered in a cooing contralto that it was a Thai joke. She smoked and watched as he stripped for his beating, taking off Leda's frilly white thong (giggles), and this time Woaw, in turquoise bra and panties, took him face down on the bed. She had a rubber quirt of nine thongs that she had made specially (he thanked her, his offer to pay being accepted, the stated cost no doubt including a generous mark-up), and lashed him hard till the pain made him squeal, then made him turn over and whipped him on the nipples and belly, the thongs dancing perilously close to his stiff penis. Ouan thought it satisfying.

Woaw said he was to make love to Ouan while she watched, and he agreed. How could he not? They thought this enormously funny, but he was entranced as the girl stripped naked: a slim muscled body, firm breasts, surprisingly bulbous on her svelte form – he suspected silicone – flat belly, and boyish hips, with a pubic forest of sleek black hairs. As a livener, Woaw sat on his mouth, knowing he liked it, and he tongued her moist panties, gorgeous with her rank aroma, while Ouan swooped to perform an expert fellation. Woaw's buttocks, crushing his face, writhed gently as she rubbed her cache-sexe. Soon, Ouan ceased the caress, and crouched on the bed with her buttocks up. Woaw released him and ordered him to take her friend in the anus, since she liked that best, and she knew he did too.

He penetrated the clinging channel, enculing her slowly at first, then faster and harder as she responded to his thrusts, her supple back writhing and her mane swaying on her shoulders. The squeezing of her rectum was as expert as her tonguing, and soon he climaxed, vaguely aware that Woaw brought herself off too, for her cache-sexe was wet. In his spasm, he clutched Ouan's pubic fleece, probing for the crevice and not finding it. After ejaculating, he kissed the bony skin of her spine, still trying to get his fingers into her sex.

'Wow! That was good,' he panted.

There was a faint swelling of what should be a vulva, but the pouch wasn't there. What the hell?

He withdrew, to see both girls laughing, and sank back on the bed.

'You're a katoey,' he gasped. 'Oh, God.'

Ouan shook her head earnestly.

'Real girl,' she said indignantly. 'I have money for snip, but not for pussy.'

'You not recognise On, from the Lucky Strike?' Woaw said, with mischievous glee. 'Before the snip, she was boyfriend of lady O.'

He looked at the ladyboy he had just fucked. She was beautiful, her previous maleness certainly false, her body now in full flowering as a girl. In the soft light, she looked the most seductive of whores, more girl than a real girl.

'You not like me?' said Ouan/On, in a hurt tone.

'Sure, I like you,' he said. 'Here, you can have these panties as a gift.'

She held them up, delighted.

'Expensive! Thank you,' she purred.

'Come and work for me and you'll save enough for another operation.'

Woaw said a complete sex change cost two thousand dollars, more than a year's wages. He gave them their tips, and they clapped their hands, hugging him, with cries of 'good heart'. Watching Ouan dress, after sliding Leda's panties over her mysterious crotch, he marvelled at the delicacy of her feminine gestures; truly, she was a girl. *What am I, though?*

200

25

Smackers

In the end, impatient with a fruitless search for alternatives, they bought the Schoolgirls bar from Lancelot and Goong and spent time and money on a makeover, toning down the neon, shifting the central stage to one side to make it cosier, less like a clip joint, and splitting the upstairs rooms into tiny cubicles, some as living quarters, for girls who had no other lodging. If anyone asked, they were massage facilities. What sort of massage was up to the client and his masseuse. There were no seats directly under the stage, so as to deter arseholes who wanted to get up and dance or maul the girls. Lancelot wanted to spend more time at his educational business, opening a new school, that's where there was real money, but he and Goong seemed pleased their bar was in safe hands.

'British,' said Lancelot. 'Most important. Show them how things are done.'

Goong offered to work as extra mama-san without pay, at least just for tips, and Leda accepted. Pink was to be the chief mama-san, with the proviso that she could entertain clients. The permits and lease were in order, payroll and taxes taken care of by the accountant, and the cops paid off, with Lancelot's contacts helpful there, notably the suave police colonel Plodprasop, deputy chief of the Pattaya constabulary, who warmly shook Mitch's hand and made a *wai*, wishing him very good luck for his new bar, so refreshingly high class and different.

Lancelot admitted he made a profit on the key money, but a small one, for a quick sale, not what he would have charged some greenhorn. He was helpful, too, in recruiting, with Plodprasop's help, a trio of heavy off-duty cops as bouncers. Mitch wanted a party, with balloons and publicity and hoopla, but Leda said that was not the way here. You got the thing built, and as soon as the dust had cleared, you were opened for business. Word got around. You didn't want too much publicity; a fetish gave the excluded faction of cops yet another excuse for a shakedown. Jeffrey was at the opening, with Lancelot and Goong, but Chuck demurred.

'Spanking, that's a British thing. But there are too many freaks in this town already. Used to be a nice honky-tonk place. Pasties and sequins and tassels. Healthy fun.'

How old-fashioned the Americans were! Mitch explained that it wasn't perversion, saying pointedly that he would buy a couple of dildos (Chuck's hypocrisy!) and Chuck wished him good luck, but with a certain weariness.

He had a posse of girls. Woaw was there, with Ouan, O and Lemon, along with a couple of O's submissive friends, like gorgeous little Lin, and those of the Schoolgirls crew who understood real corporal punishment. He dreamed Nampoong would arrive, as if by magic, seeking a job. In the back room there was a selection of whips and canes in a glass showcase, not on full view, but shown to the customer after he had bar-fined a girl. Leda and Mitch had had them made, in wood, leather, rubber, and he had tested several on O's bottom. Dildos were kept under extra-special security. O was excited, but he said she was not to take part in the action, though she could work for tips as a dancer. She was not to service customers, for she was his property. She promised that she and her katoey On, or Ouan, were now best friends again, meaning that no one owed anybody money.

Whips and canes decorated the walls, with framed drawings from old English books and magazines, cribbed from flagellant websites, showing school discipline: a 'beak' with mortarboard and gown, or a starched matron, flogging a schoolboy on the bare. Sometimes the victim was 'horsed', carried on piggy-back by a larger boy with his trousers comically dangling in mid-air: part of becoming a gentleman, and fun for the onlookers. There were pictures of schoolgirls bending over, bloomers down, for a bare-bottom tanning, and Parisian ones, with semi-draped midinettes at caning games, which he liked the best, though he displayed them more discreetly; caning boys was harmless fun, but girls meant immodesty in puritanical Thailand.

Woaw was helpful in finding girls with her own secret tastes via the Thai grapevine, while Leda recruited some of her lesbian amours; interviewing was just as awkward and polite as interviewing salesgirls for Strips. Smackers would be a switch club, for he had both girls who would cane, and subs who would take cane (at a huge tariff). There was a fixed price list, and no bargaining, the girl to split the fee with the bar, but keep any extra tips. Once in the massage cubicle, full service must be rendered for an hour, the same tariff for light or heavy punishment. That included *chak wao*, but not penetration; a girl who fucked must negotiate her own tip. The dances were adapted from Schoolgirls, and while they kept some fetish routines, like hot wax and razor blades, the tricks with eggs and bananas and darts were dropped.

The rule was, a completely shaven pubes, except for very hairy girls – unlike most Thais, graced with a mere sliver – who were forbidden to trim at all, as men tended to like either jungle or desert. Woaw classified herself and Ouan as hostesses, and they would not dance, although paid the same as dancers. Neither must they obey the 'ten bar fines' rule, but could pick and choose their clients. That way, Woaw imagined she appeased her grandfather. Most whores in Pattaya told their families they worked as hotel receptionists; as long as the money came in, no questions were asked.

Goong and Ouan, as katoeys, at once became allies, and Leda said it was a good idea to have a discreet katoey presence, for matelots and oil-riggers and showerbath towel-flickers (what Mitch called rugger buggers) really went for them. Stuff they wanted at home, but didn't dare.

It was important to keep a mix, slightly genteel, otherwise the place would be taken over either by screaming fairies or tattooed chavs. A bar fine was exacted if a punter took a girl home. It was the way things were done. He said that made him a pimp.

'What did you think you were?' Leda replied.

She was relying on his experience, for she knew whoring, but not the uncharted waters of BDSM. More and more, she deferred to him in decision-making, saying she thought Danny would be pleased, but must not learn they had already fucked. He retorted that an English gentleman never told tales and, anyway, they hadn't fucked. They had *acted*.

'So when is a duck not a duck?'

There was no happy hour for the beer-swillers, and no TV blaring football. Jeffrey said they should have a TV, show movies, you know what I mean. He added a DVD player to his new computer (nifty for stock control), with a wide-screen TV at the back of the bar so that a punter's line of sight crossed the girls (the stock), and tested the video of himself, Cheetah and Leda. It was superb; he told Jeffrey he was the new Fellini.

'Yeah, right,' said Jeffrey. 'More like a fucking Carry On film. Remember those silly sods? They're all dead now, of course.'

On opening night, the room was festooned with balloons for good luck, and the girls made their obeisances before the Buddha, tucked away with his candles, beer and biscuits, amid the fetish toys. Woaw and O had their fortunes told by *moh-doos*, and were assured of prosperity. This helped him in the perplexing skein of relationships and jealousies in Pattaya, where everyone seemed to know everyone else. Woaw and O knew about each other, for they were friends, but each pretended to ignore his adventures. There was always a face-saver: O thought he was whipped by Woaw, but did not fuck, and Woaw thought he fucked O, but did not whip. No one believed that he and Leda were just good friends. Neither, really, did he, amazed she could treat the invasion of her person as casually as a male sticking his penis into a short-time girl, or a mango.

The girls touting outside were to sit demurely. If they smoked, though, they were to let their cigarettes droop sluttishly over their schoolgirls' uniforms. They were not to squawk 'welcome', but nod, a little primly: not whores eager for short times, but masseuses, to teach naughty boys a lesson. The first punters included the predictable beery oafs, but were mostly those who had known Schoolgirls, and were delighted to find it changed for the better. Lancelot and Jeffrey stood amiably, swigging jack-coke, while Goong flirted and smiled; Woaw sat serene, a goddess, stroking an imported English riding crop, and watching O, Pink, Lemon and the others mime flogging on stage.

The first evening, there were plenty of enquiries about services on offer, but no takers; the second night, a few furtive takers, then, on the third, many. They sold a lot of drink, too. Thereafter, the place was full, as word got round that Smackers played fair, gave good value, you got what you paid for. The girls were not to hustle for lady drinks, and if they got one, it was a proper drink, not coloured water. They showed spanking videos from England and Denmark on the TV screen, but not yet the one with Mitch and Leda. He was nervous.

They learned as they went along. Mitch and Leda masqueraded as customers (sometimes he was Marc), and in response to any query, said they were friends of the owner, keeping an eye on things. They opened in mid-afternoon, which proved a brisk time for those who wanted a daytime spanking as a livener for their more conventional evening adventures. The dancers, at first, appeared not in the full nude, but wore strings, removing them for the whipping mimes, the high point of the act.

On the second day, he staged a little scene where Jeffrey bought a girl's cache-sexe from her on the spot. That started the hoped-for trend; rule was, if a punter wanted to buy her string (wildly expensive), the girl stripped it off at once, wiped it extravagantly on her sex, kissed it, and

205

draped it over his face, *after* he had produced the requisite banknotes. The bar got half the price he paid, and she got a new garment out of Mitch's ample stock. When a girl joined a punter to sit on his lap, there was to be no surreptitious wanking as in other bars, sometimes to public climax. Her role was that of sadomasochistic masseuse, and the squelchy part began only in privacy.

Leda was often, but not always there, discreetly dressed, and nursing a tequila and beer chaser. Soon, when O was not present, she suggested that they stage another little scene: Mitch should get Woaw to spank him. The cubicles were built so that the sound carried, thus satisfying the exhibitionist nature of masochists. Woaw was game; he put on a loud laddish act for the customers, phwoarr, let's give it a go, bet she can't hurt me, and followed her wiggling bottom upstairs.

'I really want to beat you,' Woaw said, amused at the escapade. 'I like beating you, and it must sound real.'

She used a slipper, which made a good resounding crack on his bare, and Leda turned off the cacophonous music system for a minute so that her whacks and his whimpers echoed through the bar. There was no sex between them although, after a hard fifty, his buttocks were crimson; Woaw put her hand out and demanded her tip.

'Why, you cheeky slag,' he said, but agreed to pay her the going rate; she curtsied, then stuck out her tongue.

He returned to the bar, rubbing his arse and grimacing horribly, to be welcomed by applause. The cheerful Scene spirit.

'What a sadistic bitch!' he exclaimed. 'The rotten cow! I'm not doing that again!'

At once, Woaw had the first of four customers that night, and every other girl had at least two. The bar was full after dark, with a youngish crowd, the middle-aged preferring daylight hours. There was no trouble, as he had expected, smackers being an amiable lot, and the bouncers sipped their beer, smiling vacantly. Since the crowds were so great, he wanted to hire extra bouncers, and suggested female cops complete with sticks and cuffs. It was arranged through Colonel Plodprasop. Three nyloned cuties in bottom-hugging uniform from the local tourist police proved an instant attraction, even without their guns. They were useful, too, in stopping tiffs and cat spats amongst the dancers, which led to ripped bras and thongs, without, thankfully, progressing to beer bottles.

Leda suggested *refusing entrance* to people, as in the snobbiest European clubs. A male and a female bouncer framed the doorway, checking dress and intoxication, and waving a stern finger at undesirables: the beginning of the masochistic experience. Soon, the queues stretched across the street. Many couples came, and often it was the girl who went upstairs for a spanking from one of Leda's *tom dee* recruits. Ouan was popular with men, and Goong turned a few tricks as well, while Lancelot nodded acceptance through the bubbles of his jack-coke.

'She sucks them off,' he said philosophically. 'Or they do her up the arse. Keeps her happy. Doesn't matter who she goes to bed with, as long as it's me she wakes up with.'

Mitch learned that girls tended not to stay in one bar for long, however well treated; there was a constant flux, and he constantly received new referrals from the grapevine. At first, he tried to eliminate girls with tattoos, but half of them had them, buttocks, breast and hillock being the favourite locations, often with piercings of nipples or clito. Those girls did brisk business. His notion of meetings for pep talks soon foundered. Lancelot said it was bullshit, you were lucky they turned up for work at all. Information was conveyed, as always, by hints and nods and whispers. That was how he kept track of the girls caned by the customers, about a fifth of all bar fines. The caned girls were happy, since they got huge tips, and liked to exhibit their scars on stage, like battle honours. *As long as they feel approved, safe, obeying the rules . . . nice girls.* A hierarchy soon grew, of those who took and those who were afraid to.

He increased the number of katoeys, and had a special ladyboy glamour stage show; they were happy to provide their own frilly flouncy costumes. Katoeys had to be the

207

svelte feminine ones, like Ouan, not the honking bull dykes who infested the sea road. Some were snipped, some not, the unsnipped (but silicone-breasted) proving most popular with hairy-chested customers. They must speak English, for often a couple just wanted to chat, but the katoeys were ready for caning, fellatio, or anal sex (preferred), and often returned from a massage staggering theatrically and rubbing their bottoms, to peals of laughter. Leda said that since the katoeys were so popular, the cream on the whore pudding, Mitch should dress in her clothes. Well, he already had her knickers.

'Oh yeah, ha ha.'

'I'm serious. It would be such fun. I might even like you lots.'

One evening, a ravishing girl cop was pestered by a German, who wanted a thrashing with her nightstick. She looked flustered, trying to be polite, with her eye anxiously questioning Mitch. Discreetly, he told Leda to tell Goong to tell Pink to tell the girl it was okay, and they wouldn't grass to her boss. The girl cop disappeared happily up the stairs in a slither of slinky nylons. Lancelot said they should call the place 'Cop Girls', and wished he had thought of that. Or 'Bouncers' – hey, that could be Mitch's next one, a titty bar for breast-mad Americans. But he didn't regret selling out, as it was too arduous hanging round the bar every night, being the boss. Now he just hung around the bar every night. What else was there, in a country full of fucking savages? He slugged at his jack-coke. It was a long time since he had been able to get it up for normal doings, he said. That's why Goong was so good. Ladymen understood fellatio. So what if she fucked around. Who didn't?

26

Ladyman

The months slid past, drenched in heat. There was rain, or not rain; many tourists, or few; the squawk of girls, the sultry humid air, the smiles, the ocean. The days blending into one another like a rainbow, the colours all the same. Like his trips to the border for a passport stamp, Mitch's life with O became routine, the whip helping to keep their physical passion alive, and his visits upstairs with Woaw, in O's absence, serving to thrill and chasten him with her inventive beatings. Sometimes, for a lavish tip (*the greedy cow!*), she would queen him, sit on his face with or without panties, and let him lick her chatte; if she felt generous, she fellated him, and swallowed his sperm.

She would only let him fuck her when she boasted she had already serviced one or two others, making him burn with jealousy, as was no doubt intended, and usually chatting to Lin or Ouan, or both, while he pumped (*the slag!*), but lending power to his penis, for he wanted to show her who was best, and there was an exhibitionist thrill in having other girls watch. He still marvelled at the nonchalance of Thai venery, Woaw's nearly-nude companions casually eating, or doing their nails, while conversing, no doubt about him, with the humped Woaw. *They are all fockin whores.* Seeing him eye Lin's succulent young body, Woaw hissed that she would bite his balls off (explicit gestures), if she caught him fooling with the tiny girl. O was putting on weight, and she complained about being *ouan*, but he said that, curiously, chubbiness was a normal reaction in bodies regularly whipped. He worried he was getting chubby himself.

Once, Leda gave him a beating, for she was in a good mood; her husband Danny had arrived, visited the bar, and was pleased, liking Mitch, and thinking it all great sport, a typical pom perversion. He slavered, watching his wife embrace Ouan, or a girlfriend, and would select a girl for a threesome at their lodging. Danny was younger than he had expected, early forties at most, muscled and fit. He grinned a lot, didn't say much, groped the girls, friendly fashion. Mitch greeted him with the disdainful sympathy of a man who has cuckolded the other.

Leda had wanted to whip him onstage, but he demurred. That was a bit too far, especially as Danny loved the spectacle of an olaf squirming in joyful shame, a spectacle they now staged just before the grand finale most nights. He accused her of wanting to humiliate him, and she extended his dozen (mysteriously, with Woaw's rubber flail) by a further four strokes. Suddenly, panting, she ordered him to fuck her, and, astonished, he obeyed, erect at the sheer audacity of the thing, like doing it on Brighton beach or somewhere. The little cubicle rocked to the sound of their coupling, and he came very quickly, then asked what *that* was all about.

She shrugged, hopelessly; she had not orgasmed. 'I don't know,' she said. 'I just wanted it. From you, or anybody. To feel free. Danny's at the dangerous age, a man in his forties thinks he's still young, can still do press-ups, and can start over, get rid of wife, home, the lot, and set up with a Thai whore. He's done it already, for me, and I'm afraid he'll do it again.'

Smackers was busy when other bars in the street were not, and, as the winter season began, it became packed. He recognised customers' needs, over and above the prescribed whopping and *chak wao*, so the alcove contained a dispensing machine for fruit-flavoured condoms at three times the store price, strawberry being the most popular. The bouncers were still turning people away at the door, and the girl cops routinely serviced customers upstairs.

Beating by a uniformed policewoman! That was one big draw, another being the katoeys, for few bars featured ladyboys as part of an eclectic mix: it was generally either all or nothing. The ladyboys seemed almost in a trance, enchanted with their own femininity, while whirling and glittering in their frocks, and loved to show off their long legs, or spangled panties, in glistering nylon.

Happily, this period was one of Thailand's frequent lapses from puritanism, when the cops would cease harassing, and settle back to enjoy their bribes, and Smackers was untrammelled in lubricious display, although the rules were still strict: no public display, except onstage, where lesbian and katoey acts were popular, especially buggery with a strap-on dildo. Woaw, doyenne of the whippers, had suggested early on that since masochistic farangs liked their sufferings overheard, some would like it even more, and pay accordingly, if they were whipped onstage, especially if they could go home with a video of their performance.

For this information, she expected (and got) a tip. She needed money for her grandfather, who was not well. Jeffrey thought it a diamond idea. Despite murmurs from the katoeys, who feared being upstaged, every other night a selected customer would strip off in the back room. Wearing a girl's thong, he would waddle on all fours behind a whip-cracking girl in bra and panties, who flogged his bare arse on stage. Usually, she was joined by one or two other girls who shared the work while Jeffrey's vidcam purred. The whooping reverently hushed, as the strokes landed; *that could be me*.

One evening, Mitch stood before a mirror in the back room, accompanied by O and Leda.

'I'm not sure. I feel awfully nervous,' he said.

'You look divine,' Leda said. 'No one will guess.'

He looked in the mirror at his own body, balls hidden by Leda's pink cache-sexe, and his shoulders hidden by a long wig of shiny black Asian hair. Some peasant girl had fed her family with those shorn tresses. She ordered him to sit and straighten his legs while she rolled her stockings up

to his thigh, shimmering ten denier pink nylon. They wer
a tight fit, encasing him snugly. Leda snapped on crimso
garter straps while O, looking on with approval, fastene
a frilly crimson suspender belt around his waist. She wor
a pink thong, like his, preparing to dance, with the mark
of the previous night's strapping emblazoned on he
bottom, which, she fretted – like all girls – was too big. H
had beaten her the night before, after she had cried *I lov
you too much*, and he snarled she must not say that. Mayb
this was revenge, or thanks.

'Is all this necessary?' he asked. 'I mean, no one's goin
to see.'

Leda said it added to the thrill of secrecy. Why else di
girls wear sexy underthings to the office? And whom wa
he trying to kid, if not himself, with his collection of girl'
thongs? They showed off his buns to advantage. He ros
and looked in the mirror again, feeling a surge of strang
excitement. O applied eye shadow and lipstick – it taste
horrible – and then fastened a padded bra around hi
chest. She dabbed perfume behind his ears and between hi
breasts.

'Oh, really,' he sighed.

Leda helped him into a pleated grey-and-pink tarta
skirt which clung to him, the hem just above his knee
then into a loose white blouse, camouflaging his breast
Only the shoes were bought specially, high heels, pink, i
the largest possible size, and still pinching. He sat, practis
ing crossing his legs with a deliciously tingly slither o
nylon, and sluttishly pulling up his skirt, in a vamp'
come-on.

'You have nice legs. Sexy, like your bottom,' Led
murmured.

He thrust his false bosom forward, with a coquettis
pout of his lips, camping it up. But the girls were serious
and said he looked lovely. He mustn't joke, a katoey wa
a precious animal. Leda said they were made for eac
other. He was ready to appear as her friend *Mee Cham*
which, as far as he could tell, meant 'sneezing wife' o
'worm bowl'. He stood at the mirror, patting his wig

posing and preening, twirling so that his skirt flew up, and smoothing down his crotch, worried that his bulge was apparent.

'Come on,' Leda said, pulling him.

They entered the crowded bar and sat in the back alcove where girls were chewing on fried locusts and combing their hair. No one appeared to pay him much attention, although he got a few bleary curious looks. Goong was aware of his imposture, but he wasn't sure if Lancelot or Jeffrey knew. Leda wasn't sure either.

'How can you not be sure?'

'Look, it's just fun. There are other things to bother with.'

The TV screen was showing the video of him, Cheetah and Leda in Kuala Lumpur. Months had passed since then, and since the opening of Smackers; the video seemed an archive from eons ago: the man in a stage play, fucking Cheetah, gorgeous and writhing, Leda overpowering him, and there was the strange male, clenching under a woman's lash. It wasn't him, surely, for he was a girl just now, serene and swaddled in the fortress of girl-clothes, the straps and elastic and nylon that make a girl's seductive armour. In the raucous bar, he felt secure in female clothing, both provocation and shield. Now the man in the video was fucking Leda; beside him, Leda breathed rapidly, clutching his hand.

'Hasn't he a big cock?' she said impishly. 'How can the girl take it without screaming?'

'*Bagwan*,' he replied.

'Go on, walk around,' she said, signalling for another tequila. 'Strut your stuff, girl.'

He waited until O danced, then gingerly moved into the throng. His cover was, he was Leda's Australian friend. There were Jeffrey, Lancelot, Danny, Goong; only Goong gave him a wink, the others casting a brief glance, like the other males, intent on O's buttocks wriggling onstage. He grew bolder in the shadowy light, mingling with the crowd, and oddly pleased at the looks of appreciation, and the few pats to his arse, at which he wiggled, with a little simper –

acting was such fun. He smoothed his skirt, looked in the glass, and fussed with his hair, like girls who, though half-naked, instinctively tugged their hems, to prevent an extra millimetre of skin from showing.

The evening passed without incident. After a super grand finale, with a customer taking ten cuts from Woaw's cane, then a katoey sucking another volunteer to noisy orgasm, he slipped gratefully back into male attire. Again, the girls fussed over him; taking off girl's clothes seemed almost as complicated as getting into them. Everything was so fiddly, the hooks on bra and garter belt, zippers that got stuck, buttons in stupid places, wobbly heels, the weird garter clips that kept slipping. Clothing designed by men to oppress women so that, in willing bondage, they had no time to think of anything else. Yet they connived in their own submission, teetering on high heels, and encased in delicious carapaces of nylon, silk or satin. Even the corsets sold at Strips to slender girls, who didn't need them, were an exquisite form of self-mutilation.

He repeated the experiment the next day, in a vivid outfit of green and yellow; a few evenings later, he wore blue, and then black, then mauve. He had his hair cropped very short, to accommodate a wig. He liked sitting with the other girls, finding he could share their wistful, bitchy, funny talk in a way impossible as a male. Incredibly, they accepted that he was the boss's cross-dressing 'sister', or perhaps they were just being polite – up to you. The katoeys treated him with sly hilarity, knowing he was the boss, but amused he was one of them. Their waspish tongues and high camp were wearisome, though; he preferred real girls. Leda began to hint that she should buy his own bloody dresses. One night she fucked him again, in a cubicle, with the groans of spanked customers all around. She did not let him disrobe, but roughly pushed up his mauve silk dress and, bouncing on his erection, forced him to service her while she rubbed her clito. It was no *bonk de politesse*, she was asserting ownership rights. This time she did orgasm.

'Another sudden urge?' he said.

'Don't think I'm going to make a habit of it,' she snapped. 'I still prefer girls. Danny watches me making love with one and he jerks off. He's usually too pissed to get it up the usual way.'

It was not clear from her moue whether this amused or disgusted her. He was growing annoyed at Danny and his blatant flirting with Goong: lots of pawing and bum-patting. Yet his pleasure at parading in girl's attire outweighed any irritation, and it excited him that Lancelot and Jeffrey seemed unaware of the deception. He over-heard them mention him as 'that bird of Leda's, pretty classy for a flaming dyke.' Clothes made the man, all right, add a bit of slap, a wig, nylon stockings, and you were a whole new self.

He did not object when the drunken Danny sat beside him on a banquette and offered him a drink. Why not? He had a tequila, not his first, and they clinked glasses. God, everyone was drunk here. Drivers were drunk, barflies were drunk, a guy marrying some venal honeypot half his age was drunk. How could you put up with the place unless soaked in alcohol? He raised his voice to a fluting contralto, imitating an Australian accent, but said as little as possible, relying on simpers and smirks. That's what girls always did.

'I know you get it on with Leda,' Danny slurred, nodding his head upstairs. 'I'd like to watch, sweetheart.'

He wouldn't really. Shit, perhaps he would.

Danny's hand was on his stockinged knee, and, curious, he did not resist, although he worried about getting a ladder in his nylons. So this was what it was like being a girl, fussing about your clothes, annoyed at getting mauled all the time, but offended if you weren't. He jumped as Danny's paw slid all the way up his skirt and suddenly groped his penis and balls. His stomach turned in revulsion. He was seething, but aware of Leda's amused eye on him.

'No, no . . . please . . .'

He clawed the hand out of his skirt.

'Haven't had the snip, eh? That's quite a package you've got. I don't mind. Let's go upstairs. Do you take it up the arse?'

215

'I only give whoppings.'

Danny lowered his voice to a whisper.

'I bet you *give* it up the arse.'

'Just whopping.'

He shrugged, then winked, showing disbelief.

'Of course, darling. Okay by me.'

He was being watched by curious girls. Apart from Ouan and Woaw, they had to oblige a customer who wanted thrashing. He rose.

'All right. Just whopping.'

'Sure, sure.'

Stomach turning, he pointed Danny upstairs with the stoutest cane from the rack. What the hell am I doing? Then he laughed, it was so perfect. The dolt thinks I'm a real katoey, he doesn't know I'm just pretending. *Can't you join in a joke, you beery fucking cunt? You'll regret this.* He pretended to lock the cubicle door, but left it on the latch.

'I've never done this before. But the missus likes it, says it puts lead in your pencil. I reckon if you get me going, we can make a threesome. The missus likes you a lot, Mee Cham. What do you say?'

He flexed his cane.

'I shall make you suffer for that. Get your pants off and lie on the bed, face down, you animal.'

'A real tigress, eh? That's the spirit.'

When Danny's arse was bare, he really lashed into him. No cooing and stroking and tickling, or whatever it was the girls did to satisfy the customer. Just whop, whop, whop, the cane leaving harsh stripes on the man's buttocks, which jerked and squirmed frantically.

'Oof!' Danny gasped. 'You really lay it on, don't you?'

'Shut up.'

Vip! Vip!

'Ahh! Christ! That hurts!'

He gave him a dozen stingers, and his arm was sore. Afraid the welts would turn to blood, he put the cane down, and stood beside the door, but flight wasn't necessary; Danny turned over, revealing his erection, which he began to rub. He delved under Mitch's dress and

216

grabbed his bare bottom, stroking it as he masturbated. Mitch shut his eyes, feeling the massage of his buttocks; the tickling sensation, in itself, wasn't unpleasant, if you could separate it from its source, imagining the arse floating in space. But for real pleasure, as with spanking, you had to know a girl was in charge, otherwise it was sterile, like a buzz from an electric toothbrush. Danny groaned and ejaculated, thankfully not over Mitch. *God, men are disgusting.* He tugged a banknote from his pocket and shoved it down Mitch's cleavage.

'Next time, you, me and Leda, eh? It'll be even better when you've had the snip.'

He managed to flee, with some female excuse, for a girl always had to powder her nose, or something, part of the defensive armoury. Back in the bar, he tried to appear unruffled, and in fact did not feel the shame or loathing he had feared. That is what service girls did several times a day, spanking a customer, helping him spurt his load, like milking a cow, or wiping a baby's bottom, just another grubby meaningless chore. Danny reappeared, and button-holed Leda.

'That was fuckin' A, Leda,' he bellowed. 'She gave me what for. That's a girl and a half!'

Leda smirked at Mitch.

'Isn't she?' she drawled.

217

27

Bad Luck

High season over, the rainy months came. He was drinking more, smoking too much. Must cut down. Since he had begun to masquerade as a katoey, straight coupling excited him less. Goong flirted with him, and, friendly fashion, sort of keeping up the troops' morale, he enculed her twice, *like fucking a mango*; she said cock made her fake pussy too sore, and he wondered if there were ladyboys with fake arseholes as well. He enjoyed chewing her breasts, and spanking her trim tight bottom, but would certainly not go down on her. She didn't mind, for she masturbated in some obscure way while he was buggering her. Lancelot didn't know, or, if he did, didn't care.

He paid one further visit to Nit, which was less than successful for she wouldn't spank, or be spanked, and he left, having tongued her to climax, but, losing appetite, without his own consummation. Someone else could mess up her innocence, as would surely happen, and in a year or two she would be a raddled squawker. The vision of her skirt, fluttering in the breeze, was enough to haunt his dreams, but you could never go back. Just as with Sylvie, of whom he sometimes dreamt, an avenger, at the prow of a ship, crushing him as he swam in grey Channel waters. Once, she cut off his penis with a sword, and once, he was being guillotined, only the wrong way round, with his erect penis under the blade, and Sylvie bewigged and moustachioed, in a frock coat, as *Monsieur de Paris*, the executioner. Strangely, the 'snip' did not hurt, but each time he woke up sweating and babbling, knocking away O's worried caress. She said a bad dream meant bad luck, and he did not say that all his dreams were bad.

His nocturnal prowlings diminished; with O, his erotic torments became crueller and more inventive, trying to goad her into begging for release: scalded with hot wax, bound with tight cords, immersed in mud, forced to wear painful anus plugs and dildos, for harsh caning, and, finally, penetration. But she never pleaded for mercy, taking whatever punishment he inflicted with trembling lip and tear-stained cheeks in silence, and in her eyes a misty gleam of satisfaction. He could not break her, however cruel his beatings.

'You want kill me, up to you,' she whispered.

Thais spoke casually of death, for they always came back, reincarnate, or at least as a ghost. There was no heaven or hell. It was no game, but real punishment and, after a session, she would lick his feet, thanking him. Except that the sessions never really stopped: everything she did, every household task she performed, was in submission. She had dreams of his abandoning her, *have new lady*, which increased her submissiveness. It didn't matter if he took a girl for a short time, it was the disappearance of the meal ticket which terrified.

He took her on a week's holiday to Ko Lanta, the coming resort island in the south, of which he had vaguely heard. It was not wholly successful; too much cowboy construction, too many villainous taxi drivers, too expensive, for, like everything else in Thailand, it was run by various mafias. O was out of her element, not understanding the southern dialect, and subdued. She didn't like boat trips, or the southern food. It rained all the time, the locals were scared of a tsunami. They had a nice beach bungalow in a swank resort hotel, but cut short the visit and arrived back in Pattaya in the small hours, during a thunderstorm, which had O praying fervently to the Buddha to avert bad luck.

Leda interrupted his breakfast omelette the next morning. She had the shakes: pale, shivering, nauseous-looking, a candidate for the DTs.

219

'You look like death. You need a drink,' he said.

He poured her a tequila with soda to help it go down, and took a beer for himself. Sun's over the yardarm. She gulped the drink, lighting a cigarette with trembling fingers and spilling half the packet on the floor.

'Christ,' she said. 'Oh, Christ.'

She ignored the cigarettes, letting O pick them up. Blearily, she saw the naked girl rubbing her scalded croup, and smiled.

'Nice,' she said. 'We should have that in the bar. A restaurant section, eat off your girl. If we still have a bar. I feel like the sky's fallen in, like a fucking coconut falling on your head. Bloody Danny, the fucking bastard shit. Damn him. And not just that. Oh, Christ.'

He poured her more tequila, which she swallowed and, after a while, she stopped shaking.

'You want to cut down on that stuff,' he said.

'Don't we all? You too.'

'Start the day as you mean to finish it,' he said, waving at O, who prettily cracked open another beer with her sex.

'Ordinarily, I'd be turned on,' said Leda, grimacing.

The news was bad. All the girls – those left after the increasing 'slippage', besotted olafs whisking them away as brides – had departed en masse. There had been a fight, over money, boyfriend, whatever, and Pink had stabbed her rival in the face and groin with a broken bottle. She died in hospital; had she lived, disfigured, she would never have worked again, or married. Pink was in jail, Plodprasop unable to help. The girls had consulted *moh-doos*, to learn that Smackers was cursed, and the ghost of the slain girl would haunt it.

Woaw had quit, for grandfather was dying, cirrhosis of the liver, and Woaw knew her immoral life was to blame. Another girl, who had 'Helmut' tattooed on her right buttock (more slippage), had thrown herself from a tenth floor balcony, for reasons unknown, possibly to do with Helmut. On top of that, Danny had deserted Leda for Goong, whom he had been fucking in Lancelot's absence.

Just another day in paradise, Leda said bitterly. Mitch poured himself a stiff tequila along with his beer.

'We'll have to recruit some girls in a hurry.'

She shook her head, with her breathing calmed, and face softened, as the drink took effect.

'Don't you understand? Word gets round. No girl will work for an accursed place. Shit, shit, shit. Anyway, how was Ko Lanta?'

'Less than thrilling.'

'Shame. I remember it was quite pretty. I stayed on the beach, with a fun crowd. You could have a good time in those days. There was one English girl I was hot for, Zelda her name was, pretty little thing, and boy, could she fuck. I mean fuck *me*. She fucked everybody else, too, boys and girls lining up to pull a train. And whip shit out of that cute little bum. She loved the whip, especially when we tied her up. And she loved pulling a train, twelve cocks, one after the other. Some girls like that, look at the Hell's Angels and their mommas. Girls are basically masochists, I think. Her boyfriend was a real shit, an Aussie, Greg or something, used to charge a few dollars for people to fuck her. He said she was screwed up because her dad raped her. A bloody policeman. Anything's possible.'

He did not respond: out here, there were no coincidences. Zelda seemed so far away, in space and time. They sat, smoking and drinking, until Leda's shakes went, and a plan formed: he would go upcountry, to Udon, and recruit some greenhorns. Meanwhile, Smackers would announce a week's closure, for staff holidays. It would be okay, a temporary hiccup, everything would be back to normal.

'Normal?' she spat. 'What the fuck is normal?'

And that night, O dreamed of ghosts and monsters, telling him there was worse to come.

The overnight train from Bangkok deposited him in Udon: a pretty, sleepy little place, only fifty clicks from the Mekong river and Laos. There were not many tourists, but the place was full of whorehouses masquerading as

221

karaoke bars, hairdressers, or plain hotels, at one of which, the Hotel Chulalangkorn, he found himself staying. Full in-house service for the Thai travelling salesman. Across the road was the shabbier Hotel Asia, a six-storey barrack block with whores waving from their windows; girls who couldn't get jobs in the factory, some of them not legal age, and chained to their beds at night. Truck drivers went there. He would give it a try.

It was cheap and cheerful, with some tasty meat on offer, all young. Om, On, Porn, Foon, the usual names, the usual honey skin, soft eyes, and fragrant chattes. They knew about condoms, but did not use them: they were so expensive. He had short times, the squalid surroundings an excitement, tipped lavishly, then told them of a possible job in Pattaya. They lit up, for Pattaya was the promised land, its streets paved with gold. But he would have to buy them from the mafia owner, for they were slaves, a slave costing a few hundred dollars. They spoke a little English, making them desirable merchandise; most had been schoolgirls in Bangkok before being sold. Some demurred when he explained spanking, but some were keen, and applied it to his own arse. A few, hearing of a sub's rewards, nervously accepted a light strapping, for *sanook*.

He telephoned Leda to say his trip would be longer than expected. She told him rather mysteriously to be as fast as he could, for O was unhappy without him. He prowled the shopping malls and the bus station, when the 'bar-girl express' buses to Pattaya set off, and was able to recruit a dozen girls. Money talked. He took them back to his hotel, 'broke them in', and weeded them down to four, sending the selected girls to Pattaya with an advance of money and the promise of lodging. All said they were escaping from jobs at the big new clothing factory, its long hours, low pay, and air that made you sick, *mai sabai*. Girls died from the noxious dye fumes and the dust particles that choked the air. Many of the living would seize a job in Pattaya.

He found an old Strips business card in his wallet and went to see the factory, posing as a buyer, and was welcomed by the unctuous manager, Mr Sawaddipong. It was hell. There, in the factory, girls with breathing masks cut, sewed, and dyed delicious frillies, corsets and thongs like those Strips sold. The air was foul, stinking, almost unbreathable. Mr Sawaddipong said that, by coincidence, another English buyer had just left, a Mr Dern: did Mr Barnett happen to know him? He said he did not. As a reward for a big order, Mr Dern had had his choice of floor girls. They came back very sore, and unable to sit at their workplaces. Mr Sawaddipong laughed uproariously. Of course, he had to fire them, for a girl who could not sit could not sew. Small matter, they would not need to sit, picking rice, and would not die from the factory air. Mr Barnett, too, could avail himself of the girls, Udon girls being the most beautiful in Thailand. He lied that he would come back.

He had been in Udon two weeks when he ventured to the top floor of the Hotel Asia, finding that the higher one went, the less desirable, and cheaper, were the girls. Their hair was dull, their skin blotchy, faces drawn from malnourishment, and there were few prowling truck drivers. At the very top he found a girl in a red dress whose body and lips might once have been ravishing, but now looked scrawny and wasted, with sagging breasts. She flung herself at him.

'Mr Mitch! Why did you leave me? I love you too much!'

It was Nampoong. No coincidences in Buddhaland. Quickly he shut the door and sat on the bed, hugging her in the wretched cubicle while she told her tale of woe. Another same story. After he had deserted her in London (*his* fault, of course), her heart was broken, so she freelanced on the seafront in Pattaya, calling herself Lek. A customer offered her work as a dancer in his own go-go bar. She had to take it anally, and smoke him, which she hated (oh, sure), for she was a good girl. She described her boss in Pattaya, married to a katoey, and it could only have been Lancelot. When the wife found out, and threatened them both, proposing to cut off his penis, and Nampoong's breasts, he had sold her, along with some girls from a school in Bangkok, to the owner of the Hotel

223

Asia, a Pattaya policeman called Plodprasop, who was also a supplier of pills.

'Please,' she murmured, 'we have bouncing?'

She hoisted her dress, showing him an untrimmed hairy sex, her pouch dull red between the furred brown lips. He turned away.

'Please?'

'Not possible,' he stammered. 'No power.'

'You do not love me any more,' she said softly, her eyes misted with tears. 'You said you loved me.'

He had wanted her, but never said he loved her.

'Nampoong, darling, too much has happened.'

She wasn't curious why he was there. People, like money, just fell inexplicably from the sky.

'You have another lady.'

Well, of course I have another lady. This is bloody tits-out-for-the-lads Thailand. He nodded, and her face was a picture of misery. Suddenly, she brightened, with a whore's false smile. It was an amphetamine mood swing; her stinking breath and unearthly eyes were plain.

'*Mai pen rai,*' she chirped. 'It doesn't matter. You are a sexy man, on holiday. You take ladies, it's up to you.'

He told her it was not the same, and told her about his own bar.

'I'll work for you!' she cried.

He did not say she was spoiled, not the same person, bad merchandise. But in his heart, the old longing welled, the vision of her in the past, of what might have been. He had to get her out. Impossible to imagine her rotting here, or in the poisonous factory.

'I'll dance, fuck, smoking, everything. I whip, and take whip, no problem. I can cook and clean for you, and you can beat me if I am lazy. I shall be your slave.'

'All right,' he said, heavy of heart, and she wept with joy, embracing him, kissing him full on the lips.

'Darling Mitch, good luck for Lek!' she cried. 'I love you too much.'

He turned away to wipe his mouth, trying not to think where her lips had been.

28

Slap and Tickle

Smackers picked up again as if nothing had happened, the Thai way, the past a dream. The Udon girls, young and raw, proved a powerful attraction. He put Nampoong to work as a cleaner and general skivvy (in a sort of French maid's uniform), lodged upstairs with the others. Off the dope, she rapidly put on weight and health and resumed some of her old cockiness, hinting that she would like to turn tricks for extra money. He agreed, no longer loving her, a replica or wax model of the girl he had known in England. She proved a good cook, making hot snacks, served, as Leda suggested, on the bare buttocks of a crouching girl: another crowd-pleaser. Leda drank more and more, but didn't have the shakes for she confessed wanly that she started the day with a slug of tequila before getting out of bed. Danny and Goong were an item, enjoying themselves elsewhere, Jeffrey had departed, and when Lancelot appeared unexpectedly, Mitch was in drag, wearing only a bra and panties, with nylons, stiletto heels, suspender belt and a long wig, but, recognising him, Lancelot didn't seem to care, barring a nod of appreciation.

'Very pretty. We all get what we want, eventually.'

He said thank you: he liked people ogling his costumes, liked playing the teasing unapproachable vamp, part of the theatre. He went bar-hopping alone, in full drag, and found the girls he took were delighted by his subterfuge. He had revisited the Sexy Girls, looking for Nit, to learn she had married a US marine and had gone to live in Okinawa. He told Lancelot that fucking a girl was only half the equation: cross-dressing meant you could feel like a girl, really know her, as your penis touched her womb. He didn't know how to tell him about Goong's desertion, but, jack-coke at his lips, Lancelot said he knew. Of course.

'It's a mistake seeking happiness outside the self, in material possessions, or abstract things such as religion, a cause, or a woman. All are destructive, and women are the most destructive of all:'

He sighed, draining his drink.

'You know by now, life here is a constant struggle not to admit you hate it. These people have a mental age of nine, and soon you become like them. The brain turns to mush. It disproves evolution, the survival of the fittest. Thailand is survival of the stupidest. But you get addicted to the fatuous bloody pleasures, you can't help it, and end up hating yourself, same as an addict hates his booze or pills. Didn't Nietszche say that no man ever does evil, he always thinks he's doing right? Whatever you do, Asia shafts you in the end.'

That was the last time he saw Lancelot. Meanwhile, he was uncertain what to do about O. She seemed as loyal and submissive as ever, but there was a distance in her eyes. At home, he learned from Leda, after filling her with tequila, that in his absence she had been seeing other men. The coy euphemisms of women.

'You mean, fucking around?'

'More than that.'

Leda groped for words, as if the booze, and Danny's desertion, were stripping the Australian patina from the tough Ukrainian hooker.

'How do you say, pulling a train. Gang-bangs. I fucked her, too, couldn't help myself. She wanted it.' As if wanting something made it all right. She smiled blearily. 'She is very good.'

He looked at the naked, kneeling O. Hell, what did it matter? Should he beat her for it? That was surely what she

226

wanted. He told her to fetch the wooden snake, then whipped her while Leda watched nervously, the beating as much her punishment as O's. Afterwards, O burst into tears and cried that she needed punishment, for she was an evil girl. She had killed her sister, fleeing Udon for the bright lights of Pattaya, leaving her twin to work in the clothing factory, to support the family. There, she had become sick in her kidneys, her arms and legs swelled up, and she died. It was her fault for being selfish and, since then, she hoped that the pain she endured would appease her twin's ghost. So the girl died for a pair of panties. It would be comic, if it wasn't real.

He visited the Lucky Strike, looking for Chuck, and found Woaw, dressed primly in a white business suit, with glassine white nylons and white shoes: the colour of mourning. Her grandfather was dead, she said, died of drink, cirrhosis of the liver. The hotel now belonged to her.

'*Chuck* was your grandfather?'

She nodded, and clutched his arm.

'But I am scared of his ghost coming to punish me for my bad deeds. I need a man to defend me and help me run this place. I scared of mafia. I know you are good heart, Mitch. Will you join me? We can be married in the temple, by the monks.'

'It's very sudden! I need time to think.'

'Not too much time. If you do not like me, we stop being married. Up to you.'

Nampoong was overjoyed when he allowed her to dance, her body newly voluptuous. He felt no attraction for her himself for that had died, seeing her in the ratty northern brothel, but wished her good luck when she turned her first trick, a beery olaf taking her upstairs to spank him. Close up, he saw it was *the* Olaf, first met so long ago, in Walking Street. He did not recognise Mitch in drag, but leered, perhaps contemplating a threesome.

'I have this girl many times before,' he slurred. 'She is fockin good. I have not had the spanking here, but in Norway we have the best spanking girls, strong as a fockin ice bear.'

After beating O in front of Leda, he found that his sexual appetite for her increased, as his desire to hurt her diminished. Penetrating her sex, lately visited by so many alien cocks, was a savage turn-on. When she danced at the bar, he allowed her to go upstairs and turn tricks, but demanded she hand over all her tips. That way, he thought grimly, he knew she was fucking for fun, or to please him. After she had serviced customers, his lust for her was fierce, and he would take her in the same cubicle, moist with her sweat and the stink of her submission. He demanded all the details of her coupling as he thrashed her, then tupped his buttered bun. He took to cross-dressing at home, too, amusing the neighbour women. Why did everything in this blasted place have to be funny?

Ouan, having seduced him before, returned from Bangkok, newly equipped with a vulva, and seduced him again. This time he took her in her sex, the first to penetrate her new crevice, an honour for the boss. It was dry and rubbery, and of course didn't go anywhere, so it was really like having a wank, but it clung like a glove, and he seemed to bring her off, as there was some sort of clitoral arrangement, fashioned from the frenulum of her former penis, which he preferred not to scrutinise. She was pleased that her new device worked, but begged him not to tell Woaw of their coupling. Little hole was no cause for jealousy, lady hole was. Of course, she wanted a tip.

Not long afterward, final disaster struck, as O's dream had forecast. Plodprasop said they must vacate the premises at the end of the week, for it transpired that Lancelot and Goong did not have title when they sold it. The land belonged to the government, that is, the police. Goong was unreachable in Perth; Plodprasop showed him the local paper, turned to the suicide page, and there was Lancelot, stretched out dead in some crummy hotel bedroom. He had died from an overdose of pills, with an empty bottle of Jack Daniels beside the bed. His real name was Kevin Barrow. He and Leda were wary of renting another venue after losing their key money, although the profits were some compensation. Meanwhile, they would carry on to the end, with a rousing grand finale, as if nothing was amiss.

Wearing green bra, thong and nylons, with black stilettos, on their last evening, after a realistic whipping routine onstage, he heard a familiar reedy voice.

'Hello, Mitch. What a marvellous place you have! The girls take whip most convincingly. You do look divine in that get-up. Took a trip to Asia to find the real you, eh?'

He turned to see Derek Wantrill with three women – one Chinese and one English, with the delicious pert-breasted Lin, whose ripe young pears had just now been whipped onstage. The Englishwoman, licking her lips with a coy but lecherous smile, had her hand stroking Lin's bare buttocks.

'*Chance* magazine did you proud with all those photos,' said Derek. 'Repeated them in three issues. And a cracking video. Shannon and Gav loved it. They're an item now, as I suppose you know. I believe Shannon wants a divorce. Shall I tell her where you are?'

'No. Tell her I've disappeared. Done in by ghosts. Lost my mind.'

'Still, you can't be short of squirt.'

'Derek, please,' pouted the Englishwoman.

'Hello, Derek – Jane,' he said, remembering the name of Derek's mistress.

'I don't know any Jane,' Derek replied frostily. 'This is my wife Amanda, and our friend, Tara Lee.'

He patted the elfin Chinese girl's bottom.

'Tara likes it both ways,' he said, rather nastily, 'and so does Amanda.'

'Funny, having to come to Thailand, to be introduced to, you know, spanking,' Amanda said. 'I always hated that awful Scene thing, but here . . . well, it's such *fun*. Like the Garden of Eden.'

He gave them drinks on the house, then Derek bought a round, then Tara Lee. When Derek suggested he join their foursome in his room at the Lotus Court, he was already fairly drunk, and said why not have it here. It was nearly time for the grand finale, anyway. They could make it a party; O and Nampoong and Leda would surely join in.

229

He had a vague idea of 'let's all be friends'. They went upstairs to a cubicle to get ready; O and Nampoong were there, clad in thongs, and he stripped to his own thread, keeping his wig, but as the others stripped, and began to lick and paw, he couldn't get an erection; his control had deserted him, even when Nampoong lowered her thong and parted her quim lips to show them 'Olaf' daintily tattooed inside.

One of the girls suggested they do it onstage. Before he knew it, he was hustled into the spotlight, pinned, unresisting, face down, and stripped completely naked. O sat on his head and Lin on his thighs, and his penis was stiff. The crowd cheered. Leda said they should offer drinks on the house, drink the place dry, and he agreed; they both knew it was the last act. He shuddered as he felt the first whipcrack on his naked arse. It was heavy, savage, not in play, and was followed by a stroke with a whippy lethal cane. Tears blurred his eyes as the girls lashed him without mercy, their hoots and cackles of glee echoing in the hushed room. He took a dozen cuts, two dozen, like white-hot spears searing his buttocks, yet his erection did not wilt. Twisting his head, he gazed through moist eyes at the nude girls, teeth bared in exultation as they flogged him. *Isn't that what you want, Mitch?* Zelda had said. Derek's camera whirred.

'*Chance* magazine will love this,' he said.

The whipping stopped and he smelled a feline young body straddle his, breasts pressing to his back. Who was it? Leda, Nampoong, Ouan? Small matter, for he shrieked as deft girl's fingers parted his buttocks and a massive dildo penetrated his arsehole. God, it hurt! He writhed as the unseen girl buggered him for a minute, two minutes, then gasped in relief as his enculement was over. But it was not; another girl took the strap-on and recommenced the torture, then another.

'Go on, Amanda,' he heard Derek say.

'This is fun,' Amanda panted.

After her, he smelled a katoey, an unsnipped one, and the tube invading his anus was real flesh, while he writhed and shrieked, moaning, *stop, please*, with his penis rock-hard. Then Leda buggered him savagely. They paused to whip him again, and then continued his enculement, lovely little Lin proving most cruel. His rectum smarted with white-hot pain. Finally, it was O who wore the dildo, and his arse rose towards her as he bucked in the agony of his humiliation until he felt his seed well up in his balls and he groaned, *yes, yes, fuck me*, and spurted in orgasm, ejaculating a flood of sperm.

'I knew you could do it, Mitch.' Leda said. 'You're one of us, really.'

She kissed him on the lips, a proper kiss, and he wept in agony and gratitude, for it had been so long since a woman had kissed him.

Months later, he sat in his favourite beachside bar – Declan grumbling as usual about his aching telephone arm, and 'those cheap fucking yankee shitkickers' – reading from the memoirs of Marc Delatour, written in his cell as he awaited the guillotine. It was mostly an *apologia*, justifying his libertine existence.

How we sublimate or express our life force, that is, the sexual impulse, is the prime concern of all humans, and all activity whatsoever is fundamentally sexual. Animals rut, but only humans have imagination. Some make love, or, like me, explore the most unspeakable perversions, in pursuit of self-knowledge, some make paintings or music, some go to war, rule kingdoms, or accumulate money, to awe and possess others. But despite our tears, love, greed and cruelty, we can never truly know another being, only, fitfully, ourselves.

Smackers was ancient history now, the bar reborn as 'Bouncers', proprietor: police colonel Plodprasop. You learned your lesson: Asia always wins. Leda sent an occasional postcard from Perth where she was living *à trois*, and sober, with Danny and Goong, who protested, alleging herself a victim, that she had lost more money than anyone in the Smackers disaster. O danced at the Troika on Walking Street where her piercings were much appreciated, not least by her alcoholic Russian pimp, who beat her, according to Woaw, with a homemade knout, and devised frightening uses of her nipple rings. O was not unhappy. She had buggered him, hurt him, payback, transaction annulled. Pink was in jail, hoping for a royal amnesty, Lemon whoring in Hamburg. Lin was living in Norbiton, as au pair to the Wantrills. Nampoong was in Norway, amid the fockin big prawns. However long any of it would last.

He was married to Woaw, and lived with her in the penthouse suite of the Lucky Strike. It was rewarding, for little effort, acting managerial, and drinking in his own bar, still called the Up Chuck, for respect. They married in the Buddhist temple, smoke and mirrors, just a ceremony, with no legal validity outside Thailand, and probably not even inside. Meaningless, like everything else. Woaw would please him, dressing all in turquoise for their love-making, letting him adore her nylons, her panties, her buttocks; she let him dress in her underwear, though he no longer wore full drag, and she scourged him, with deft, loving cruelty, while he wore her panties. To his pleasure, she eventually trusted him to shave her mound every day, once she understood it was an act of worship. He gave up his fruit-flavoured condoms, and of course his collection of other girls' panties. But he kept Sylvie's pink ribbon after all these years, and would press it to his lips.

That was the essence of fetish: knowing a woman by adoring the cloth that touched her, the garment a mere inert thing, yet symbolising her, imbued with her smell, her spirit. A girl's panties, the ribbon fragrant with her hair, were the *idea* of her. Like her secret swaying buttocks, a fetish. Just as Thailand, with its brown girls, was itself a fetish. Maybe everything on the planet was a fetish of the ideal platonic form.

Sometimes Woaw wanted a spanking, for she felt guilty about Chuck's death, even though it had brought her good luck. Too much good luck attracted the malicious envy of ghosts, and must be diluted by suffering. He loved spanking her young buttocks, delicately, for it seemed like

232

spanking precious porcelain. He must love her, after a fashion. She let him fuck and tongue her during her monthlies, a practice he found more and more joyful, swimming in her crimson love, but she murmured about babies, for she was that age. Perhaps he would give her a designer brood, pale skins for success. A dizzying prospect, little Thai Mitches, breeding and evolving down through the eons, until the very last one was some armour-plated lizard, rutting in hundred-degree heat, before the exploding Sun burned Earth to a cinder. Well, let it be.

He idled away time, playing solitaire on his computer. The cards didn't suffer, nor answer back. The magic, as the kings obediently cascaded! Woaw's American swain, he was certain, had been an invention to make him jealous. She was his Thai dragon wife, scolding him if she suspected him of being a butterfly. Which he was. He loved taking a girl, furtively, a cheating, beery husband, *nom de guerre* Marc, belly thickening and hair thinning. A grimmie. He sometimes *focked* one of the olaf girls from Walking Street. Sucked her filthy toes. His sleep was dreamless. It was all good.

But what was it all for? The tears and romance and fantasies, a corny deceit, it was just power, money, mindless spurting, fear of the dark. The orgasm, even as you swooned, announced its own end. Fucking, trying to get back to the womb, how fine to stay there forever and never leave. Warm, fed, and contented, brain function minimal, just like Thailand, a life of bearable emptiness. All the years of rutting and sweating and grunting, squirting into warm wet holes, until the slap and tickle was suddenly over, and your lights went out. Swinburne knew, supping in the Rose and Crown, wanting the girls to cane his wrinkly old arse.

And love, grown faint and fretful,
With lips but half regretful
Sighs, and with eyes forgetful
Weeps that no loves endure.

Might as well die here as anywhere else. Away from the cold damp fantasies of England, frustrated libertines pawing through bloody magazines to gaze at images of paradise. He thought sadly, fondly, of Shannon, of Zelda, of Trudi, of sweet little Wendy Ruminaw. All shadows in the wind. God, he was past thirty, getting too old for it. Luscious brown honeypots, always the *same* luscious brown honeypot, so hard to tell them apart. Had one, you've had them all. Burned out. Turn to religion, become a Buddhist monk.

A teenage honey strolled past, met his wandering eyes. She was supple, lithe, ripe of breast and bottom, well spankable. Lovely jubbly. She smiled, and he crooked his finger to beckon her over. She approached and demurely sat down, crossing luscious brown thighs with a cheeky wiggle of her toes. *She fancies me! I'm in with a chance, here.*

nexus

The leading publisher of fetish and adult fiction

TELL US WHAT YOU THINK!

Readers' ideas and opinions matter to us. Take a few minutes to fill in the questionnaire below and you'll be entered into a prize draw to win a year's worth of Nexus books (36 titles)

Terms and conditions apply – see end of questionnaire.

1. Sex: Are you male ☐ female ☐ a couple ☐?

2. Age: Under 21 ☐ 21–30 ☐ 31–40 ☐ 41–50 ☐ 51–60 ☐ over 60 ☐

3. Where do you buy your Nexus books from?

☐ A chain book shop. If so, which one(s)?

_____

☐ An independent book shop. If so, which one(s)?

_____

☐ A used book shop/charity shop

☐ Online book store. If so, which one(s)?

_____

4. How did you find out about Nexus books?

☐ Browsing in a book shop

☐ A review in a magazine

☐ Online

☐ Recommendation

☐ Other _____

5. In terms of settings, which do you prefer? (Tick as many as you like)

☐ Down to earth and as realistic as possible

☐ Historical settings. If so, which period do you prefer?

_____

- ☐ Fantasy settings – barbarian worlds
- ☐ Completely escapist/surreal fantasy
- ☐ Institutional or secret academy
- ☐ Futuristic/sci fi
- ☐ Escapist but still believable
- ☐ Any settings you dislike?

_____

- ☐ Where would you like to see an adult novel set?

_____

6. In terms of storylines, would you prefer:

- ☐ Simple stories that concentrate on adult interests?
- ☐ More plot and character-driven stories with less explicit adult activity?
- ☐ We value your ideas, so give us your opinion of this book:

_____

_____

_____

7. In terms of your adult interests, what do you like to read about? (Tick as many as you like)

- ☐ Traditional corporal punishment (CP)
- ☐ Modern corporal punishment
- ☐ Spanking
- ☐ Restraint/bondage
- ☐ Rope bondage
- ☐ Latex/rubber
- ☐ Leather
- ☐ Female domination and male submission
- ☐ Female domination and female submission
- ☐ Male domination and female submission
- ☐ Willing captivity
- ☐ Uniforms
- ☐ Lingerie/underwear/hosiery/footwear (boots and high heels)
- ☐ Sex rituals
- ☐ Vanilla sex
- ☐ Swinging

☐ Cross-dressing/TV
☐ Enforced feminisation
☐ Others – tell us what you don't see enough of in adult fiction:

_____

_____

_____

8. Would you prefer books with a more specialised approach to your interests, i.e. a novel specifically about uniforms? If so, which subject(s) would you like to read a Nexus novel about?

_____

_____

_____

9. Would you like to read true stories in Nexus books? For instance, the true story of a submissive woman, or a male slave? Tell us which true revelations you would most like to read about:

_____

_____

_____

10. What do you like best about Nexus books?

_____

_____

11. What do you like least about Nexus books?

_____

_____

12. Which are your favourite titles?

_____

_____

13. Who are your favourite authors?

_____

_____

14. Which covers do you prefer? Those featuring:
(tick as many as you like)

☐ Fetish outfits
☐ More nudity
☐ Two models
☐ Unusual models or settings
☐ Classic erotic photography
☐ More contemporary images and poses
☐ A blank/non-erotic cover
☐ What would your ideal cover look like?

_____

15. Describe your ideal Nexus novel in the space provided:

_____

_____

_____

_____

16. Which celebrity would feature in one of your Nexus-style fantasies? We'll post the best suggestions on our website – anonymously!

_____

THANKS FOR YOUR TIME

Now simply write the title of this book in the space below and cut out the questionnaire pages. Post to: Nexus, Marketing Dept., Thames Wharf Studios, Rainville Rd, London W6 9HA

Book title: _____

TERMS AND CONDITIONS

NEXUS NEW BOOKS

To be published in October 2006

BRUSH STROKES
Penny Birch

Amber Oakley is dominant and beautiful. But just a little too beautiful for her own good. As far from accepting her sexuality as she seeks to portray it, her fellow enthusiasts almost invariably want to get her knickers down, usually for spanking. In *Brush Strokes*, her attempts to resist the attentions of the firm and matronly Hannah Riley quickly come to nothing, and Amber is once more back over the knee, behind-bared as a hairbrush is applied to her well-fleshed cheeks. Rather than give in, she tries to resist, but only manages to get herself into even deeper trouble.

£6.99   ISBN 0 352 34072 X

CORRUPTION
Virginia Crowley

The greater the degree of purity in a person, the darker the taint on their soul if they succumb to temptation. Not even the men and women of the holy orders are safe from corruption as Lady Stephanie Peabody and her host of greedy, voluptuous collaborators engage in the most sinister forms of seductive manipulation. Not even the Prior, the nuns at the convent, or Stephanie's principled stepdaughter, Laura, are safe from the threat of spiritual corruption.

With the aid of a powerful aphrodisiac, Stephanie's coven of cruel, demanding harlots tempt the righteous with the tawdry delights of the flesh – at the expense of their immortal souls.

£6.99   ISBN 0 352 34073 8

THE DOMINO QUEEN
Cyrian Amberlake

Wherever dark pleasure reigns, there the Domino Queen keeps her court.

Whether she's initiating a lonely peasant girl or training a trio of eager slaves, Josephine deals out tenderness and cruelty with an even, elegant hand.

Meanwhile Cadence Szathkowicz, the lover Josephine abandoned on Dominica, is searching for her. From pulsating Los Angeles to the strict discipline of Madame Suriko's house in Chicago, Cadence travels on an odyssey of pleasure and pain.

All she has to guide her is the sign Josephine wears between her breasts: the tattoo of the domino mask.

£6.99   ISBN 0 352 34074 6

If you would like more information about Nexus titles, please visit our website at www.nexus-books.co.uk, or send a large stamped addressed envelope to:

Nexus, Thames Wharf Studios,
Rainville Road, London W6 9HA

nexus

This information is correct at time of printing. For up-to-date information, please visit our website at www.nexus-books.co.uk

All books are priced at £6.99 unless another price is given.

------------ ✂ --------------------------

Please send me the books I have ticked above.

Name   ....

Address   ....

             ....

             ....

             .... Post code ....

Send to: **Virgin Books Cash Sales, Thames Wharf Studios, Rainville Road, London W6 9HA**

US customers: for prices and details of how to order books for delivery by mail, call 888-330-8477.

Please enclose a cheque or postal order, made payable to **Nexus Books Ltd**, to the value of the books you have ordered plus postage and packing costs as follows:

UK and BFPO – £1.00 for the first book, 50p for each subsequent book.

Overseas (including Republic of Ireland) – £2.00 for the first book, £1.00 for each subsequent book.

If you would prefer to pay by VISA, ACCESS/MASTERCARD, AMEX, DINERS CLUB or SWITCH, please write your card number and expiry date here:

....

Please allow up to 28 days for delivery.

Signature ....

Our privacy policy

We will not disclose information you supply us to any other parties. We will not disclose any information which identifies you personally to any person without your express consent.

From time to time we may send out information about Nexus books and special offers. Please tick here if you do *not* wish to receive Nexus information.   ☐

------------ ✂ --------------------------